COURAGE FOR THE COUNTRY NURSE

KATE EASTHAM

Boldwood

First published in Great Britain in 2026 by Boldwood Books Ltd.

Cover Design by Colin Thomas

Cover Images: Colin Thomas

A CIP catalogue record for this book is available from the British Library.

Paperback ISBN 978-1-83656-226-9

Large Print ISBN 978-1-83656-227-6

Hardback ISBN 978-1-83656-225-2

Trade Paperback ISBN 978-1-80625-849-9

Ebook ISBN 978-1-83656-228-3

Kindle ISBN 978-1-83656-229-0

Audio CD ISBN 978-1-83656-220-7

MP3 CD ISBN 978-1-83656-221-4

Digital audio download ISBN 978-1-83656-222-1

This book is printed on certified sustainable paper. Boldwood Books is dedicated to putting sustainability at the heart of our business. For more information please visit https://www.boldwoodbooks.com/about-us/sustainability/

Boldwood Books Ltd, 23 Bowerdean Street, London, SW6 3TN

www.boldwoodbooks.com

For Ann Hall (1936-2023)

Hope is the thing with feathers
That perches in the soul,
And sings the tune without the words,
And never stops – at all

— EMILY DICKINSON

1

INGLESIDE SURGERY, LANCASHIRE, JANUARY 1937

It was Sunday morning; Lara was off duty. And despite the gathering of cold that nipped at her nose, she was up early, bright-eyed and ready for what the day might bring. The village practice housekeeper, Mrs Hewitt, had hinted at a lazy morning in the sitting room listening to the radiogram but Lara thought she'd probably make her excuses because she wanted to get out to the country lanes for a good walk.

Last night around the kitchen table as they'd sat chatting after their evening meal, her nurse colleague, Marion Wright, had pleaded for Lara to join her and their junior doctor, Angus Fitzwilliam, for pre-Sunday lunch drinks at the pub across the road. Not wanting to upset Marion but knowing it wouldn't fit with her plans, Lara had politely declined. But in an overly dramatic display of sorrow, Marion had pleaded, 'You must come, Lara. You know what Angus is like when he's had a few drinks. Particularly if your young fella me lad vet comes in or he sees his mate from the sawmill. They're off together, huddled at the bar like men do.'

'I know,' Lara had said gently, mustering a smile and

reaching out to her friend across the table. 'But I have to get out into the fresh air... I'll come with you next time, I promise.'

Marion had twisted her mouth with disappointment, but in moments she'd lifted her head and offered one of her lopsided smiles. Then reaching across the table to Lara, she'd said, 'Our time off is precious, so do what you need to do.'

There was another reason to get out of the surgery. It was important not to be in striking distance of their senior doctor, Henry Bingham. He'd been more irritable than ever recently. Downright snappy, in fact. Mrs Hewitt had told her in confidence she'd heard a rumour over the festive season that the woman from Ridgetown he'd been seeing had broken up with him. Well, that's what Lara had already assumed because just before new year, he'd come back from a night out in a very foul mood. He'd growled and grumbled, then slumped onto his chair at the head of the table and cracked open the bottle of whisky Angus had gifted him for Christmas. Then he'd sat silently boozing until he'd almost slumped face first on the table. Mrs Hewitt had ushered her and Marion to their rooms saying she'd need to get him sorted. And they'd had no choice but to leave the housekeeper to it. Lara had listened out though, just in case Mrs Hewitt had needed any help. But beyond Bingham's slurry, mournful singing which had floated up the stairs and made her and Marion giggle, all seemed to have been well.

Thankfully, in the bitterly cold weeks since then, Bingham had rallied. He still had his outbursts of temper but those were his norm, particularly when it came to the management of Angus. The young doctor had always been on shaky ground regarding his excesses in the pub and there'd been several loud confrontations. But this time, after more tense exchanges around the kitchen table, Angus seemed to have taken some heed of Bingham's warning. In fact, he'd even been seen staying in of an evening drinking cocoa. Lara thought it was probably the colder, icier weather that was keeping him at bay, but she was prepared to give him the benefit of the doubt.

Trotting down the stairs in her thick blouse, woollen slacks and a fluffy lambswool cardigan, with her white-blonde hair clipped back, she hurriedly pushed her feet into her sturdy walking shoes. As she straightened up, she caught the puttering sound of a vehicle from the cobbled street. Vaguely wondering who was out and about on a Sunday morning, she was ready to head to the kitchen for a quick cup of tea when a high-pitched screech of brakes and the heart-wrenching howl of some injured creature came right at her. Her heart jumped into her mouth as Mrs Hewitt ran from the kitchen shouting, 'What the heck was that?'

'Sounds like an animal's been hurt,' Lara called, already running up the green-tiled corridor. As soon as she had the front door open, she spotted the tousled head of Leo Sullivan, the young vet from the surgery down the road. His face was ashen; he looked distraught as he scrambled from his van which had stalled skew-whiff across the road.

'Oh my God, I've hit a dog,' he yelled, his voice tight with pain.

Lara launched herself into the road, shouting, 'Oh no! Have you? Where is it?'

Leo fell to his knees, glanced under the van. 'Nothing there.'

At another blood-curdling howl, together they saw a blood-stained bundle of white fur with brown ears and a patch of darker brown over one eye, lying on the far side of the road.

Leo let out an agonised groan, then leapt up and ran straight to the creature, throwing himself down onto the cobbled street, almost sobbing. 'You poor little blighter, I'm so sorry. I just didn't see you.'

He tried to reach out to the injured dog, but it was growling and snapping at his hand. Then it emitted another heart-rending, sorrowful howl.

Lara felt the mournful screech pierce her heart and she was more shocked by this than some of the human casualties she'd attended. As a hard bubble of anxiety tightened in her throat, she fell to her knees beside Leo.

Clearly, he was rattled and upset, and he moved a bit too fast to grip the dog. The suddenness caused the animal to snap harder, catching him with its sharp teeth and grazing his hand.

He sucked in a sharp breath, muttered, 'I deserved that,' as drops of blood dripped onto the road. Lara was about to pull her folded handkerchief out of her pocket to press against the wound, but he roughly wiped the back of his hand on the leg of his trousers. Then he was shouting instructions. 'We need to move the little fella, get him to the surgery. Stay with him, Lara, while I grab a blanket from the van to move him.'

As Lara continued to crouch by the dog, she noted the distorted angle of his back leg and knew it was badly broken. It wasn't an open fracture but there was so much blood all over his fur and on the road; she needed to check the source. Quickly, she saw that most of the blood was coming from the torn flesh on the dog's snout which had probably borne the initial brunt of the collision. 'We'll soon have you stitched up and mended,' she said gently, trying to soothe, but her words made the dog howl even louder. And as a fist of anguish closed around her heart, she felt desperately sad because there was no reassurance she could give in the way she'd so often done with a human casualty.

Mrs Hewitt shouted to her from the surgery door, 'Don't get too close, Nurse Flynn. The poor little blighter will snap your nose off.'

'I'll be careful,' she called back, noting the housekeeper's pale, stricken face.

Leo had returned with the blanket and a pair of thick leather gloves, and he seemed to be rallying. 'Right, so if you can help, let's get the little fella loaded onto this blanket and carry him down to the surgery. Then I can give him a whiff of anaesthetic and get him patched up.'

'Righto,' she replied, feeling that certain set of her mouth with her lips pressed together that came during an emergency.

Once Leo had the gloves on, ever so carefully he picked up the dog, still growling, then howling with pain and snapping at his hands in their thick gloves.

'The shock's setting in,' he said, an urgent note to his voice. 'We need to get him treated right away.'

'I'll move your van off the street, Leo,' a male voice shouted, and Angus emerged through the surgery door to slip into the driver's seat.

'Cheers, mate,' Leo called as Lara took one side of the blanket to help carry the dog very carefully down the hill to the vet's surgery.

Other folk were out of their cottages now after hearing the commotion, and Lizzie Cronshaw was in tears over the poor, injured dog. Even some of the big, burly fellas who worked at the sawmill were full of concern for the helpless creature.

'At least the poor little beggar got run over by a vet,' Sam Collins called from the door of his butcher's shop as he unloaded his van. But Lara could tell by the shake of Leo's head that he hadn't gained any solace from that remark.

Lara held open the door to the vet's as Leo walked through cradling the dog, who appeared to be rapidly weakening. The little fella was shivering violently and seemed to be on the verge of collapse.

When Leo spoke, his voice was so full of concern, it made her heart almost melt. 'We need to treat him right away; he's not much more than a puppy and he's in shock. He's lost a fair bit of blood from the wound on his nose and probably much more internally around that fractured back leg.'

They were straight into the treatment room and as Leo lay the little dog gently down on the examination bench, Lara glanced around for clues to where the equipment they needed to stabilise their patient was stored.

'I'm thinking some towels, dressings, sutures and a whiff of ether,' she said firmly.

'Yep,' he replied, pointing in the direction Lara had already headed. 'It's all there on the shelves, apart from the jar of ether. I've got that here next to the bench.'

Lara quickly found and began to gather the materials one by one then she headed briskly back to Leo, placing them for easy access on the bench.

'Thanks,' Leo breathed as he twisted the lid off a glass bottle of ether and gave a tiny whiff of anaesthetic. The dog was knocked out in seconds.

'Are we tackling the fractured back leg or the deep laceration to his nose first?' Lara asked.

'The nose, I think. It's the same for dogs as in humans; the internal blood loss around the fracture will be slowing up by now, so it makes sense to sort out other bleeding points first.'

She nodded. 'Right. So what do you need me to do?'

'Support the little fella's head while I stitch him up.'

Lara was already there, her hands slicked with blood, undeterred by what she was about to do given her experience of attending human casualties.

It perhaps felt wrong to be surprised at Leo's expertise but as he leaned over the dog, an untidy lock of dark-brown hair falling over his forehead, and began to suture while she watched his slim, agile fingers make the best possible job of it, she felt impressed. She'd never imagined when it came to the nitty-gritty, the young vet would be so adept and professional. It didn't marry with the almost lackadaisical, jokey approach to life Leo had often displayed when he'd been on a night out in the pub. But this pleased her, and she was already revising some of her previous thoughts about Leo Sullivan. She forgave herself though for her earlier opinion because it stemmed from an incident on her first day in Ingleside when she'd been called to assist a local farmer with the delivery of a calf because Leo hadn't turned up on time. So inevitably it had led her to feel unsure of his professional standards.

Once the stitches were done, Leo handed her a wodge of clean swabs to apply pressure to the suture line on the dog's nose. Then he pulled a stethoscope from his jacket pocket and furrowed his brow as he leaned over to listen to the animal's heart. 'The little fella has a racing heartbeat, but you'd expect tachycardia after blood loss and shock. His ticker sounds steady enough and it's strong.'

'Good, that's good,' Lara offered, still pressing the swabs against the dog's nose, easing off intermittently to check for seepage of blood. The wound was looking good; the sutures were perfect.

Leo moved on to the dog's broken back leg; it was twisted wildly out of shape below the hock. 'No mistaking what's happened here,' he murmured softly, then he furrowed his brow and drew a slow breath as he felt with his slim fingers for the degree of displacement. Lara couldn't take her eyes off his hands; she'd never noticed them before but now they seemed like the most beautiful hands in the world.

Smoothly, he clicked the bones back into alignment. 'Right,

so, Lara... that suture line on his nose seems to have stopped oozing blood so could you switch now and hold on to his leg to keep the fracture aligned. I'll soak some plaster of Paris, and we'll get on with applying a cast.'

'Right you are,' she replied, quickly stepping much closer to Leo so she could position her hands as he gently let go. As she leaned in, she felt his warm breath on her cheek and her heart gave a gentle flip. Instantly, she dismissed it as heightened emotion from seeing a helpless creature injured.

She was glad she had transferrable skills and experience that were of use for this non-human casualty. Nevertheless, she was surprised by the relative ease of her transfer from human to dog. She supposed it might be because she'd had to get used to dealing with barking dogs, stray livestock and the wild creatures she regularly encountered out on the country lanes. So now, as she assisted the young vet, she felt reasonably confident. And when he murmured a thank you and told her how well she was doing, she felt her heart expanding with satisfaction.

Glancing to Leo, she noted the scrunch of his brow and the determined set of his mouth. She saw the professional side of him again and she was impressed. And once more, her heart skipped and she knew she needed to distract herself, so she asked, 'What breed of dog is this one?'

He glanced directly at her as he pulled the plaster bandage from the mixing bowl, his hands slaked with white paste. 'Oh, he's mostly Jack Russell with maybe a bit of mongrel mixed in. Many of the farms keep these lively little dogs because they're good ratters and they're likeable creatures apart from the ones that nip at your ankles.'

'Oh, so if that's the case and he's from one of the farms, we might stand a chance of finding his owner.'

Leo waggled his head as he began to apply the plaster.

'That's debatable, and from what I've been hearing, there's a new wave of poaching. The men in those gangs use these Jack Russell terriers to go down rabbit holes. It's possible this little fella wasn't up to scratch, so they dumped him. But he might just have got lost or found himself stuck down a hole or something. I'll be asking around the farms, see if anyone's missing a Jack Russell. And I'll get my dad onto it; he knows everybody from here in the village right up to the fells.'

Lara had already fallen for the little dog with his brown patch over one eye and it dismayed her that he might be sent back to a careless owner. 'So what if his owner can't be found, what will happen? Will you keep him?'

He drew a slow breath, made his final turn of the plaster bandage, then glanced up with a mischievous twinkle in his dark eyes. He left another beat and held her gaze before he answered. 'Yes, of course I'll keep him.'

Lara felt relief flood through her. 'I'm so happy to hear that,' she gushed.

'Steady on, Nurse Flynn.' He laughed. 'I've never seen you like this. Do you get so het up about your human patients?'

'Oh yes, most definitely. But, like you, I'm a professional so I don't let just anyone see.'

He raised his eyebrows, fixed her with a direct gaze. 'So when you say you don't let just anyone see... does that mean I might be a someone?'

She felt flustered. 'Well, I suppose it's just we're sort of doing the same kind of work in a way.'

He was still gazing at her, his eyes bright, that untidy lock of hair falling onto his brow. Then quite unexpectedly, he took a step towards her. And when he spoke, his voice sounded breathy. 'I don't care if you think I'm a someone or a no one... every time I see you, I can't help myself. I feel drawn to you.'

'Well, we're kind of in the same line of work so—'

'So, nothing. I've never felt this way about anyone ever before, so that doesn't wash.'

His eyes locked onto hers and seemed to draw her in, and with his next step, he was right there, reaching up to place a warm, gentle hand against her cheek. She could feel his breath on her face, hear the beat of her own heart. And when he leaned in to kiss her gently on the mouth, his lips tasted of salt, and the tenderness of the moment blew her heart wide open. She couldn't speak, she could only feel, and her instinct was to kiss him back. But the little dog let out a yelp of pain and showed signs of waking, so they were both caught back up with his care. Then gazing down to the dog, still with his bloodstained fur and those black silk sutures running the length of his nose, she felt again the heightened emotion of the accident and wondered if that was what had sparked the kiss.

As Leo administered a painkilling injection to settle the little dog, her thoughts lurched back and forth. She felt heightened and conflicted all at the same time and her instinct was to get back to the surgery.

'I'll be off now,' she said as soon as the dog was settled and sleeping. 'Mrs Hewitt will be wondering what's happened and how the dog's doing.'

'Right, yes.' He smiled, as he reached out to place a gentle hand on her arm. 'Thank you for helping me with this little fella. And before you go, I just need to tell you that I've wanted to kiss you since the first time I saw you in Tom Douglas's shippon when you helped deliver that calf.'

She giggled. 'I see where you're coming from with the smell of manure and all that messy birthing.'

He laughed. 'Well, you're a nurse, you know what it's like; it's our bread and butter, isn't it?'

'It is.' She smiled, feeling drawn by his warm gaze, but unable to say anything more or hint at what that kiss might mean because right now, with the shock of the injured dog and the heightened emotion between them, she felt overwhelmed. The feel of his lips had been so gentle, yet she still felt the tingle of it. All adding to the confusion she now felt over this man who, with switches and turns, infuriated her then melted her heart with his tenderness. She cleared her throat. 'I need to get back to the surgery but no doubt I'll be seeing you around.'

He offered a slow smile, his eyes burning into her. The dog whined and Leo was distracted, then flustered. 'Yes, I feel sure we'll be bumping into each other, given I'm here and you're just up the road... Right, so when all this happened, I was just on my way up to Ingleside Hall to attend one of Sir Philip's horses... So I need to hand this little fella over to my dad and get on with that.'

'Yes, right. The work still needs to be done,' she replied, already gathering herself. Then as she turned to walk away, she called over her shoulder, 'I hope the dog does well... See you soon, maybe?'

'Yes, of course,' he replied, sounding flustered.

By the time she was opening the door, she was desperately trying to work out if she was still reeling from the dog being run over or what had happened with her and Leo. She hadn't been kissed like that since her ex from Liverpool, Patrick Kavanagh, and it felt a little overwhelming, especially given they'd broken up because he'd cheated on her. She quickly pushed those thoughts aside and thankfully, now she was out in the street, the cold air sent a shiver through her body that helped to steady her.

'Is everything all right?' Mrs Hewitt called, bobbing out of the kitchen as soon as she was back at the surgery.

Lara hesitated for a split second, wondering how the housekeeper knew something had happened with Leo. With her next breath she realised of course that Mrs Hewitt was referring to the little dog. 'Yes, all fine. We got him sorted and it wasn't much different from treating a human casualty once we had him anaesthetised.'

'Good, that's good,' Mrs Hewitt replied as Lara followed her into the kitchen. Then, as the housekeeper reached the Aga and began to pour steaming water into the teapot, she called across, 'It's strange isn't it, when a helpless little creature gets injured, almost the whole village turns out. I saw grown men with tears in their eyes. And Ed Cronshaw, you know how he always comes across as such a tough guy, he was fighting to hold it back. But he's such a big softie under all that manly swagger.'

Lara heard the words 'manly swagger' repeat in her head, and it took her straight back to that kiss. She needed to suck in a sharp breath and Mrs Hewitt glanced to her with concern.

'Are you sure you're OK, Nurse Flynn?'

'Yes, of course,' she replied too quickly. 'I was just recalling what Leo was like after Vic Taylor had that go at me in the summer. He physically rose very strongly to my defence, but he also showed his gentle, protective side.'

Mrs Hewitt narrowed her eyes. 'But wasn't it Ed who came to your rescue that day, not Leo?'

Lara's cheeks flushed as she quickly offered, 'Yes, of course I meant Ed, not Leo. Sorry, I'm just a bit discombobulated by the little dog being run over.'

Mrs Hewitt was nodding but she had a shrewd, questioning look in her eye.

Lara knew she needed to distract the housekeeper, so she asked, 'Did anyone out on the street have any idea who the dog belongs to?'

The housekeeper sighed. 'No. And you know me, I got right in there and asked around but there was nothing beyond some rumour he belonged to poachers.'

'Yes, that's exactly what Leo was thinking,' Lara replied, drawing a sharp breath to stop her cheeks from flushing again.

Mrs Hewitt narrowed her eyes. 'I know you keep telling me you're fine, Lara. But I hope the whole thing with the dog hasn't upset you too much.'

'No, honestly. I'm fine.'

'Well, hopefully Leo will be able to find the dog's owner and explain that the whole thing was an accident. It's horrible to see a defenceless creature injured but when they run out right in front of you, there's nothing you can do.'

'Yes, let's hope he can find the owner,' Lara was saying, starting to feel more settled and able to control the flush of blood to her cheeks. 'Leo said he'll make enquiries in the pubs and around and about the local area when he gets back from Ingleside Hall.'

Mrs Hewitt raised both eyebrows. 'Ingleside Hall, hey. I suppose he's off up there to see Miss Philippa Harrington and one of her horses.'

'Well, he mentioned a horse, but he didn't say anything about Miss Harrington.' Then as Mrs Hewitt pursed her lips, Lara asked, 'What's that look for, Mrs H? I know when you're trying to hold back some gossip.'

'Oh, it's nothing really...'

'Mmm, I've only been working here six months and not six years, but I know you well enough by now to know it's not nothing.'

The housekeeper twisted her mouth. 'Well, it's just that there's a rumour going round the village that Leo isn't just going up to the Hall to see the horses.'

Lara felt the dull thud of her heart and when she tried to speak, she needed to clear her throat. 'Well, Leo is a grown man so he can do want he wants. But given he and Angus are so close, and we both know Angus can't ever keep anything to himself, I feel sure if there was something going on between Leo and Miss Harrington, our young doctor would have spilled the beans by now.'

Mrs Hewitt waggled her head as she considered what Lara had just said. 'Well, Angus has made one or two mild comments, but nothing substantial. And you know what the village is like for rumours. So yes, I agree, our young doctor can't keep anything to himself, so we'd definitely know by now.' The housekeeper had a faraway look in her eye as if she were still mulling things over. And not wanting any further discussion, Lara waited for the moment to move on.

Mrs Hewitt shrugged, pushed a strand of black hair from her cheek, and looked Lara straight in the eye. 'Anyway, lass, you finish your tea before it gets cold, and I'm just wondering if you'd like to sample one of my freshly baked ginger biscuits?'

'That would be very nice indeed,' Lara said a little too loudly, still trying to push back what had happened with Leo. But the feel of his lips lingered, sending a gentle pulse through her body. 'Oh for goodness' sake,' she breathed.

'What was that?' Mrs Hewitt frowned as she placed the biscuits on the table.

'Ooh, ginger biscuits,' Marion called as she bounded into the kitchen, immediately swiping one off the plate. 'Mmm, delicious,' she said through a mouthful of crumbs as she walked to sit opposite Lara.

'Stop eating those. You've not even had your breakfast yet,' Mrs Hewitt scolded good-naturedly.

'It's all right, ginger biscuits are just the thing with toast and coffee,' Marion replied through a mouthful of crumbs.

'Well, I'm amazed you slept through all that kerfuffle out on the street.'

'What kerfuffle?' Marion asked, wide-eyed with mischief as she reached for another biscuit.

'You tell her, Nurse Flynn. I can't seem to find my toasting fork... I bet Dr Bingham's had it in the front room; he's recently taken to making toast over the fire in there. It's like something from the olden days.'

Marion began to chuckle. 'Well, if that olden times thing takes off, we nurses will be wearing big skirts and extravagant starched caps.'

'Nothing wrong with the olden days. We had strict discipline and no messing back then,' Mrs Hewitt called over her shoulder as she strode past the table on her way to the sitting room.

Lara tried not to giggle as she reached for her cup and called across to Marion. 'No messing, what does that even mean?'

'No sex,' Marion replied with a wicked grin.

Lara coughed, and almost choked on her tea.

2

The weeks had flown by since Philippa Harrington, the daughter of Lord Harrington of Ingleside Hall, had invited Lara and Marion to dinner. Even though the invitation had been moved to the new year, they'd been so busy at the surgery that it seemed to have come upon them too quickly. And with the pressure of work, and the thought of sitting down to dinner in a formal way with a young woman who could switch and change her moods like light and shade on a blustery day, Lara was almost hoping an urgent call would come in to give her an excuse not to attend. Marion, of course, was very excited about attending and had already been planning what to wear. Lara knew she'd be able to manage; she could always play her part even if her heart wasn't in it, but what riled her was the way Philippa had framed the invitation as a way of thanking her and Marion for attending the victims of a car crash in the autumn: two young men who had been visiting the hall. Tragically, one of Philippa's close friends, Quentin, had died at the scene and the other man had been badly injured. But now with the distance of time, it didn't feel quite right to use a poor young man's death as a reason for an invitation to dinner. And it made Lara wonder if Philippa was struggling with her friend's death and perhaps needed some support.

Maybe it was something else entirely; her current thoughts were shot through with the intimacy she'd shared with Leo when they'd been attending the little dog. After all, at the Harvest Ball, Philippa had danced many times with the young vet and glared at Lara with every turn of the dance floor. It wouldn't take a genius to work out that the young lady of the manor had a thing for the vet. And given the tenderness of Leo's kiss, she felt sure Philippa's feelings for Leo weren't fully reciprocated... but then, she knew romantic entanglements could be tricky. She'd tried to take what had happened with Leo with a pinch of salt; they'd both been in a heightened state after attending the dog... and she'd told herself many times it was just that. But even as she thought over it, a warm flush crept up her neck.

She heard her Irish nurse friend, Maeve's, voice in her head. *Don't be getting too bogged down in the detail. Go with your heart, not your head.* It made her smile, but she still felt a little apprehensive knowing Leo would also be attending the Ingleside Hall dinner. She hadn't told anyone, not even Marion, that Leo had kissed her. Even at the thought of it she felt her skin prickle.

'Oh for goodness' sake, you just need to get yourself ready and go to the flipping dinner with her ladyship,' she muttered to herself as she sat alone in the empty kitchen, cradling her second cup of tea. Marion had already gone up to her room to change into her going-out clothes; she was off-the-scale excited about tonight and it had made Lara even more aware that she needed to make the best of it, for Marion's sake if nothing else.

As she got up from the table, Mrs Hewitt bustled into the kitchen. 'Ah, Nurse Flynn, I was just thinking about the arrangements for your night out. I know Angus has volunteered to drive you and Marion in the little blue Austin, but I'd rather you ask Dr Bingham to run you in the Rover, or we could telephone Percy Smith at the garage and see if he could chauffeur you. It would be more appropriate for a visit to the hall.'

Lara recalled their erratic journey to the Harvest Ball with the aged Mr Smith at the wheel of the charabanc. 'Oh no, Mrs H, we'll be perfectly fine with Angus... Marion was quite scared by Percy's driving. And even though Angus tends to speed, I'm sure Marion would rather go with him.'

'Yes, of course, I'd forgotten about Percy's driving... Although as far as I'm aware, he's never killed anyone. But maybe not Angus – perhaps Dr Bingham would be more appropriate.'

'No, honestly, it's fine, and given Angus isn't going to the pub as much these days, he'll be sober, and he'll probably enjoy a run out.'

Mrs Hewitt nodded. 'We need to encourage that, don't we? Especially now he's steadying up.'

'Yes, indeed,' Lara replied. But she also knew it was way too soon to make any sweeping assumptions regarding the young doctor's drinking habits.

* * *

Lara was ready in plenty of time and as she emerged from her room wearing a tailored skirt and a blue, silky blouse, Marion stepped out into the corridor in her culottes and the bright-pink blouse she'd worn for the Harvest Ball. With her red lipstick and mass of curly black hair, she looked stunning.

'Well, look at us two, all dressed up.' Lara smiled.

And as Marion walked up the corridor, she called, 'Well, Nurse Lara, what's not to like about us stepping out together in our silky blouses.'

'Nothing whatsoever.' Lara giggled, as Marion linked her arm.

And as they trotted together down the broad, red-carpeted stairs, Angus emerged from the kitchen, ruffling his fluffy, dark-blond hair. As soon as he saw them, he stopped in his tracks, his eyes shining. 'You two look very lovely indeed,' he called as they passed by to pull their coats from the hooks in the hall.

'Thank you, chauffeur.' Marion beamed.

'Right you are, ladies,' Angus called as he strode up the corridor to hold the front door open in mock-formality.

Mrs Hewitt stepped out of the kitchen. 'Let me have a look at you both,' she said as they both stood with their coats over their arms. 'You look smashing,' she said, her breath catching and her eyes shiny with tears. She raised a hand and called after them to have a good time as they slipped into their coats. 'And don't be worrying about any emergency calls. We have two doctors here, ready and waiting.'

'Please don't struggle though, if it gets busy. Telephone the hall and I'll come back,' Lara said as Marion pulled on her arm to get her through the door.

'It's fine, we've got it covered,' the housekeeper said firmly, offering a swooshing motion with both hands. 'Off you go and have a lovely time.'

The little blue Austin was parked out front and as Angus slipped into the driver's seat, Lara clambered in the back with Marion up front. As soon as Marion had the door closed, she twisted in her seat. 'I wonder if we should have offered Leo a lift?'

'Oh no, I'm sure he'll have made his own arrangements,'

Lara replied, feeling her breath catch, instantly pushing the suggestion aside because the thought of him squashing in the back of the car with her was far too unsettling.

'No, he said he'd already be there,' Angus called over his shoulder. 'Something about needing to check on that Arabian stallion of Lord Harrington's. The one with the sprained fetlock.'

'Mmm, so he says,' Marion offered with what felt like a nudge in her voice.

Lara drew a slow breath. It wasn't so much the thought of Leo and Philippa having some kind of flirtation; it was what had happened at the vet's surgery that she needed to fight against. But all thoughts of Leo passed in seconds as Angus revved the engine and roared down the cobbled street at some speed. And as they hurtled towards the humpbacked bridge, Lara gripped the leather seat in front as the lights from the cottages at either side whizzed by. When Angus anchored on the brakes before crossing the bridge, she was thrown side to side in the back of the car as he vigorously twisted the steering wheel. Her heart was pounding, and she almost shouted for him to slow down.

But Marion was there first. 'Steady on, Angus. We're not rushing to an emergency.'

He cackled then. 'That's as may be, Nurse Marion, but this little car loves to go fast. Especially at night when we can hardly see where we're going.'

Lara's stomach did another flip as they headed away from the village. But thankfully, Angus did slow down a little to counter the effect of driving along pitch-dark country lanes. Fortunately, the weather had been wet rather than icy in the last few days, so at least there wasn't much risk of skidding out of control. Just as she thought it, she felt the car twist and slide, and it made her breath catch. Angus righted the vehicle, but her heart had already picked up a staccato rhythm, and with her whole being she wished she could take over the driving.

Thankfully, she knew it wasn't too far now to the hall. In the autumn, she'd ridden this route many times on her bicycle to visit Robert Thompson, a young gamekeeper who'd sustained a nasty leg injury from a poacher's trap. And as they bounced along the rugged country lane, she distracted herself with thoughts of how satisfying it had been to see him healed and back to work. She'd told him of the invitation to the hall and with a twist of his mouth, he'd said, 'Good luck with that.'

She hadn't questioned him further because she'd known from her own brief encounters with the young lady of the manor that she could be tricky. Nice as pie one minute then she could switch and turn. She didn't want to prejudge however, so as Angus turned sharply into the long drive that led up to the hall, she tried to push aside her previous opinions.

As they arrived in a slow scrunch of gravel, the young doctor pulled up smartly outside the heavy wooden door graced by stone pillars. Marion slipped out of the front, while Lara scrambled from the more cramped back seat, and with a broad grin, Angus pipped his horn and skidded away. It felt suddenly quiet, even serene, as Lara linked Marion's arm and they walked to the door. They glanced to each other, almost giggly, as Lara rang the bell and they waited to be admitted. Then, at the sharp clip of heels inside the house, the door swung open and they were greeted by Mrs Stewart, the housekeeper, in her pristine black uniform and spotless white cap. 'This way please, ladies,' she said, walking ahead as Marion nudged Lara with her elbow and offered a wide-eyed glance. After the housekeeper had indicated for a young maid with tousled hair and a cheeky smile to take their coats and hang them on the hooks beside the telephone, she beckoned for them to follow.

The crystal chandeliers sparkled and the whole place felt light and warm, and it took Lara back to the Harvest Ball. She'd enjoyed a wonderful evening with plenty of dancing and champagne, until her ex from Liverpool, Patrick had turned up and caused a rumpus. She swallowed hard to push back those thoughts and hoped Patrick was now gone from her life for good.

'Ah, there you are, my nurses,' Philippa called as they were shown into a wood-panelled dining room with a highly polished table set with starched, white napkins and silver cutlery.

The young lady of the manor's use of 'my nurses' sounded possessive, and it irritated Lara, but she swallowed it down as Marion walked ahead to take Philippa's hand in greeting. 'Nurse Wright, thank you so much for coming. It's so lovely to see you again,' their hostess gushed. Philippa glanced in Lara's direction. 'And you, Nurse Flynn,' she said, her voice tightening.

Lara took her proffered hand, squeezing it firmly. 'Thank you for inviting us,' she said politely.

'Well, it's the least I can do after what you both did for my friend Alastair.' She snatched a breath. 'And of course dear Quentin.'

Lara couldn't help but feel for Philippa, especially when she saw the glisten of tears in her eyes and how hard she was working to keep them at bay. In that moment, Lara recalled how distraught, how traumatised the young lady of the manor had been at the scene of the accident and how she'd tried but failed to hold her back from seeing Quentin crushed to death in the driver's seat of the mangled car.

She was about to offer some gentle words, but Philippa smiled brightly, too brightly, her voice high-pitched as she directed her guests to their seats. 'I thought we'd use this, our small dining room, instead of the grand one, for our cosy get-together.'

'Yes, it's lovely,' Marion offered, glancing back to Lara with a split-second, wide-eyed flash of her eyes that said, *She thinks this is small.*

Philippa stopped, turned to them, looked first to Marion, then to Lara. 'Please take your places,' she said, gesturing to either side of the table. 'And I do apologise on Leo's behalf, but our young vet is still attending Samson – my father's stallion – so he might be a little delayed.'

'No worries,' Marion replied breezily as Lara's stomach twisted at the mention of Leo.

'So, we might as well make a start; I'll ring for the aperitifs,' Philippa said briskly, as Lara and Marion slipped into the seats at either side of the table and their hostess picked up a brass bell to ring for the maid.

Once the white-aproned, starch-capped young maid had delivered the drinks, she offered a bow and retreated.

Philippa picked up her crystal glass and raised it in a toast. 'Here's to us, ladies… and before Leo arrives, I just want to offer another most sincere thank you for what you did that day of the accident.'

Lara and Marion muttered their usual responses about it all being part of the work.

But Philippa offered a piercing gaze, first to Marion, then to Lara. 'No, this is when you nurses need to accept credit where credit's due. Your actions that day undoubtedly saved my dear friend Alastair's life.'

Lara felt the hairs at the back of her neck prickle at the warmth in Philippa's voice. And when she thought of how devastated the young lady of the manor had been that day of the accident, she felt sympathy for her as well. So she raised her glass to Miss Harrington and said, 'Well, as a profession, we nurses aren't good at accepting praise. So maybe it's time we did just that. So I propose a toast to you, Miss Harrington, and all of us who came through that awful day.' She raised her glass and Marion and Philippa followed suit, and it felt as if the three of them had a moment of unity.

The cheers seemed to break the ice and the three women chatted then, back and forth, across a range of safe topics. Philippa even enquired about the details of their nurse training and the work they'd done elsewhere. And she seemed amazed at Marion's account of nursing in the Highlands of Scotland, riding her motorcycle up mountain tracks to get to her more isolated patients.

'Well, ladies, if another war does come, we'll certainly know who to call, won't we?'

'That'll be us.' Marion grinned, raising her glass in another cheers.

All their drinks were finished by the time the tall, carved oak door opened abruptly and Leo strode in wearing a smart suit and white shirt but still tying his tie. He blew out a breath, then he was brushing the sleeves of his jacket. 'Sorry about that; the examination of the stallion took much longer than expected. But he's all strapped up now – just needs to rest that foreleg.'

'Excellent,' Philippa gushed, gesturing for him to sit at the opposite end of the oblong table.

As he sat, he nodded to Marion on his left, then to Philippa at the head of the table, but his eyes grazed quickly over Lara. It was enough though to make her breath catch. She felt ridiculous and knew she had to take a grip of herself. So she deliberately made eye contact with him, unflinching as she asked him to tell them more about the horse he was treating.

He smiled and seemed to relax as he gave the detail of the case. And as Lara nodded and asked pertinent questions, she had to fight to hold back a giggle at the stray pieces of straw in his dishevelled hair.

As time moved on, the meal was served and glasses were topped up first with sparkling white wine, then with red, and Lara began to relax despite the unsettlingly warm glances Leo regularly shot in her direction.

Even though Philippa had had many glasses of wine by the time the chocolate mousse dessert with a delicate dusting of icing sugar was being served, she was barely slurring her speech. But a little worryingly, she had begun to narrow her eyes at Lara and she almost scowled when Lara responded to some question Leo was asking. And as the young vet leaned back in his chair and began to tell the story of his and Lara's shared experience of treating the little dog he'd run into and had named Lucky, Lara felt the young lady of the manor's eyes burning into her.

In moments, Philippa was glaring, breathing heavily. Leo fell quiet and Lara focused on her white, porcelain pudding dish as she ate her dessert one tiny spoonful at a time. And as she felt the thick, dark chocolate mousse with its edge of bitterness slide down her throat, she knew the rest of this evening would not go well.

They were all eating silently and the scrape of silver spoons on porcelain felt unbearable in the heated silence. She could hear Leo's breath, sense him at the end of the table. It had begun to feel agonising.

Suddenly, Philippa shouted out, not words exactly, but a strangled scream. She jumped up from her seat, knocking over her wine glass.

In that split second, Lara gasped with shock, shot a glance to

Marion, who was wide-eyed, stupefied. Then Philippa screamed again, picked up her pudding dish and hurled it with some strength right down the table, straight at Leo. He deftly slipped sideways to avoid it. Then he was up from his seat, genuine concern in his voice. 'Philippa, are you all right?'

'No, I am not,' she raged.

Lara and Marion shared a startled glance.

Leo pushed back his chair, moved to Philippa at the head of the table. 'What is it? Are you unwell?' he asked gently.

'No, of course not,' she blurted angrily.

'Do you want us to leave?' he offered.

'No, of course not,' she repeated, her voice cracking on a sob.

Lara was standing up now, trying to work out a way of helping. Philippa glowered at her. 'Sit back down. I know what you're up to, Nurse Flynn, with all your nice chit-chat with Leo. Just so you know, Leo and I have been seeing each other all summer. And you come here thinking you can take him from me.'

'*What?*' Lara and Leo said at the exact same time.

Philippa turned to Leo. 'You know how close we've been. And now you're denying it because of *her*.' She thrust a hand in Lara's direction.

'Now, look here,' Leo said, glancing to Lara then back to Philippa. 'I've been here helping with the horses but—'

'But. Everything,' Philippa purred, but when she spoke again, her voice cracked at the edges. 'I know we've not made it public, Leo. But we have something special, you know we do.'

Leo glanced to Lara, knotted his brow, tried to speak but the words wouldn't come at first. Then he said quietly, steadily, as if he were trying to calm a skittish horse, 'I'm so sorry if there's been a misunderstanding here, Philippa. But what you've just said... it's news to me.' And Lara couldn't be exactly certain, but it did sound as if he were genuinely shocked.

Philippa narrowed her eyes, then she was shaking her head. She tried to take a step towards Leo but needed to grab the table to steady herself. And as a silver knife clattered to the polished wooden floor, she jabbed a finger in Lara's direction, and spat, 'She's the one who has poisoned you against me.'

'No, Philippa, honestly. Me and Nurse Flynn, we've never so much as talked about you.' He glanced to Lara, mouthed a sorry.

'I think we need to leave,' Lara called gently but firmly across to Marion.

'Yes, right you are,' Marion breathed as she pushed her chair back and rose from the table, her eyes bright, almost gleeful. Clearly, she was savouring the dramatic outburst.

'That's it, you go,' Philippa threw at Lara.

'I don't think we have any choice,' Lara said gently. 'But thank you for inviting us.'

'Yes, thank you,' Marion chimed as she pushed back her chair.

And as Lara raised a hand to Leo and mouthed, 'Good luck,' Marion trotted behind as Lara walked briskly to the door, her mind rapidly going through what had just happened. Maybe it was all down to too much wine. But Miss Harrington's outburst had come from somewhere and it might be a place where she had strong feelings for Leo which may or may not be reciprocated.

Out in the hallway, Lara went straight to the telephone she'd used previously when she'd been here in a professional capacity. She dialled the surgery number and when Mrs Hewitt answered, she requested a pickup. After she'd replaced the receiver with a firm click, then pulled their coats from the hooks on the wall, she steered Marion out through the stately front door. And just as she was pulling the door to, she heard Philippa emit another spine-tingling scream and hoped Leo was safe in there.

Marion glanced back with a wry smile, then she began to giggle. 'So much for posh folk and their formal dinners.'

'So much indeed,' Lara replied, already picking up on the absurdity of it all.

She would have liked to have started to walk back to the surgery, but Angus would need to turn the car anyway, so it was best to wait. And it felt peaceful now out here, with the heavy, carved front door firmly closed behind them. As they huddled together, their breath steaming in the bitingly cold air, Lara was already straining her ears for the sound of the little Austin. Then Marion began to chuckle, and Lara had to work hard not to pick up on it because once they were both caught, they could laugh till tears streamed down their faces. It would be unseemly and the last thing she wanted was to attract any attention from inside the hall, so she fought to keep a straight face by mulling over just what, if anything, was going on between Leo and Philippa. It made her feel uneasy about that kiss they'd shared, even though she'd already put it down to the heat of the moment after the dog was injured. But that didn't stop it being real. And now Leo was in there trying to defend himself when, of course, he knew full well what had happened. It all felt like a mess, and she didn't know what to think. Maybe Leo was good at lying to himself and he was far too casual about his relationships with eligible women. But his shock at Philippa's outburst had seemed genuine. And as Lara began to assess and reframe what had happened that day in the vet's surgery, the logical part of her told her it would be best to keep her distance from the young vet, at least for the time being.

She sighed involuntarily and Marion linked her arm and pulled her close. 'What a to-do,' her friend murmured, her voice holding the edge of another giggle. It made Lara feel warm inside and she snuggled up to Marion, their steaming breath mingling in the cold air. And as she gazed up to the ink-black sky and saw the twinkle of the bright stars, it felt as if she were just one microscopic fragment of something so huge, it could hardly be imagined. And in that moment, nothing seemed to matter.

3

Lara was feeling very cold and a little shivery by the time they heard the putter of the Austin in the distance. Even Marion seemed subdued and had fallen silent as they waited. Lara spoke then, keeping her voice low. 'Given Angus knows Miss Harrington on a personal level from their connections at boarding school, I think it best we keep what happened tonight to ourselves, don't you?'

'Yes, that makes sense,' Marion replied. 'That thing with him and Philippa is something we shouldn't get involved with. And we don't want to be responsible for spreading rumours. You know what Angus is like; he revels in that kind of thing. And when he's had a few, he'll be telling everybody in the pub.'

Lara was relieved by Marion's response. But when her friend spoke again, she felt thrown out. 'So, Lara. I've been mulling over that drama around the dining table. And I know it's probably all in Philippa's imagination... but is there anything you need to tell me about you and Leo?'

Lara had never lied to her friend, and she knew Marion would know if she did. So she swallowed hard then said, 'Well, there was a fleeting thing in the vet's surgery after we'd worked on that little dog Leo ran into. But it all feels confusing right now, so I'm not getting involved with any of it.'

'Ooh, what kind of "fleeting thing"?'

'I don't want to say.'

Marion was almost jumping up and down with curiosity. 'Did you kiss him? Did you?'

Instantly, Lara knew she should have stayed silent, but it was out now and there was no stopping Marion once she latched onto a tasty morsel of gossip. She knew she was closing the door after the horse had bolted but she had to try and limit the damage. 'Look, I gave you the information because I didn't want there to be any secrets between us. So yes, we kissed – it was brief, and it came out of a heightened situation with that poor little dog. And that's all there is to it.'

'Aw, you and Leo, what a lovely—'

Knowing Marion hadn't properly grasped what she'd just said about what had happened being fleeting, Lara spoke firmly. 'Stop right there. It was an "in the moment" thing. That's all. You're my best friend and I trust you; that's why I told you. So to make it clear, the kiss was something and nothing. Let's leave it at that.'

Marion was still smiling, then she nodded, slightly drunkenly. 'Right you are. And of course I'll keep your secret.' Then she was jigging up and down on the spot, emitting tiny squeaks of excitement.

'You need to stop that, right now,' Lara said, a note of exasperation creeping into her voice. But Marion was still jigging up and down. And as soon as the glint of headlights came at them from the Austin, she told Marion again, more firmly, 'You can't tell anyone. You need to promise.'

'I promise, Lara.' Marion giggled. 'Cross my heart and hope to die.'

As the car approached, catching them in its headlights, Lara reinforced what she'd just said. Then she added, 'And not a word about the bizarre twist of events that was served with dessert.'

'You mean Philippa throwing the pudding.' Marion cackled.

'Yes,' Lara said firmly, but even as she spoke, she felt a tickle of amusement in her belly and had to work hard to keep it at bay.

'How was dinner?' Angus called over his shoulder as Lara and Marion slipped into the back of the car. Lara mumbled some platitude about having a nice time, while Marion stifled a laugh.

Then, maybe because Angus didn't get a detailed response to his question, he launched into a monologue. 'Well, I bet the Harringtons put on a good spread. In fact, I've heard they have a new French chef who worked in one of the top-notch restaurants in London before he came up to Ingleside Hall.'

'Oh really?' Lara replied, nudging Marion when she clamped a hand over her mouth to hold back a laugh but snorted loudly instead.

Then Marion whispered with a delightful tickle of amusement in her voice, 'I'm just wondering if that was one of those restaurants where the guests throw chocolate mousse at each other?'

Lara fought to hold back a giggle as she clung to Marion in the back seat. Then the situation began to ease as the car bumped and lurched, and Angus launched into telling them about the evening he'd spent at the surgery with Bingham and Mrs Hewitt. 'The good old Doc was on fine form tonight; he was tucking into his malt whisky and holding forth on the advantages of being a single man. I mean, I can understand it myself, given I'm at an age now where my friends from boarding school and medical school are all getting married.'

'You toffs don't still have arranged marriages, do you?' Marion croaked from the back seat, clearly trying to distract herself from the chocolate mousse.

'Hah, no, at least not officially. It's just that they all seem to marry eligible young women from the families they know.'

'Oh, I see,' Marion replied, leaning forward, her interest piqued. 'So Angus, do you have an eligible posh woman waiting for you?'

'Not that I'm aware of. And as you know… I'm happy to spend my time going out with the lads right now. It's good to be with Ed and Leo doing all that man stuff in the Fleece, or should I use the pub's affectionate nickname, the Dorchester, given I've been identified as a "toff".'

'Well next time you see your friend, Leo, he might have had his wings clipped a little.'

Lara gave Marion a nudge.

'What do you mean? Has he finally got together with Pip, I mean Philippa?'

Lara nudged her again. Hard.

'Oh no, I'm not saying anything like that,' Marion replied, nodding as she gazed to Lara. 'It's just that the time might come in the near future… you know what I mean.'

'Yes, indeed,' Angus called over his shoulder. 'In other words, make hay… or should I say roll in the hay, while the sun shines.'

'That sounds a bit coarse, even to my ears,' Marion replied.

Angus laughed out loud as he crunched the gears to negotiate a corner. 'Sorry about that,' he said, dropping his voice.

'And we need to make the hay first, before we can enjoy the rolling in it.'

'I think that's enough,' Lara offered firmly. 'So why don't we change the convers—'

Angus rammed on the brakes then, shouting, 'What the hell was that?'

Lara and Marion had been thrown violently forward against the front seats, and the car engine had stalled. They were now skew-whiff across the country lane.

'Are you both all right?' Lara called, reaching for Marion.

'Yes, no harm done,' Marion croaked as she pushed herself back in the seat.

Angus called breathlessly, 'Yes, no harm done. I just can't work out what happened... It felt as if there was something in the road.'

In the next second, something bumped hard against the roof of the Austin and a face loomed at the passenger window. Lara shot back with shock as Marion screamed.

'Well, if it isn't our lovely nurses,' a rough voice shouted. Lara knew right away it was Vic Taylor, the man who'd threatened and attacked her in the summer.

Angus sat rigid at the wheel. Clearly, he had no clue what to do.

'Just get going, Angus,' Lara said firmly.

He nodded, but when he tried to restart the car, the engine emitted a depressingly slow response that fell far short of kicking the vehicle into life. The Austin was fully stalled and now there was ragged laughter from what sounded like other men.

Lara felt something click inside her. 'I'm not having this,' she said firmly.

Without even thinking of the possible consequences, she

pushed open her door and stepped out. Instantly, she made out the shapes of three men and there were dogs too that she saw in the light of the headlamps: thin, lurcher types.

She couldn't make out Vic's expression but when he spoke, his voice was lairy. 'So, nursey, of course you're the one who's being chauffeur driven around the country lanes.'

Lara raised her chin. 'There's no harm in that. In fact, we're expected back at the surgery urgently, so Dr Bingham has probably already set out to find us.'

'Has he now?' Vic smirked, calling back over his shoulder to the other two men whose vague outlines she could see in the gathered gloom. Vic leaned in so close, she could feel his stale breath warm on her cheek. 'I haven't forgotten we've got unfinished business, Nurse Lara. And now my wife and children have sold up my home and are living all nice and cosy in the village,' he dropped his voice then to an even rougher tone, 'something that I've been reliably informed was encouraged by you... Well, I'd take a bit more care if I were you, when you're out and about on the country lanes in the dark.'

Angus was opening his door now, but Vic was already walking away. Calling back over his shoulder, 'I'll no doubt be seeing you around, Nurse Flynn. Don't get too cosy at your doctor's surgery.'

Lara heard his words but the fury she felt overrode all of that. 'I'm as cosy as can be and nothing you or anyone else thinks they can do means anything at all.'

'She's got more balls than you, Taylor,' the gruff voice of one of his companions shouted.

Angus grabbed her arm. 'Come on, Lara. We need to get off.'

Sensing the panic in his voice, she had no choice but to climb back into the car.

'You've got some courage to speak to Vic Taylor like that,'

Marion said. 'But please be careful. I can't bear the thought of anything happening to you, Lara.'

'Don't you be worrying,' Lara replied, making her voice strong. But as the shock of the encounter hit her, she had to brace her body to stop herself from shaking.

Angus tried valiantly many times to restart the engine but the more he tried, the slower the engine made that sluggish, depressing noise as it turned over but didn't catch.

'Looks like we'll need to make the rest of the way on foot,' Lara offered.

Angus emitted a heavy sigh. 'Yes, I'm thinking the same. But we'll need to push the car to the side of the road otherwise somebody might run into it.'

Marion huffed and puffed as she began to get out, muttering, 'I wish I had my motorbike right now.'

'Come on, it's not too far to the village: maybe ten or fifteen minutes,' Lara said, lifting her voice to give encouragement.

Marion responded positively. 'Right. Come on. Let's get this lump of metal shifted.'

They were all out of the car now, Marion at the front, pushing with one hand and steering with the other, while Angus and Lara shoved hard from the back. The little car felt stuck at first, until they remembered to release the hand brake. Then it was easy to move along the lane as the light of the headlamps slowly died.

'Heave,' Angus ordered as they pushed one final time to get the car clear of the lane and into a gateway.

'I hope no one comes and veers sideways into it,' Lara said quietly, feeling uncomfortable at abandoning the little Austin she loved to drive whenever she got the chance.

'It's unlikely there'll be any other traffic at this time of night,'

Marion said. 'And we can send Stan Smith out from the garage first thing to rescue it.'

'Yes, that should be all right,' Lara said, making her peace with it because there was nothing else that could be done right now on a dark country lane.

Angus piped up then, his voice tight with anxiety. 'I hope Vic and his fellow poachers have moved right away and they're not going to cause any more trouble.'

'Nah, they're all talk, those sorts,' Marion replied.

Lara was just about to remind her friend how Vic had attacked her and tried to strangle her in the summer, but Marion grabbed her arm and hissed, 'No, don't remind Angus of what happened to you. He's afraid of the dark, so don't make him worse.'

'OK,' Lara whispered, feeling protective of the young doctor.

Then she remembered the torch in the boot of the little Austin, one she'd insisted on taking when she drove the car. She ran back, clicked open the boot and retrieved it. It wouldn't switch on at first, until she smacked it hard against her thigh. Then it offered a reassuring beam of light.

'We're good to go,' Marion called, as she linked Angus's arm and pulled him close. 'Don't worry, young Dr Fitzwilliam, we'll soon see the lights of the village and have you back safe and sound.'

Lara led the way with the torch as Marion and Angus followed. It felt strange to be out here on foot at this time of night and when a flying creature swooped low overhead, Angus startled and called out in fright.

'It's alright, just an owl,' Marion soothed.

Angus began to laugh. 'I'm sorry I'm so jumpy. As the only man present, I should be the one who leads the way and offers protection.'

Marion replied instantly, 'Well, we all know that's a bit of a myth. In my experience, it's usually the women who fearlessly take charge.'

'Fair enough, I won't argue with that.' He laughed. 'And it lets me off being the knight in shining armour.'

Lara glanced back to him and she was just about to speak when Marion shouted excitedly, 'Ooh, I think I can see a glint of light up ahead. It must be the village.'

'I hope it's not the torch of a poacher,' Angus said, an almost indiscernible quaver in his voice.

'No, it's definitely the village. Hurrah!' Marion replied, bounding forward.

* * *

'Whatever's happened?' Mrs Hewitt called as she strode up the corridor as soon as they burst in through the door.

Angus ran a hand through his hair. 'The car broke down; it stalled and wouldn't start. But we weren't far from the village, so we walked.'

Mrs Hewitt blew out a breath. 'Well, I can see you're all a bit muddy,' she said, glancing to Lara and Marion's going-out shoes and the bottom of Marion's culottes. 'But it's a good job you didn't run into Vic Taylor and his gang. They've been back causing trouble.'

'We did see them briefly out on the lane. But what's been going on here?'

'Well, there was a right rumpus in the middle of the street. Vic causing trouble with two of his ne'er-do-well pals. He was hammering on his wife, Alice's, door and they woke up the children. In fact, it's only just settled down after Dr Bingham threatened to call the police.'

'Oh, what's wrong with that man?' Lara hissed.

Mrs Hewitt was shaking her head. 'He's wrong, through and through. Little Lucy Taylor was terrified, and if it hadn't been for Alice's Uncle Josh coming straight out of the Old Oak to stand up to Vic who knows what might have happened.'

Lara groaned. 'I can't believe Vic's still hanging around. Clearly, he isn't welcome in the village.'

Mrs Hewitt sighed wearily. 'Well, I'm thinking you won't have much sympathy with this, Lara. But Dr Bingham did say, and I suppose he does have a point, Vic is still the father of Alice's two children, Lucy and Robin.'

Lara was about to reply with something along the lines of him not being fit to be their father, especially after he'd put his daughter's life at risk by compromising her recovery from a nasty leg injury. But she had to concede that Mrs Hewitt did have a point. Not that she'd ever want to see Vic have full access to the children. But yes, he was still their father.

'It's a complicated world, isn't it?' Mrs Hewitt sighed. 'Then again, Dr Bingham told Vic, and he made it clear, that although he was perhaps entitled to see his children, it wasn't right for him to come to the village at night and wake them up to do so.'

'Yes, quite right,' Angus said. Then he asked, 'Did Vic see sense?'

'Not at first, but he did in the end. That tall fella he brought with him though, I didn't like the look of him one bit. The other was just a young lad, a teenager, and he was scared to death. But we don't want men like that hanging around the village. I mean, they had those big dogs with them and Vic didn't hide the fact that he was now part of some gang in Ridgetown.'

Lara heard Marion suck a sharp breath and she felt sure she was about to tell Mrs Hewitt about their own encounter with Vic and the poachers in the lane. Lara nudged Marion and nodded to Angus, then whispered, 'She's worked up enough as it is without telling her what happened to us.'

Angus put an arm around the housekeeper's shoulders and led her to the kitchen. 'Come on, Mrs H. I think it's time for a hot cup of cocoa laced with brandy.'

'Ah, that sounds nice. Just what the doctor ordered,' Bingham quipped as he walked up the corridor from his room. Catching up with Lara, he murmured, 'I suppose Mrs Hewitt has told you about the shenanigans in the village tonight.'

'Yes,' Lara replied. 'And we stand united.'

'Steady on, Nurse Flynn, anybody'd think he'd been rattling at your door.'

There didn't seem any sense in trying to keep it quiet from Bingham as well, so she dropped her voice to speak in confidence. 'We've not told Mrs H; we didn't want to worry her. But we did encounter Vic and his cronies on our way back from Ingleside Hall... I think they laid something out on the road to stop the car. Anyway, once they'd gone, we couldn't restart the Austin, and we had to walk back.'

Bingham's brow scrunched hard. 'Are you OK? Did they threaten you in any way?'

'Not directly. But there was a definite sense of menace, and it scared the living daylights out of Angus.'

Bingham emitted a low growl. 'If they ever try anything like that again with any members of my team, I'll—'

'Lara,' Marion called from the kitchen. 'What the heck are you doing out there? We've got a stack of buttered crumpets here. Hurry up.'

'Righto,' Lara called with a single nod to Bingham, leaving him in the corridor, his forehead still scrunched with concern.

Then, as she took her seat opposite Marion, Angus helped Mrs Hewitt serve the brandy-laced cocoa which he insisted on sprinkling with grated chocolate. Bingham walked in and slipped into his seat at the head of the table. And once they were all sipping their cocoa and Marion had a sheen of butter from the crumpets all the way around her mouth, their chat turned to the visit to Ingleside Hall – without the detail of Philippa's pudding slinging, of course. And as the gentle rhythm of their conversation punctuated by laughter played back and forth across the table, Lara felt her mind and body begin to relax.

4

A few days later, on a crisp, bitingly cold morning with the village rooftops outlined pin sharp against a clear blue sky, there was an urgent call from a local farmer, Tom Douglas. Two of his children had fallen ill with a fever and he was very concerned about both, but especially the youngest, Poppy, who had a heart murmur. Lara was despatched right away and as she pushed hard against her bicycle pedals, she shivered inside her thick district nurse's overcoat. Knowing Tom was a level-headed farmer used to dealing with all kinds of animal ailments and emergencies, she felt her stomach twist at the realisation there was real cause for concern here. Her head began to swirl with potential diagnoses and in the end, all she could do was cycle hard until her legs hurt to stop herself from getting het up even before she laid eyes on the children.

The call from Tom Douglas felt frustrating because she'd promised to ride up to his farm for a brew of tea and a slice of cake every time she'd seen him since her first day as a country nurse, when she'd helped him deliver a calf. But her busy schedule had never allowed any time, and she felt sorry now that this visit had been sparked by the Douglas's two young daughters, Emma and Poppy, falling ill. As she approached the whitewashed shippon and turned right onto the farm track, her heart twisted at the prospect of what she might find. In the dark and cold of winter, the nastier childhood ailments could spread like wildfire, and she'd seen the tragic consequences during her work at the Liverpool Royal Infirmary and out on the district. Hopefully, this call would lead to a diagnosis of nothing more than a simple fever that would come and go in a few days, leaving the children unscathed.

But even as she parked her bicycle against the gritty stone wall of the farmhouse, she sensed the untoward quiet of the farm. The house had an unusual, closed-up feeling that sent a shiver of unease through her. And as she walked over the cobbles to the farmhouse door, the chained-up yard dog offered a sorrowful whine as it poked its nose out of the kennel. It filled her with apprehension and she needed to steel herself to knock on the door as she stood with her leather medical bag gripped tightly in her left hand. Almost immediately, she heard brisk footsteps inside the house and the moment Tom opened up, she felt a dull thud of shock at his pale face and harried expression. Gone were the smiles and the rosy cheeks of the man she'd seen out and about on the country lanes with his dog.

'Thank goodness you're here, Nurse Flynn,' he breathed, running a hand through his pale wisps of hair and for a moment, he seemed unable to say or do anything else.

'Can you take me to the children?' she prompted gently.

'Yes, of course. This way,' he replied, gesturing for her to follow.

As they climbed the steep, carpeted stairs, Lara noted a selection of children's drawings pinned to the wall: images of sheep and cows and one of a dog.

'Looks like you've got a budding artist in the family, Tom,' she offered, trying to reduce the steely tension that held the farmer's shoulders rigid.

'Aye, that's Emma, our eldest girl. She's a dab hand with a pencil and crayons.'

He came to a halt abruptly at the sound of a hacking cough and the mournful wail of a small child. Then came the murmur of a woman's voice from an open door along the landing. Tom began to move, picking up his pace as he called back to Lara, 'That's Poppy, the youngest. Poor little mite, she's been struggling all night long with a nasty cough. And she's the one with the dicky heart.'

As Lara followed Tom into the dimly lit room, she saw two white-faced little girls lying side by side in a double bed: the older one, Emma with an arm flung out to the side; Poppy, the three-year-old with the same light-brown hair as her sister, curled on her side as if she were still in the womb. Their mother, Moira was kneeling beside the bed, her face white and drawn.

'Thank goodness you're here so quick,' Moira called, her voice breaking as she stood up from the bed. 'This didn't seem much to worry about last evening, but now, with this fever, runny nose, sore throat and cough, Poppy's like my sister was all those years ago with the diphtheria.'

Lara's throat tightened, the timbre of that choking cough, the listlessness of the child, already supported Moira's theory.

She placed her medical bag firmly down on the floor beside the bed, then glanced over to Moira and spoke gently. 'So, just as a precaution, and this is something I do for all potentially infectious cases, I'll get a gown and a face mask from my bag.'

She heard Tom gulp back a sob.

'Just routine practice at this stage,' she said, glancing to him as she pushed her arms into the white cotton gown.

He cleared his throat, nodded, but Moira was stricken, her face drained of colour. Diphtheria was better managed now with the antitoxin that could be administered but it was still a killer of tiny children. Lara had had a mild dose as a child and she had a fleeting memory of a very sore throat, feeling shivery, and lying awake all night. And something that would always stay with her: the feel of her Aunt Matilda's hand as she sat by her bed and held vigil. No birth mother could have given better attention to a sickly child, and her aunt had shown her mettle again the next year when Lara had been struck down with scarlet fever. She knew from her experience on fever wards that it was often potluck as to whether children survived or succumbed to these nasty infections. But given Poppy's underlying heart condition, the youngest girl was at increased risk here.

Once she'd donned her white cotton gown and mask, she explained the need to first take a reading of pulse and temperature. After this was done and she'd recorded her findings – low-grade fever and rapid pulse for Emma, high fever and worryingly quick pulse with missed beats for Poppy – she took Tom and Moira gently aside and told them about the throat swab that each of the girls would need. It would involve the use of a tongue depressor and would be uncomfortable, but it was key to diagnosis. And if this was diphtheria, it was also crucial to check the back of the throat for the white membrane that could form and obstruct a child's airway.

Moira swallowed hard, nodded, while Tom drew some slow breaths.

The two girls in the double bed looked even more vulnerable now.

'So, I'll start with Emma, if that's all right. And, Tom, if you could hold her for me and try to soothe her, it might make things easier.'

He was straight there, already speaking quietly to his eldest daughter, telling her exactly what the nurse was going to do.

Lara stooped over the bed and spoke gently. 'I'll be as quick as I can, but just for a few seconds, this will feel bad. But if you keep still while your daddy holds on to you, that would be so good because it will make it easier. Are you ready?'

Emma's eyes were brimming with tears, but she nodded bravely.

Lara felt her gut twist with sympathy for the girl and instantly, she was speaking softly to her. 'You cry if you need to, Emma. Your throat must be very sore. But I'll be as quick as I can, I promise.'

'All set, blossom?' Tom said gently, on his knees now by the side of the bed and cradling his daughter.

Emma gave a single, determined nod.

'Right then,' Lara said, leaning over the bed, right next to Tom as he held his daughter in position. 'Now open wide, say ahh for me. That's good, Emma. So good.'

Swiftly, Lara inserted the tongue depressor, and as Emma gagged, she flashed the light from her torch to see a very inflamed throat. Then she grabbed the throat swab and went straight back in. Emma gagged again, harder this time, and as Lara withdrew the tongue depressor she began to retch.

'Well done, Emma. Good girl,' she offered, as Tom released his hold on his eldest daughter. And as Lara slipped the swab into a glass test tube and applied a cork stopper, she spoke softly to Emma. 'Your throat looks red, and it must be very sore, so you need to stay in bed for now. Get plenty of rest and keep taking as many sips of water as you can.'

'You'll do that, won't you, blossom,' Tom said gently. Then he straightened the bed covers over his daughter. 'You snuggle down now.'

Emma nodded, swallowed hard. 'Thank you, nurse,' the sweet little girl croaked, and it made tears prick Lara's eyes.

Focusing her attention on Moira now at the far side of the bed, she noted the tense set of her shoulders as she knelt beside her youngest daughter, Poppy.

Lara took her equipment and a fresh swab and walked around the bed. As Moira opened her mouth to speak, Poppy began to cough, then she howled with pain and grabbed at her tiny throat.

'Her throat is so sore, I can't bear to see her like this,' Moira sobbed.

Lara stooped down to Poppy, smoothed back damp tendrils of hair from her fevered brow, offered some soothing words. Then right away, her stomach lurched when she noted the fine, telltale rash over the little girl's face and neck. Even without the swab results, she was certain that this was diphtheria. And this youngest child, the one with the heart murmur, she had a much nastier dose.

Lara was already aware that taking the throat swab from this little one who was just three years old would be much more challenging. And she'd probably already been subject to scary medical procedures at the hospital due to her heart murmur.

'She doesn't like white coats or any hospital uniforms,' Moira offered with a quaver to her voice. 'So do you want to put my pinny over the top of your white gown? I've been wrestling with these two girls all night long, so it won't be clean. But I suppose you'll need to launder your own gown as soon as you get back to the surgery.'

'Yes, that makes sense,' Lara said as Moira stripped off her brown apron and handed it over.

Lara knelt beside the bed and spoke softly to the little girl,

'Hello, Poppy. I can see you're feeling poorly. Is it all right if I take a little look at you?'

'Nooo,' the child wailed, her voice tight and very hoarse.

Lara gulped back a breath, her heart going out to the tiny child, but she knew she had to perform the examination and take that swab because this little girl's life was hanging in the balance.

She drew a slow breath, dropped her shoulders, spoke in her most soothing of bedside voices and Poppy did quieten. But as soon as Lara made to move closer, the tiny girl with soft, tousled hair coughed and squealed in distress. 'No, Mummy! Don't let her hurt me.'

Moira had tears streaming down her cheeks, but she swallowed hard, spoke firmly. 'Poppy, you have to let the nurse have a look at you. She's here to help.'

'No,' Poppy tried to shout but her voice gave out.

Tom walked around from the far side of the bed and spoke quietly to Moira. 'We're going to have to hold her, like we do with the lambs.'

Moira hiccupped a sob, but she nodded. She knew what had to be done.

'Now, Poppy,' Tom called gently as he leaned down to her, so tiny in the big bed. 'This nice nurse needs to look down your throat to see where it's sore. And then she can start to make it better.'

He moved carefully as he slipped an arm under his daughter and cradled her gently in a position where she could be held.

Lara prepared her spatula, torch and swab.

Tom glanced to her and spoke quickly under his breath. 'When she starts to howl, do what you need to do.'

Lara nodded. She was ready.

'So, Poppy, can you open your mouth very wide for the nurse?' Tom asked.

'No,' Poppy croaked with all her might and that's when Tom strengthened his grip on the child as she began to fight against him.

The moment she opened her mouth to scream, Lara was straight there with the tongue depressor and torch, then in and out with a quick swab.

'All done, little one,' she called as she broke off the swab and corked it in the glass test tube, making sure to pencil in the child's name right away so the specimen wouldn't be confused with her sister's.

Poppy was sobbing, coughing, hiccupping, as Tom cradled her, his own voice breaking as he tried to soothe her.

Moira turned to Lara. 'So, what is it? What have they got?' she asked urgently.

Given the directness of the question, Lara had no choice but to reply openly. 'We'll know for certain when the results come back from the swabs. But based on the examination alone, I'm pretty sure your daughters have diphtheria. And as you are no doubt aware, Poppy is more poorly than her sister. Thankfully, I can't see any sign of the white membrane that can form at the back of the throat. But as you will no doubt know, if the infection does progress and the membrane forms, it is a very serious complication.'

Moira clamped a hand over her mouth, nodded gravely. When she spoke again, her voice broke. 'Yes, I'm very much aware of how serious this is… My sister had diphtheria, and she was struggling to breathe, and the doctor came and made a hole in her throat, just here…' She pressed her fingers to a place just below her Adam's apple. 'It was awful; there was blood everywhere. But she survived.'

Lara nodded. 'Your description is spot on, but let's hope it doesn't come to that for either of your girls. And I'm sorry we need to have this conversation now, but parents must know all of this when they're nursing their children. So any signs of breathing difficulty or further weakening, or you're just plain worried, call the surgery immediately and we'll come straight out, day or night.'

Moira nodded and when she spoke again, her voice was steadier. 'Thank you, Nurse Flynn, for all you've done already and for being straight with us.' Then she reached instinctively to where her apron pocket should be for a handkerchief.

'I think you might need this back,' Lara said gently, untying the brown apron and handing it over.

Once she had her equipment collected and the throat swabs neatly labelled and secure in her medical bag, Tom walked with her back down the stairs. As they entered the kitchen, Lara noted the carved marks of the children's heights on the door jamb, each name carefully inscribed with pencil at every measuring. Of course the eldest, Richard, was way above the two little ones, especially Poppy, who was tiny, even compared to Emma. It made Lara's breath catch and when Tom turned with a flash of concern in his eyes, she needed to force a steady expression.

As soon as they were within reaching distance of the back door, Tom turned to her and said, 'Can I ask a quick question, Nurse Flynn?'

'Yes of course, Tom. Fire away.'

'Our eldest, Richard, he's at school today. But given the girls are infected, should we keep him at home from now on? He's had his share of fevers, like all children do, but this diphtheria, do you think he's at risk of catching it as well?'

'So, let me say first that I'll be speaking to Dr Bingham as soon as I get back to the surgery and if he thinks it's necessary, we'll be advising all schools within a radius, and especially the one in the village, to close immediately. And with regard to Richard, I can't say for sure, and diphtheria can affect older children, but in my experience, it's mainly the younger ones who suffer the worst of it. And some cases aren't particularly symptomatic so it's possible he's already had it. Has there been a diphtheria outbreak in Ingleside before?'

'Yes, but it was before the girls were born and we escaped that one... but maybe Richard didn't and like you say, he fought it off.'

'Exactly so,' Lara replied. She reached out to place a gentle hand on the man's arm as he stood pale and harried, and so desperately worried about his children. 'So, all you can do, Tom, is keep going as best you can. If this is diphtheria, I'm certain you won't be alone; this outbreak will affect many other families. So we need to stand our ground and one way or another, we'll come through this together.'

She heard him hold back a sob, then he nodded. 'Thank you, Nurse Flynn. And how long will it be before we know the result from the swabs?'

'It can take a few days but from what I've just seen, with the fine red rash over Poppy's face and neck, I feel confident in diagnosing two cases of diphtheria.'

He swallowed hard. 'Right you are. So what do we need to do now?'

'You need to keep the children isolated; don't allow contact with anyone apart from you, Moira and Richard. Just keep nursing them as you are doing... but, and I'm sure you know this already, if there is any difficulty breathing for either of the girls, call the surgery immediately. I won't lie to you, Tom, this could be a bumpy journey... so all we can do is get the antitoxin into them as soon as we can, isolate the affected children and close the school. The whole community have to work together but we will get through this.'

Tom blew out a breath, nodded. 'Thanks for being straight with me,' he croaked.

'It's the best way to be,' she said firmly. Then she patted his arm. 'Chin up, Tom. Let's just keep going. And you tell Moira I'll be back tomorrow morning unless you need me before.'

As Tom said his goodbyes and closed the door, Lara felt her body slump. So much for her strong words – she knew this was going to be a hell of a fight. But even as she thought it, she heard the voices of the senior nurses she'd worked with telling her to stand firm and get on with it.

Lara had other planned visits but right now, she needed to cycle straight back to the surgery and report her findings. There were strict protocols to be followed, and it had to be done swiftly and properly to hold back the spread of infection. She knew from her previous experience in Liverpool that inevitably, now the first cases had been identified, there would be many more. At least for the families living out here on the farms, it would be easier to isolate the children. The village, however, might be an entirely different story. As she pushed hard against her bicycle pedals, she prayed the infection would be confined to the farms. But then, the farmers' children attended the village school, so it was probably too late for that.

She gripped the handlebars tightly with her leather-gloved hands, oblivious now to the clear blue sky and fresh nip in the air. After reporting back to Bingham at the surgery and handing over the swabs to be sent to the hospital laboratory in Preston, her first stop would be straight to Ingleside School to inform the head teacher, Mr Armistead. What a facing that would be for the young headmaster, new to the village.

5

Dr Bingham visibly blanched as Lara relayed the detail of the diphtheria cases and explained why she was sure of the diagnoses even before the throat swab results came back. He'd seen many cases over his long career and had witnessed the loss of several children, so he was in full agreement that quarantine measures needed to be applied immediately. It felt reassuring to know he supported the bold move. Facing this was daunting but the sooner they stopped the infection spreading, the better the outcome. She'd only worked through one outbreak in Liverpool but during that time, she'd sat by the beds of children who'd died from the nasty infection. So as she made her way on foot to report to Mr Armistead, the new, young headmaster of Ingleside School, she gathered herself, worked through the detail of the organised response which had been forming in her head. The first step of which was to close the school.

She found Mr Armistead in the corridor outside the classroom.

'Hello, I'm Nurse Flynn, one of the nurses from Ingleside

Surgery,' she called to him. 'I'm sorry to interrupt you during school hours but I need to speak to you urgently.'

He scrunched his brow, narrowed his eyes, already picking up on the gravity of her tone. 'Yes, of course, that's absolutely fine. Do you want to come to my office or are we all right here?'

'If we stay here, will the children hear us?' she asked, glancing to the classroom through the half glass door to see it full of children of mixed ages: tiny ones through to early teens. Because in a small village school, all are taught together.

'No, we're safe. The door's solid so even the pupils with the sharpest ears won't be able to hear.'

'Well, I'm sorry to come here today with troubling news but I need to let you know immediately that two cases of diphtheria have been diagnosed on a nearby farm.'

He blew out a breath, doubled over slightly. 'Oh dear, that's not good,' he said, shaking his head, then running a hand through his wavy, brown hair. He fixed her with his pale-blue eyes. 'We have a few children off sick at present; are the affected ones of school age?'

'Yes, one is – Emma Douglas.'

He tutted, then muttered, 'She's a lovely little lass and a very good pupil. Will she be all right?'

'I'm sorry, Mr Armistead but it's too soon to say. But she's doing better than her little sister.'

'Yes, that'll be Poppy. Is she the one with the heart murmur?'

'Yes, she is.'

He swallowed hard, visibly upset. Then he ran a hand around his face and spoke firmly. 'Right, so Nurse Flynn, tell me what you need.'

She opened her mouth to speak but they both startled at a harsh, rasping cough that came from inside the classroom. 'I'm hoping that's the lad who's always coughing.' He glanced into the classroom, his face relaxing a little when he'd identified the boy. 'Yes, that's him... Thank goodness for that.'

The cough had settled but Lara's senses still felt heightened as her body fizzed with anxiety. Then Mr Armistead spoke softly and fixed her with a gentle gaze, and she was soon running through the detail of the plan. The first step of which was to close the school from going home time today.

Once he was done, the headmaster cleared his throat, and said quietly, 'This is going to be a very challenging time, particularly for you and your team. But thank you for coming straight here. We had diphtheria in my previous school and two children from the reception class – a bonny lad and his twin sister – they both died.'

Lara swallowed hard. 'I'm sorry to hear that. And I know how daunting this will be. But all we can do is put strict quarantine measures in place as soon as possible.'

'Yes, of course. I understand.' He nodded solemnly, still running a hand through his hair. Then he glanced protectively into the classroom of children and she could see how harrowing this was for him. She followed his line of gaze to see young Robin, Alice Taylor's son. When he spotted her, he smiled as she raised a hand to him. And on the next desk was Michael Lennox, the young lad she'd worked closely with when his mother had been diagnosed with puerperal psychosis. He and his younger brother and sister were still living with their father at the big house of an elderly spinster, Miss Dunderdale, who'd taken the family in. And the new baby of the family, Jamie, was being cared for by a kindly neighbour, a farmer's wife. So the Lennox family had had a lot to deal with, and Michael had been so excited about starting school, it unsettled her now to think of how the closure might disrupt him.

She sighed, switched her attention back to Mr Armistead.

He looked distracted. 'My teaching assistant is off today so I need to get back in there, give the pupils some reading or colouring so I can get to the office to telephone the school board.'

'Right, yes, of course,' she said, sensing the tension in him as he took her proffered hand and squeezed it very firmly.

She walked briskly back to the surgery and was about to cross the cobbled street when she almost collided with Leo as he dashed up the hill with the Jack Russell terrier in his arms.

'Aargh, sorry,' he cried. Then: 'Oh, it's you, Lara...'

Instantly, she saw the dog wasn't doing well. 'What's going on? Has he taken a turn for the worse?' she almost shouted.

'Yes, I think so... He was making a good recovery. But now he's lethargic and on the point of collapse. And I'm looking for my dad because we've run out of ether in the surgery and I need to give him a whiff and remove his plaster cast, so I can examine for infection.'

'I see,' she breathed, glancing up and down the street for any sign of Mr Sullivan senior.

'Damn it, he said he was going up to the Fleece to check on the pub cat and he took the van because he's got a bad knee, and he can barely walk. But now there's no blithering sign of him or the van.'

The little dog let out a thin whine and Lara felt her heart clench.

'Look, I can't guarantee this will be allowed, but we've got a jar of ether in the clinic room. Why don't I ask Dr Bingham if you can use a whiff of that?'

Leo's face brightened. 'Yes, good thinking,' he said, already crossing the street beside Lara with the dog still whining in his arms.

* * *

Just in through the surgery door, she motioned to Leo and said, 'Wait there. I need to speak to Dr Bingham first.'

Luckily, the senior doctor emerged from his clinic room and, quickly, Lara explained the situation.

Bingham frowned hard, pursed his lips, then the dog whimpered pitifully once more, and he motioned for Leo to follow. 'Come on, young vet… Just a quick whiff of anaesthetic, then you need to take the little fella back to your surgery for the examination.'

'Yes, of course,' Leo replied, glancing over his shoulder to mouth a quick thank you to Lara. And in moments, he reappeared with the dog limp in his arms. He offered a nod, then walked briskly towards her and planted a gentle kiss on her cheek.

'What the heck,' she hissed, feeling her face flush. He turned to stride away but she grabbed his arm. 'This can't go on, Leo. Not with everything you're involved with up at the Hall.'

'Don't worry about that. It'll get sorted,' he said, then he was heading towards the door with the little dog resting like a baby in the crook of his arm.

It felt frustrating not to have a firm line drawn under what had happened with Leo in the vet's surgery and then up at Ingleside Hall. But right now, with all she had going on professionally, she had no choice but to push it aside.

'Leo,' she called urgently after him. 'There's a new diphtheria epidemic; the school will be closing, and we'll have to impose isolation. So spread the word if you ever find your work van and you can get out to the farms.'

His eyes flashed with alarm. 'Sorry to hear that and yes, of course I'll do that. I had a mild dose as a kid but one of the lads from school died.'

'I know, it's grim,' she replied, feeling the weight of it again.

Leo frowned deeply and when he spoke again, his voice was uncharacteristically sombre. 'I'm sorry for what you doctors and nurses will be facing. And if there's anything we at the vet's can do to help, just say the word.' Then, with a fleeting twinkle in his eye, 'And if I don't see you for a while, let's hope we can pick up where we left off when you helped me with this little fella.'

She was already shaking her head, and she growled under her breath, 'Not now, Leo. It's not the right time.'

He threw her a smile as he strode away with the dog still sleeping in his arms. Then, struck by concern for the creature, she called after him, 'When you open up that leg wound, make sure to irrigate thoroughly with plenty of carbolic acid solution.'

He turned with a grin, briefly saluted. 'Will do, Nurse Flynn.'

Then, he was gone, out into the street.

Her heart was beating fast, and she needed to draw a slow breath to collect herself. 'I've no time for this,' she muttered under her breath as she walked towards the kitchen.

Mrs Hewitt shot her a stricken glance as soon as she was in through the door, but then the housekeeper lifted her chin. 'Dr Bingham filled me in on the diphtheria cases. So, anything you need – ordering of supplies, telephone calls, whatever – you come straight to me.'

'Righto, Mrs H,' she replied briskly, her mind whirring over plans.

The housekeeper was already pouring a cup of tea and motioning for her to sit down.

'What, no. I mean yes, thank you. I'll have the tea, but I won't sit down. I need to catch up with my remaining visits, then over lunch, as a team, we'll firm up plans for managing any further cases of diphtheria.'

'Sounds like you're well on with it already,' Mrs Hewitt said encouragingly.

Lara drew a slow breath. 'I hope so, Mrs H. I truly do.'

* * *

Later, after she'd caught up with her visits, and Angus and Marion had been briefed on the outbreak, the telephone began to ring loudly on the table at the bottom of the stairs. Knowing Mrs Hewitt was busy assisting Dr Bingham with the ordering of supplies to cover the diphtheria epidemic, she picked up the receiver.

'Hello, this is Nurse Flynn, Ingleside Surgery.'

'Oh, Nurse Flynn, thank goodness it's you,' a woman's voice called raggedly. Then all she could hear was a succession of deep sobs.

Lara spoke gently. 'I know you are distressed but I'm here and ready to listen. So when you feel able, tell me what is wrong.'

'Oh, Nurse Flynn,' the woman croaked. 'It's me, Moira Douglas... My little Poppy is much worse; she's struggling to breathe.'

Lara's heart lurched painfully, and she needed to suck a quick breath. 'Are her lips still pink, Moira?'

'Nooo,' she wailed. 'They're bluish and she's making a horrible noise when she breathes.'

'Right, Moira – I'll get one of the doctors and we'll come straight out. But I'm also going to call an ambulance. You go back to her now; we'll be there as quick as we can. Is Tom with you?'

'Nooo,' she wailed again. 'He had to go out to the fields to one of the cows.'

'Try to stay calm,' Lara said steadily, listening as Mrs Haworth began to breathe more slowly. 'We're coming. I'm putting the phone down right now.'

Lara's heart was pounding as she slammed the receiver back into its cradle and ran to the kitchen. No Mrs Hewitt, what the heck? Where was everybody? There was still one patient in the waiting room so there had to be one of the doctors in surgery. She sprinted down the corridor, knocked briskly on the door before bursting through.

Angus lifted his head from the patient's notes he was reading.

'Is Dr Bingham here?' she almost shrieked.

His eyes were round; he knew this was dire. 'No, he's out to Miss Dunderdale's; she's had another fall. What is it?'

'I need you right now. Little Poppy Douglas, one of the diphtheria cases, her mother just rang. The child is in respiratory distress and highly likely to require an emergency tracheotomy.'

'Oh my God,' Angus exclaimed as he jumped up from the desk, knocking the notes and sending them scattering to the floor. He ran to the corner of the room, calling over his shoulder, 'Thank God Bingham already prepared an emergency pack for just this scenario.'

'I'll get the Austin; you bring the equipment,' she shouted as she ran from the room.

The patient in the waiting area – a middle-aged woman – jumped up from her seat, mildly out of breath, her eyes wide with concern. 'I can see you've got your work cut out. I'll come back another day.'

Lara called a thank you as she ran by. Then spotting Mrs

Hewitt in the kitchen, she relayed the detail of the case and grabbed her medical bag and legged it to the car.

As soon as she'd reversed the little blue Austin, Angus was piling in with his medical bag and Bingham's emergency pack. He sounded out of breath, then he huffed, 'I'm glad you're driving; I need to run through the emergency tracheotomy procedure in my head.' Then after sucking in more air, he said, 'I've only ever performed one on a child and that was years ago, when I was a medical student.'

Lara felt her heart clutch at his lack of experience; she'd hardly worked with Angus and certainly hadn't seen him perform surgery. But as she motored down the cobbled hill as fast as she could, she gritted her teeth, knowing there was no other choice but for the young doctor to do what he could.

As she drove the distance to the Douglases' farm, Angus sat silently in the passenger seat, checking the equipment in his bag, muttering to himself about procedure. She felt heartened that he was going over it, but she prayed his hands would be steady when he used that scalpel. Tiny children had tiny throats and there was no margin for error when major blood vessels lay close by.

He'll manage; he'll have to, she told herself. Focusing on the perfect stitches he'd applied for a young son of a local farmer, Peter Valentine, when the lad had sliced open the inside of his leg. But she hadn't seen Angus apply the sutures; maybe it had taken him ages. Instantly, she tightened her grip on the steering wheel. *No, don't go there; this is stressful enough without making it worse.*

As she bumped as fast as she could up the rutted lane to the Douglases' farm, she repeated in her head that all would be well. Pulling up sharp, she was yelling for Angus to follow as soon as she jumped out of the car. Already running, she sent a flock of brown hens squawking and flapping as she aimed directly for the farmhouse door.

Mildly out of breath as she pushed open the door, she shouted, 'Moira. It's Nurse Flynn and Dr Fitzwilliam. We're coming straight up.'

As soon as they started running up the stairs, her heart twisted at the loud, stertorous noise of little Poppy fighting for breath. The moment before they reached the door, Lara slowed her pace and turned to Angus to quickly murmur, 'Let's walk in so we don't cause more panic.'

His bright eyes shot her a glance, and he offered a single, determined nod, then followed her in through the door.

Moira was kneeling by Poppy, her face ashen, her eyes brimming with tears as she clutched the little girl's hand. 'Her breathing's terrible,' she called brokenly. 'Even in these last few minutes, it's got much worse.'

'We'll sort it, Moira,' Lara said firmly, her heart clutching when she saw Poppy's sunken eyes and the deep-blue tinge to her lips. They had moments, that's all, to save the little girl's life.

Angus was already opening his pack on the bottom of the bed, while Lara pulled down the covers, exposing the child's pale, tender throat. Gently, she opened the girl's mouth and saw the white membrane blocking her airway.

Angus was straight there as Lara spoke quickly to Moira and indicated for her to go to the opposite side of the bed where Poppy's sister lay pink-cheeked and peacefully sleeping. 'We need to make an incision in her windpipe, like the one you told me your sister needed when you were little.'

'Yes.' Moira gulped. 'I thought that's what would happen.'

'All set,' Angus called.

Poppy's lips were dark blue now; her breath was dying. Lara knew the child was seconds away from respiratory arrest.

'Ready?' she asked Angus urgently as he seemed to freeze with the scalpel in his hand.

She heard him swallow hard.

Then, as Poppy stopped breathing and her face began to turn darker blue, a voice screamed in Lara's head, *Now, Angus! Do it now*!

With an almost indiscernible shake of his left hand, he swiftly wiped the girl's tiny throat with antiseptic solution, felt for the right spot and in one deft movement, he made the incision into her windpipe. Bright-red blood poured from the wound. There was an agonising few seconds' delay that felt like an eternity, then the little girl sucked a gurgling breath through the tracheotomy.

Angus blew out a breath, swabbed the blood from Poppy's tiny, white throat as Lara passed him more swabs and a suction bulb. He used them time after time to clear the blood and mucus from the incision, then he inserted a tiny, silver, tracheal tube to keep her airway open. And as the little girl blinked open her eyes Lara swallowed hard and said gently, 'Hello, Poppy. You're doing really well.' But the child needed her mother and Moira was right there, sobbing, trying to say thank you. Then she was down on her knees beside her baby girl, speaking softly, brushing strands of pale hair away from her daughter's sweat-stained face.

Already, Lara was checking the child's pulse and respirations. Relief flooding through her as she noted the rapidly improving colour of the little girl's face and fingertips.

At the other side of the double bed, Emma began to rouse from her deep sleep and she asked groggily, 'Are you all right, Mummy? Why are you crying?'

'Oh, I'm fine,' Moira croaked. 'Your sister needed the doctor and the nurse to come, that's all.'

Poppy was coughing now as she tried to speak but the air was no longer passing through her larynx so of course her voice wouldn't come.

Moira was sobbing gently but she managed to say, 'Don't worry, my darling. You got very poorly, and the doctor and the nurse had to come and help you to breathe. So that means you can't use your voice right now.'

Remarkably, the little girl stopped squirming, then she almost smiled.

'She's a brave little soul,' Angus said, his voice husky with emotion.

In the next moment, Tom Douglas came running through the door, panicked. 'I saw the car from the surgery in the yard. What's going on?'

Moira started crying afresh and Tom looked even more distraught.

Lara was straight there. 'Try not to panic, Tom. Poppy is safe now but her breathing deteriorated and we had to come quick from the surgery to perform a procedure to help her breathe.'

'Is she all right? Is she breathing now?' he called raggedly as he walked to the bedside.

'As you can see, she's pinking up nicely.'

He slumped as if he'd taken a punch to the gut. 'Oh my goodness, what a mess. I should have stayed here with you, Moira.'

'It's fine, Tom,' Moira soothed but Lara heard the whisper of raggedness in her voice. 'Don't take on so. I rang the surgery right away; there was no more you could have done even if you'd been here.'

He blew out a breath. 'But at least I'd have been with you.'

'I know,' she soothed. 'But that doesn't really matter now,

because Nurse Flynn and Dr Fitzwilliam have just saved Poppy's life.'

He gasped, his eyes filling with tears. Then he was hugging Lara, clapping Angus on the back. 'There's not enough thanks in the world for what you've done here today.'

Lara felt her heart swell with emotion, and she had to swallow hard not to cry. 'All part of the service,' she said, reaching out to give Moira's arm a squeeze. And that's when she heard the ambulance bell in the distance.

'Here come the reinforcements,' Angus said with a lopsided smile.

Moira shot Lara a harrowed glance. 'Does Poppy have to go to hospital? Can we not look after her here?'

Lara spoke gently but firmly. 'It's absolutely in Poppy's best interest to be cared for in hospital. The tracheotomy will need to be kept open until the membrane has cleared from her throat. So she needs to be on a hospital ward where there'll be medical staff and suction equipment on hand.'

'Yes, yes, of course,' Moira said, then she leaned down to Poppy to speak gently. 'Now listen to me, Poppy. You are my little angel but you're poorly right now and you need to go to the hospital where the doctors and nurses can make you properly better.'

Poppy began to cry but Tom was beside her. 'It'll only be for a little while, sweet pea. And by the time you come home, our sheepdog, Bess, she'll have had her puppies and you'll be able to choose one.'

Emma crawled over to Poppy from the other side of the bed and knelt by her sister. 'Yes, Poppy, you can have your own little dog. So go to the hospital like Nurse Flynn says and when you come home, you'll have a puppy.'

Poppy stopped crying right away and she reached out to take her sister's hand. She tried to speak but of course, her voice wouldn't come.

'Don't worry, little sis,' Emma soothed. 'Your voice will get better when you're at the hospital. So you start thinking about names for your puppy.'

Poppy nodded, then tears were streaming down her cheeks. But her mouth had begun to gently twitch with a smile.

Lara cleared her throat and when she glanced to Angus, she saw him swiping away tears with the back of his hand.

Once the kindly ambulance men had taken the little girl on the stretcher, Angus and Lara said their goodbyes and headed back to the Austin.

'Do you want to drive?' Lara asked as they reached the car.

He was already shaking his head. 'I'd rather you do it,' he breathed. 'I'm just needing a moment of reflection.'

'A well-deserved moment, Angus. You did sterling work in there.'

He nodded, offered a tight smile. 'Thank you, Nurse Flynn, that's high praise coming from a nurse like you with such exacting standards. But I won't get above myself because we're only at the beginning of this.'

Lara blew out a breath. 'You're right, Angus. We need to pace ourselves.'

Then she turned the Austin in the yard and motored gently back down the bumpy farm track. Glancing to the young doctor in the passenger seat, she saw him preoccupied, probably still going over the detail of the case. Angus sitting quietly for once made her even more aware of the precarious times they were now facing. And from past diphtheria cases in Liverpool, she knew the whole thing would snowball from here. But she was also aware that however long it took for the infection to burn itself out, one day in the not-too-distant future, they'd be at the other side of it. And those families left unscathed would be the lucky ones.

6

Lara slept fitfully, dreaming of crying children and blood-soaked sheets. As soon as she woke, her brain was flitting over the management plan she'd worked on with Bingham yesterday. As they'd all sat together around the kitchen table last night, the atmosphere had felt quietly determined but all the while she'd been aware of the threat hanging over the children of Ingleside village and the surrounding district. Bingham had taken a firm stance and given he'd worked through many outbreaks of not only diphtheria but also whooping cough, scarlet fever, polio – all the childhood fevers that could potentially kill a child – he was an experienced and knowledgeable lead. He'd also dealt with Spanish flu while serving as an army surgeon during the war. He'd mentioned it in passing, but Lara knew from many of her former patients in Liverpool how devastating that pandemic had been, especially given it targeted young people.

Once Bingham had said goodnight and retreated to his room, Mrs Hewitt had given more detail of Bingham's experience with the Spanish flu in France during the war. She'd told them he'd had to man a makeshift tent hospital just behind the front line and many soldiers were struck down with the infection while they were serving in the trenches. There'd been a high death toll, including some of the officers he'd worked with. And when at last he'd returned to Ingleside, he'd been faced with it all over again, this time with village families he'd known his whole life. Then Mrs Hewitt's face had clouded over as she'd told them about her son who'd served in the trenches at a very young age. He'd escaped the Spanish flu, but he'd come home badly injured and still recovering from his war wounds... unrecognisable from the young man who'd volunteered and walked off down the street whistling, to sign up with his pals.

Mrs Hewitt had looked wrung out and Lara had got up from her seat to put an arm around her shoulders. Then Marion had suggested a sing-song to raise their spirits, and she'd launched into a discordant version of 'Keep Right On to the End of the Road'. Then she'd switched to 'Pack Up Your Troubles in Your Old Kit Bag', just as inappropriate and still very out of tune.

'No, my ears are bleeding. I can't bear it,' Angus had groaned. And the whole lot of them around the table, including Mrs Hewitt, had begun to laugh.

'I think it best we face our forthcoming trials without the singing,' Angus had said. Then Mrs Hewitt had suggested a hot toddy and Marion had jumped straight in and insisted she make it. It had taken her ages and had involved much cursing and swearing and when it was served, it had been so hot and strong, it had taken Lara's breath away.

Waking early the next morning, Lara snapped into action straight away as she sprang out of bed, then yelped and shivered as her bare feet touched the stone-cold floor. She hopped from one foot to the other as she got dressed. But by the time she was running down the stairs, she'd begun to warm up.

Her first visit was to check on Emma Douglas. Angus had

already promised to report back on little Poppy who had been admitted to an isolation ward at Ridgetown Hospital that had been rapidly put together by Matron Sharples. Lara wished she could go with him to the cottage hospital, but she had that feeling, a twist in her gut, which signalled things would progress rapidly from here.

First down to breakfast as always, even as Lara took her second spoonful of sugar-sprinkled porridge, the telephone rang loudly in the hallway. Mrs Hewitt moved swiftly to pick up the receiver and immediately, her tone of voice signalled concerning news. 'Yes, I'll despatch Nurse Flynn right away,' she heard.

Lara jumped up from the table, slurped some hot, sweet tea, then she was already grabbing her medical bag. The housekeeper's eyes were wide as she walked briskly back into the kitchen. Lara heard her breath catch as she said, 'That was Sally Valentine. Little Izzy has spiked a fever and she's lethargic. News has got round about Tom Douglas's two lasses so of course, she's very concerned.'

'I'll telephone from the Valentines' if I need back up,' Lara called as she ran to the hall to gather her thick, wool overcoat and district nurse's hat.

'Take the Austin,' Mrs Hewitt shouted after her.

'No, it's not far; I'll pedal almost as fast. And Angus will need the car to get to the isolation ward at Ridgetown Hospital.'

Once outside in the bitingly cold air, her breath steamed instantly as she pulled her trusty black bicycle with its white mudguards out of the shed. Placing her medical bag in the basket, she gritted her teeth as she ran with it down the side of the surgery. In seconds, she was out on the street and pushing hard against the pedals. When she'd visited the Valentine family in the autumn to attend Izzy's older brother Peter, Izzy had been very shy at first. But she'd charmed Lara with her bashful smile and quirky personality, and the thought of the bond she had with the little girl made Lara feel even more protective.

With her mind still whirring, Lara pushed on as fast as she could over a potentially icy road. As she approached the farm, a squawking, flapping, white goose burst through the bare hedge and gave her a fright that boosted her even higher. And as she drew close to the ramshackle farm buildings, she heard the low growl and angry bark of the yard dog, Fly, who was a favourite of Izzy's. Quickly, she parked up her bicycle and ran across the mucky yard towards the farmhouse. Almost as if Fly felt her agitation, his thin whine followed her all the way to the farmhouse door.

Just as she reached the house, Mr Valentine dodged out of the barn, his face white and drawn. 'Go straight in, Nurse Flynn,' he shouted, a catch to his voice. 'Izzy's in the sitting room where we nursed Peter.'

'Righto,' she called, pushing through the door. And even as she headed towards the sick room, she heard Izzy's sorrowful wail, closely followed by a harsh, choking cough, and it made a hard bubble of anxiety, painful in her throat.

Sally Valentine was by the bed, her bright-red hair sticking up in clumps. She glanced to Lara with red-rimmed eyes as Izzy still coughed and choked.

'Let's prop her up a little,' Lara offered as she moved swiftly, already removing her coat and hat.

'I've tried that. It doesn't help,' Sally almost wailed.

Lara reached out to her, briefly placed a steadying hand on her arm. 'Have you been up all night?'

Sally nodded, dabbed tears from her eyes. 'She started feeling unwell at teatime yesterday and she was very sleepy. Then she spiked a fever. I didn't know about the diphtheria till

Moira Douglas telephoned to let us know about their two lasses. Oh, Nurse Flynn, is she going to be all right?'

Lara opened her mouth to reply but before she could speak, Izzy wheezed, her voice weak and breathy but she managed to say, 'Of course I'm going to be all right.'

'There you go.' Lara smiled, her throat thickening with emotion. Then she turned back to Sally and said gently, 'I'm going to examine Izzy now – take her temperature and a throat swab. So why don't you get yourself a cup of tea and a bite to eat.'

Sally seemed to gulp back a sob. 'Right, yes. But I don't think I'll manage anything to eat.'

'So have a big cup of tea with plenty of sugar. And I'm here with Izzy now so you take as much time as you need.'

As the door clicked shut behind Sally, Lara heard Peter's voice in the corridor and a mumbled conversation. She caught the edge of what he was saying: 'Don't worry, Ma. Nurse Flynn will sort it.'

She prayed Peter was right.

Remarkably, Izzy was trying to smile, then she croaked, 'I'm so glad it's you, Nurse Flynn.'

Lara felt her heart twist at the little girl's sheet-white face, made starker by her bright-red hair. But even though Izzy was very poorly, she was clearly trying to re-establish the gentle rapport they'd shared when Lara had visited her brother.

'Hello, Izzy.' She smiled. 'I'm just going take your temperature and check a few things. Is that OK?'

'Yes,' the little girl croaked, then she closed her eyes, seemingly exhausted with the effort of speaking.

As Lara carefully performed her observations, she noted marked tachycardia, and alongside the rapid pulse, Izzy also had a high fever. Worryingly, the little girl's chest sounded tight, and her breath held a slightly sweet odour. Even as she took the throat swab, with Izzy so brave and unflinching, Lara knew without doubt this was another case of diphtheria. So far though, Izzy was lucky, because there was no hint of the white membrane at the back of her throat.

Once she was done, she knelt by the bed and held Izzy's hand.

'Are you still there, Nurse Flynn?' the little girl breathed, her voice sounding weaker.

'Yes, I'm here.'

Izzy tried to smile but she started to hack with a cough, and her voice was barely above a whisper as she croaked, 'Don't worry, Nurse Flynn. I'll get better... I know I will. And one day, I'll be a doctor or a nurse... just like you.'

Lara blinked hard to banish the tears that would come if she let them. And as the little girl drifted off to sleep, she stayed right beside her for as long as it took to be sure her airway was still clear. Then she removed her gown, checked the throat swab was secure and stood for a few moments gazing down to the poorly little girl, willing with all her heart for Izzy, Emma and Poppy, and all the other children who would be affected by diphtheria, to pull through.

As she made to walk to the door, it clicked open, and Sally stepped into the room. Her face was still pale, and she had dark smudges beneath her eyes, but she looked refreshed after taking a break. Izzy's brother Peter followed, carrying a tray with a jug of water and a ceramic cup with a feeding spout. 'I'm going to try and get some sips of water into her,' he said firmly.

'Good, that's so good, Peter,' Lara said encouragingly.

'He's an attentive older brother, isn't he, Nurse Flynn?'

'Yes,' Lara replied. 'And also an excellent nurse.'

Peter's cheeks flushed pink and he looked very pleased with

himself. 'Well, it's not long since I was a patient. Weak as a kitten, lying helpless in that bed till my leg healed. And Izzy did her share of looking after me, so I'll do my best for her.'

'Good lad,' Lara said. 'You're a credit to each other.' Then she reached out to give Sally's arm a squeeze and took her aside to sum things up. 'Right, so she has a high fever, a very sore throat and even without the result of the throat swab, I'm sure this is diphtheria.' Sally visibly slumped and Lara reached out to her. 'So the good news is there's no sign of any blockage in her throat. But if there's any worsening of her breathing, or a bluish tinge to her lips, you must contact the surgery immediately.'

Sally swallowed hard, nodded. 'Right. Yes. I thought it was diphtheria and like most families round here, I've seen it before. So I'll be in touch straight away.'

Lara offered a firm smile, then gathering her medical bag, she said her goodbyes.

As she made her way back across the yard with Fly nosing out of his kennel to offer a growl and a single yap, she took a succession of steadying breaths. It was going to be a long haul over these next few weeks and as she mounted her trusty bicycle, she had a sense of her work stretching out before her, clearly done with every attention to detail. And the challenge of it made her push hard against her pedals and steer a very steady course back to the surgery.

As she cycled into the village, she saw Ada Lightfoot, the barmaid from the Fleece, chatting to Mr Armistead at the bottom of the stone steps that led up to the pub. She raised her hand in greeting and was about to pass by when the teacher flagged her down.

'We were just wondering if there was anything we could do to help you and the medical team,' he said.

'Well that's good of you both,' she replied. 'Right now, just off the top of my head, I can't even think. But I'll let you know if there is.'

'Righto, Nurse Flynn,' they called together as she pushed off, leaving them chatting.

Even before she was back through the surgery door, Angus burst out towards her, his brow furrowed. 'I'm off to Ridgetown Hospital; there've been any number of new cases with severe respiratory symptoms, so they need me on the isolation ward.'

'Right, that makes sense,' Lara called to him.

Angus wiped a hand around his face. 'Those poor children. I can't stand the thought of how horrible this is for them.'

She reached out to him, gave his arm a squeeze. 'We'll get through, Angus. Just take it steady, one case at a time.'

He swallowed hard, nodded. 'Same to you, Lara, with all the work here. Don't know when I'll be back; Matron Sharples says poorly children are streaming in so fast, she needs me to stay at the hospital for as long as it takes.'

'You take care, Angus. And after what you did for Poppy Douglas yesterday, I know you're the man for the job.'

'I hope so,' he replied with a wave. Then he called back over his shoulder, 'Sam Collins is giving me a lift to the hospital so you lot can keep the Austin here.'

'Righto, good thinking,' she called after him.

Back inside the surgery, even as she was hanging up her coat, the telephone in the corridor began to ring and Mrs Hewitt ran out of the kitchen to answer. Then Bingham was shouting, 'If it's more cases, unless the patient has severe breathing difficulties, tell them we'll be there in due course.'

'Righto,' Mrs Hewitt replied.

'Ah, Nurse Flynn,' Bingham called as soon as she was in through the door of the kitchen. He stood up from the table and pointed to the papers spread out before him. 'I'd like you to run through this plan I've set out for managing the quarantine. Cast your eyes over it will you, while I make another cup of tea.'

'Yes, of course,' she said, walking briskly to the head of the table as he filled the kettle.

Then he was calling to her from the Aga, 'We've had news that two of the Lennox children, little Freddy and Ava, have gone down with it. Nurse Wright's gone straight out to assess. Sounds like their father, Steven, is beside himself with worry but that's no surprise given he's managing alone with his wife still recovering from puerperal psychosis. And he's only just started his job at the sawmill.'

Lara had worked closely with the family and the news rested heavily on her. 'I'm sorry to hear that; those children and their father have gone through so much already.'

'Yes, they have. Mrs H was so concerned for Steven, she had to pass the telephone to me. The poor man was almost hysterical. But like you say, he's still recovering from the shock of what happened with his wife, and the stress of those few days when the children were missing...'

Lara was shaking her head, trying to make sense of it. 'It's such a shame; the family were just starting to pick up.'

Bingham growled under his breath about nothing being fair in this world. Then he brought two cups back to the table and he was pouring the tea. 'We've got a hard road ahead of us this next few weeks, Nurse Flynn. We need to get the planning of our response spot on... So what do you think?'

'From what I've just read, it's looking good.'

'High praise indeed,' he replied with a quick smile as Mrs Hewitt came back into the kitchen, her face ashen.

'That was Alan Haworth, out at Brock Farm... His two youngest boys and their six-month-old baby sister have been taken ill suddenly. It sounds like we have three more diphtheria cases.'

Lara felt the news like a punch to the gut. Back in the summer, that baby girl had been her first delivery as a country nurse.

'This diphtheria is so terrible,' Bingham almost wailed. Then he seemed to get a grip on himself and asked, 'Are you all right, Nurse Flynn? Do you want me to take this one?'

She sucked a quick breath. 'No, I can manage,' she said firmly. 'And you need to get on with the planning – it'll be crucial to the outcome of all this.'

Mrs Hewitt's features clouded for a moment. 'But, Nurse Flynn, you've only just got back; you need to have something to eat and drink before you go out again.'

In moments, the housekeeper had spooned plenty of sugar into a cup of tea and she'd pushed two shortbread biscuits in front of her. Lara had no choice but to do as she was told.

'Good girl, that's it,' the housekeeper crooned as if she were giving medicine to a poorly child. Then Lara was grabbing her medical bag, running from the kitchen and pulling her coat and hat from the brass hooks in the corridor with Bingham's voice shouting after her to take the Austin. And as she scrambled into the little blue car, her heart was already pounding.

7

Lara sped out of the village and drove fast to Brock Farm, her mind and body already honed for facing another emergency. Back in the summer, Mrs Haworth had gone into labour abruptly and progressed rapidly, and Lara had pedalled at speed along this same road, arriving in the nick of time to run across the yard and deliver a baby girl amid the straw in the barn with hens clucking all around. She couldn't even contemplate a reality where she'd see that baby and two of her brothers struck down.

'Come on,' she growled at herself, seeing the farm up ahead, steeling herself to confront the reality of the situation.

In the same way she'd rapidly dismounted her bicycle in the summer and run through squawking, flapping hens in the yard, she re-enacted it now. But this urgency felt much more stressful; delivering a baby could be harrowing if complications set in but it was routine compared to what the ravages of diphtheria could bring.

Running by the barn where the baby girl had been delivered, she began to slow her pace, so she wasn't out of breath or looking harried when she arrived in the sick room. At the farmhouse door, she smoothed back the strands of hair that had escaped from her brimmed hat, pulled her district nurse's overcoat straight. Then she knocked.

At the sound of running feet inside the house, her heart twisted. She sucked a breath a moment before the door opened.

'Nurse Flynn. Thank God,' Mrs Haworth wailed, urgently gesturing for her to follow. And as the farmer's wife walked briskly ahead, she glanced urgently over her shoulder. 'We've been up all night... The two boys are holding their own – they're upstairs with their dad – but it's the baby, our little Daisy... She's...'

'It's all right, Mrs Haworth,' Lara offered, using the clear, steady voice she kept for emergencies. 'Let me assess the baby first, then we'll know where we are.'

'Yes, of course,' Mrs Haworth almost sobbed as she led her to the small sitting room where Lara had attended for the post-natal visits.

Lara heard the baby's stertorous breathing even before she was in through the door. And the hairs at the back of her neck prickled when she saw the basket-weave crib in which she'd last seen Daisy on her final visit back in the summer. The baby had been tiny in the crib then but now she almost filled it. Lara's heart was broken in a second when she saw how desperately the infant struggled for every bit of breath. And she already knew little Daisy was gravely ill.

Quickly, she pulled the cotton gown from her bag and donned it. Then she called gently over her shoulder, keeping her voice rock steady, 'Right, Mrs Haworth, I can see Daisy is struggling with her breathing so I need you to call the surgery right away and ask them to send for an ambulance so we can get her checked out in hospital.'

Mrs Haworth seemed to choke on a breath, then she was all action.

Lara called after her, 'And while you're in the kitchen, pop a pan of water on the hob – it's mainly what we use for croup, but let's see if some steam will help relieve this tightness in her breathing.'

'Right you are.' Mrs Haworth gulped, then stifled another sob as she ran from the room.

Lara gritted her teeth, stooped down to pick up the dark-haired infant so she could hold her in a position that might assist her breathing. Nothing worked at first; in fact, Daisy seemed to be struggling even more. But Lara forced herself to stay calm and as the steadying voice in her head murmured, *She's breathing, she's still breathing. And there's only the tiniest tinge of blue on her lips,* she sat down on the Lloyd loom chair beside the crib and cradled the baby, holding her upright. Right away, she noted some easing of the baby's stuck breath but alongside that came a murmuring sound: a deep rattle from inside her tiny chest.

'Let's have a look at you, little Daisy,' she said out loud to help steady the pounding of her heart.

In the next second, she heard footsteps in the corridor and Mrs Haworth reappeared with a pan of steaming water. She placed it on a low table beside the crib and as Lara lay the baby back down, she asked Mrs Haworth for a bed sheet. 'I don't know if creating some kind of steam tent will help, but it's worth a try.'

Mrs Haworth ran from the room, coming back moments later with a white, cotton sheet.

Lara's mouth felt dry as she assisted Mrs Haworth to position the sheet. She had no idea if this would be of any benefit, but it paid sometimes to act on a hunch. Trying something, anything, when you're terrified, was sometimes all any nurse could do. So, with her heart still pounding, she positioned the white bed sheet and sat inside it, holding it aloft. And as the steam gathered, slowly, the baby's breathing began to loosen, just a little. Lara's heart began to quieten then and she murmured, 'Come on, little one, keep fighting. Just keep fighting.' The tiny improvement helped spur her on but all she had to keep her afloat right now was hope.

She sat for quite a while inside the makeshift tent listening to every catch of the baby's breath. And once she was satisfied that the improvement in the baby's breathing was sustained, she lifted a corner of the sheet and called gently to Mrs Haworth, 'Your little girl seems a tiny bit better now. Do you want to take over from me so I can nip upstairs to examine your two boys and speak to your husband?'

'Yes, right you are, Nurse Flynn,' Mrs Haworth croaked.

Lara had only once met Mr Haworth when he'd run into the barn in a flummox shortly after Daisy had been delivered. He'd been red-cheeked and flustered that day but now his face was pale and drawn, and he had a sheen of tears in his eyes as he directed her to the double bed where the two young boys lay. Their elder brother, Frank, was sitting in the middle of the bed with an arm around each.

'This one's Gordon.' He nodded to the dark-haired boy to his right, 'And this is Bobby,' he said indicating the smaller boy with brown, curly hair who lay at the other side. Lara's heart swelled with emotion when she saw how carefully he was supporting his brothers and as they both started hacking with a cough at the same time, Frank propped them and soothed them.

'You've got a good one there, Mr Haworth,' Lara offered with a nod to Frank, as she pulled her equipment, including the throat swabs, from her bag.

'Yes, we have that,' the man replied with a glint of pride.

It was obvious the two boys had diphtheria, but she still did her full examination. They both had fevers and the characteristic tight cough but thankfully, there was no sign of the white membrane at the back of their throats. And given they'd been poorly for some days now, it felt as if they were probably through the worst of it.

As she explained her findings to Mr Haworth, he groaned with relief, wiped a hand around his face. But that's when she needed to inform him of Daisy's condition and the ambulance she'd requested.

'Righto.' He gulped, as he took on the news. 'So you're saying it's just to check, to monitor her.'

'At this stage, yes.'

Frank piped up then. 'Does Mum need any help with the baby? I can go down to her if you want.'

Lara didn't want the lad to see his baby sister so poorly or unsettle Mrs Haworth, so she said, 'Your mum's managing well at present. But if you do want to help, you could walk out to the road to flag down the ambulance when it comes.'

'Righto,' the lad replied, making sure his two brothers were comfortable before he walked to the door.

'Good lad, Frank,' his father called, pain and anxiety mixed with pride in his voice.

As Lara packed her medical bag, then followed Frank down the stairs, she heard Mrs Haworth shouting, panicked, 'Nurse Flynn, come quick!'

Frank switched round, startled, and shot her a stricken glance.

'It's all right, I'll sort it. You go outside and wait for the ambulance.'

He nodded, pressing his lips in a firm line.

Mrs Haworth was calling again, her voice rising.

Lara was straight in through the door to find her cradling Daisy. The poor little mite was trying to cough against a very tight-sounding airway.

'Put her back down in the crib, please,' Lara said firmly but calmly as her heart picked up a staccato rhythm.

Quickly, she pulled her torch and a small tongue depressor from her medical bag. 'I just need to look down her throat. Hold her head please, Mrs Haworth.'

The woman sobbed but instantly complied.

Lara's heart twisted when she noted the beginnings of a white membrane in the baby's throat. Thankfully, the airway was still clear, but she steeled herself, knowing time was running out for this tiny one. And still, they were waiting for an ambulance. Inevitably, during a diphtheria outbreak, there was heavy demand, therefore even longer waiting times.

Flashbacks came to her from back in the summer, when she'd delivered Daisy in the barn amid the hay, with hens pecking all around. What a joyous event that had been... A tragic contrast to what was happening now. She made an almost physical effort to push those thoughts away. She had to stay fully functional to use her well-honed medical knowledge to the best of her ability.

'Stay calm, Mrs Haworth. Your baby can still breathe,' she said firmly, with no hint of anxiety in her voice.

Mrs Haworth gasped brokenly, 'Thank you, Nurse Flynn.'

Lara checked the baby's temperature and pulse – and as expected, the tiny girl had a fever and her pulse was fluttering like the heartbeat of a tiny bird. She made a note of her recordings as she ran through the option of telephoning the surgery to see if Bingham could drive out to collect her with the baby and rush her to hospital. In her medical bag, she had a scalpel and all that was required to make an emergency incision into the baby's trachea. She'd witnessed the procedure many times and knew she would be able to follow it... but with such a tiny child, it would be extremely challenging.

'Why don't you go and make us all a good, strong cup of tea,' Lara asked Mrs Haworth gently, feeling the twist of anxiety in her chest pull tight as the baby offered another tight cough.

The farmer's wife snatched a breath as the baby coughed again. But this time, something seemed to loosen, and her breathing eased a fraction.

'Yes, I'll go and make some tea, now you're here with her. How many sugars for you, Nurse Flynn?'

'I usually take one, but right now, three please.'

'Right you are,' the woman called as she made towards the door.

The cups of tea were long drunk, and Lara had taken and recorded the baby's vital signs many more times and offered tiny sips of sugar water off a spoon before, at last, they heard the ambulance bell.

Frank ran in, shouting, 'They're here, they're coming now!'

The two grey-haired attendants had dark smudges of exhaustion beneath their eyes as they came quietly into the sick room.

'Ah, she's a little one all right,' the leading ambulance man said, his breath catching ever so slightly as Lara quietly relayed the detail of the case.

The other man, the thinner of the two, gulped when he saw the baby. 'Aye, and she's a bonny wee thing,' he offered with a gentle Scottish accent.

And as Lara passed across a written record of her observations, the first man gently gathered the baby in his arms. 'We'll take this little one straight down to Preston Royal Infirmary.'

Mrs Haworth sucked a sharp breath. 'So far away. Can she not go to the isolation ward at Ridgetown Hospital?'

He was shaking his head. 'I'm sorry, but because the tiny ones are much more vulnerable, our orders are to take them straight to Preston Royal.'

Then, clearly understanding Mrs Haworth's distress, the Scottish man spoke gently. 'If you want, you can come in the back of the ambulance with me. You won't be able to go into the fever ward with your wee lass, but you can hand her over at the door.'

Mrs Haworth seemed to gulp, then she said, 'Yes, I'll come, I'll do just that.'

Lara knew the baby's mother would be facing a harrowing experience. She'd worked on a paediatric isolation ward in Liverpool, and it had been heartbreaking to witness the tiny children screaming and crying as they were separated from their distraught parents at the door.

'Ask the hospital to call Ingleside Surgery with news of Daisy's progress,' Lara called after her.

'Will do,' she replied, glancing back to offer a wobbly smile.

Mr Haworth and Frank were out in the hallway, their eyes shining with tears as Daisy was carried to the ambulance with Mrs Haworth following. 'You be good for your father and look after your brothers,' she called over her shoulder to Frank.

And Mr Haworth replied, 'Don't you worry, Maggie, he's the best. And he's so good with the little ones.'

Once the ambulance was slowly bumping away over the yard, Lara went back inside to perform her final checks on the two poorly boys upstairs. They were both sleeping peacefully, their breath coming easily with no sign of obstruction. So she said her goodbyes to Mr Haworth and Frank, then she was away, back along the lane on her bicycle. And with all that she'd been required to do, just in this one visit, she felt drained of everything, body and soul. What she needed right now was to restore her energy levels and get a bite to eat before she was called out to the next case.

As she cycled by the Fleece and made to turn up to the surgery, an urgent, familiar voice called out to her. It was Leo with the little dog tucked under his arm, and knowing she was short on time, she called, 'I'm sorry, I can't stop right now... I need to get back to the surgery before my next visit.'

'Right you are. Keep up the good work,' he called after her. The little dog offering a yap as Leo turned to head back down the hill.

Then, even as she pedalled over the remaining distance, a low slung, blue sports saloon pulled up in front of the surgery and Lara's heart sank when she clicked it was Philippa Harrington. As the young lady of the manor nimbly slipped out of the driver's seat in her expensive coat with a fox-fur collar, she glanced around brightly, expectantly. Instantly, Lara knew Miss Harrington had absolutely no idea about the diphtheria outbreak they were currently dealing with.

'Hello,' Philippa called, catching Lara's eye as she slowed her bicycle to pull up outside the surgery. 'Is it OK if I leave my car here? I'm just bobbing in to see Leo but there isn't much room to park down there on the street.'

Lara already felt a little light-headed due to lack of food, and then with the effort of having to engage with Philippa, it was all she could do to stand up straight. So for a few moments, no words would come.

'How quaint, to see you out on a bicycle,' Philippa offered to fill the gap.

Lara still couldn't form a response, but given Miss Harrington had seen her with her bicycle when she'd been visiting her gamekeeper patient at the hall, she knew it couldn't be that startling.

She groaned inside, drew a slow breath. 'It should be fine to leave your car here. We're not seeing many patients in the surgery right now because of the diphtheria outbreak.'

'What was that... sorry?'

'Diphtheria. A nasty childhood fever that's currently doing the rounds.'

'You mean, here, in the village? Where we are right now?'

'Yes, here, and in the surrounding district.'

Philippa cleared her throat. 'Oh, I see. Well, is it safe for me to be here?'

Lara toyed with the idea of telling her no, it wasn't safe, and the young lady of the manor should scurry straight back to her stately home. But of course her inner professional voice wouldn't allow her to do that. 'It's a childhood fever, so it doesn't usually affect adults. Some children get a nasty dose, others barely much more than a cold. So you should be OK.'

Miss Harrington still looked uncomfortable, and Lara couldn't help but take a little delight in that.

Philippa watched as Lara dismounted her bicycle. 'So, Nurse Flynn, just to check. You think I will be all right to visit Leo, here in the village?'

'I think so, I can't really say. But like I said, diphtheria is a childhood illness.'

'Right. So I'll chance my arm then, as they say.' Philippa smiled, pulling her fur coat tightly around her body in what looked like a protective gesture.

Lara was already wheeling her bicycle towards the side of the surgery as Philippa began to pick her way down the cobbled street. And given the village was very quiet at present with folks keeping their children indoors, the tap tap of her heeled shoes seemed to be magnified in the crisp, winter air.

It felt heavenly to push open the back door of the surgery and feel the warmth from the Aga seeping out from the kitchen. And as the smell of freshly baked cake met her, Lara felt at home.

As she entered the kitchen, Mrs Hewitt glanced up from the counter where she was slicing a fruit cake. 'Ah, good to have you back safe and sound, Nurse Flynn… and I'm thinking by your expression that all was manageable at the Haworths'?'

'Yes. But the baby was very poorly and had to be transferred to the Infirmary. Her two older brothers seem to be fighting it off, though. How are things here? Have there been any more calls?'

'Yes, Marion's just run down the hill to Alice Taylor's; young Robin is showing symptoms, and he'll need a throat swab taking, but he doesn't sound too poorly…' Mrs Hewitt drew a slow breath. 'And I don't want you to be alarmed, after everything the Lennox family have already been through, but we had another call from Miss Dunderdale… The children were due to move back to Foxglove Cottage with their dad, now that Steven's been taken on as a joiner at the sawmill. But it sounds like Freddy is worsening with diphtheria and little Ava is also poorly. Dr Bingham's gone out there to assess but it sounds like Freddy will need hospitalisation.'

Lara felt it like a punch. After what the Lennoxes had been through and how closely she'd worked with them, she felt for those children.

Seeming to pick up on her distress, Mrs Hewitt quickly added, 'But Dr Bingham was thinking that little Freddy might not need to go as far as the Infirmary. If anything, he'll be transferred to the isolation ward at the cottage hospital. That's good because Angus will be looking after him. And that lovely Nurse Greenwood who worked in our clinic when Marion was off after her accident, she's the senior nurse in charge of the fever ward.'

Lara nodded, tried to offer a smile but it felt more like a twist of her mouth.

'Come on, sit down,' the housekeeper soothed. 'I'm giving you the cake first to boost you up, and I'll have a big mug of sweet tea to follow. And while you're eating and drinking, I'll be making a pile of sandwiches. How does that sound?'

'Heaven, Mrs H, it sounds like absolute heaven.'

8

As Lara wheeled her bicycle down the side of the surgery, heading out to a routine visit before more emergency calls came in, she felt replenished by Mrs Hewitt's kind ministrations. But then she spotted Miss Harrington's blue sports car still parked up and instantly it vexed her because she felt sure she'd conveyed enough information to the young lady of the manor to indicate parking was only for a short period of time. Then, almost as if she'd willed it, she heard Philippa's voice calling a goodbye and when she glanced down the cobbled street, she saw her walking slowly up with Leo at the door of the vet's gazing after her. Philippa looked downright miserable compared to how she'd been when she'd jumped out of her car. Obviously, something was up, but Lara reminded herself of the promise she'd made to steer clear of any entanglement with issues related to Philippa and Leo. So she told herself very strongly that whatever was happening was none of her business, particularly now with this diphtheria outbreak needing her full attention.

Marion's voice popped into her head... *Well, you can tell your-*

self that. But of course you want to know what's going on. It made her smile.

'I'm glad you've got something to be happy about,' Miss Harrington said a little too loudly and miserably as she approached.

Lara felt the sting of her churlish remark and offered a firm reply. 'Well, if you call being up to the eyes with visits to many very poorly children being something to be happy about, then yes, I'm beside myself with joy.'

Philippa sucked in a breath and to her credit, she did look sorry.

'Apologies,' she said immediately. 'Leo gave me more information about the diphtheria outbreak, and it does sound awful.'

As often happened with Miss Harrington, Lara felt sideswiped by her switch of tone. She tried not to let it soften her attitude towards the young lady because she already knew Philippa was mostly focused on her own world and issues related solely to that. But it needled her, and she didn't have the energy right now to work out if Philippa was genuinely sorrowful about the diphtheria outbreak, or whether it was more about what had just happened with Leo. Seeing Leo still at the door of the vet's, she thought it was likely to be about him, and it frustrated her even more as she felt the tightening of that strange hold the young woman seemed to have on those around her.

As Philippa clambered into her low-slung car, slammed the door, then skidded away, Lara was about to push off on her bicycle when she heard an urgent shout from one of the mill cottages across the street. It was Lizzie Cronshaw, white-faced, gasping for breath. 'Come quick, Nurse Flynn. It's Sue; she's not breathing.'

Lara let her bicycle fall to the ground and as she legged it across the street, she heard a shout from down the hill and Marion was running up. In through the cottage door and into the warm kitchen, Lara noted in passing Lizzie's baby boy, William, sleeping soundly in his crib. But up the narrow stairs, Lizzie was panicked and shouting.

Lara ran up, her heart clenched at what she might find.

Lizzie was on the bed cradling her three-year-old. The little girl's brown hair was dark with sweat and plastered to her head, her body limp in her mother's arms.

'Give her to me,' Lara said firmly.

Marion was right there beside her now, still catching her breath.

Lara shouted, 'Quick, let's get her across to the surgery.'

Little Sue's lips were blue; she was barely breathing. Lara flashed a glance to Lizzie, she didn't even need to speak.

'Go, just go,' the child's mother urged. And as Lara ran down the stairs with the little girl in her arms, closely followed by Marion, she heard Lizzie shout after them, 'I'll grab the baby and bring him across to the surgery. I'll be in the waiting room!'

Lara ran straight in through the door of the clinic room and placed Sue down on the examination couch. The tiny girl was still limp, her lips blue.

'Quick, Marion. She's burning up; run some tepid water so we can sponge her down.'

Even as she spoke, she was assessing the child's breathing then pressing two fingers to the side of her neck to check for a pulse. 'Respiratory effort is weak. Her pulse very rapid, off the scale,' she called to Marion, who was quickly gathering equipment.

Lara tipped the child's head back, used a torch to check her throat. 'Right, so I can see a membrane forming. But her throat isn't blocked so we might have a bit of time.'

'Good, that's good,' Marion murmured, already sponging the child's body, desperately working to reduce her fever.

The door flew open then and Mrs Hewitt was there. 'Do you need me to call an ambulance?'

'Yes, please,' both nurses replied.

Lara checked the child's airway again with her torch. 'There's thick mucus in her throat. I think it's worth trying some suction to unblock.'

'Anything. Let's try anything and everything,' Marion gasped breathlessly. Then she began to murmur to the little girl. 'Come on, Sue. Just take some big, deep breaths for us.'

Lara had the suction bulb now. 'So, Marion, if you could help by holding her mouth open for me, I'll see what I can do.'

'Right you are,' Marion replied.

Lara's heart twisted when she noted the child's body still floppy, her lips tinged with blue. She quickly inspected her throat, then used the suction bulb. Instantly, the child gagged and to see that reflex felt encouraging, but it was still scary. As she eased off the pressure on the bulb, the suction pulled a good amount of mucus out from the back of Sue's throat. Lara diligently kept going, squirting the exudate into a receiver.

Just when she was beginning to think there wasn't much improvement to the girl's breathing, Sue offered a choking cough and more mucus came up. Then she was wailing – a tight, mournful sound.

'Whew, at least she's able to make some noise now,' Marion offered breathlessly. 'What a sweet sound. Like the first cry of a newborn baby.'

'It is.' Lara nodded, tears pricking her eyes.

Even though Sue had roused, it was clear that she was still very poorly. And as Lara gently sponged her ashen face, then dried with a soft towel, the tiny girl blinked open her eyes and offered the shadow of a smile. Then, clearly feeling the raw pain in her throat, she began to wail – a miserable, heartbreaking sound.

'It's all right, little one. You cry if you need to,' Lara soothed.

'We're just glad you've got enough breath,' Marion murmured as she heaved a sigh of relief. Then Marion was slowly shaking her head. 'How much longer do you think we can carry on like this, going from one emergency to the next?'

'As long as we need,' Lara replied firmly, trying to cast her mind back to the outbreak in Liverpool when she'd nursed many children. But all she could recall now was the relief when the rate of infection began to ease and the joy of discharging those children who'd recovered. And the heartfelt sorrow that felt like a punch to the gut for the ones they'd lost.

Once Sue was more settled, Marion went to the waiting room to let Lizzie know how she was doing. And left alone in the surgery now the little girl's complexion was pinking up, Lara felt her body slump with tiredness. She'd try to get an early night in case this rapid pace didn't ease. But even as she thought it, she heard the surgery door slam open, and a man's voice was shouting. Her heart jolted in her chest. She strained her ears; all she could hear was the murmur of voices. Then the clinic room door clicked open, and Marion came through with Ed Cronshaw. His black hair full of sawdust, his work clogs ringing on the polished floor.

'Is Sue fighting it off?' he croaked, his breath coming quick, his eyes wide with panic.

'Well, she's improved markedly from when we brought her to the surgery. But she's not out of the woods yet,' Lara told him gently.

Ed nodded, swallowed hard, then he reached out with his work-roughened hand to gently stroke his little girl's face. The gentleness of the gesture was such a stark contrast to his muscular, workmanlike appearance that Lara felt her breath catch.

The three-year-old's eyes flickered open and she croaked, 'Dada.'

He gulped hard to hold back a sob, the effort almost taking his breath. 'I'm here, my little darlin',' he crooned. 'I'm right here with you.'

Lara swallowed hard against the lump in her throat, emotional with the poignancy of the scene but also knowing how far this man had come since she'd first encountered him in the summer. Out on the street, worse for wear with drink, he'd shouted at her and threatened her as Bingham had taken Sue to Ridgetown Hospital for treatment of scalds from a hot cup of tea. It made her heart swell to see what a good father he was now to Sue and baby William.

The clinic door opened and Bingham strode in, his face tight with concern. 'Mrs Hewitt told me Sue needed urgent treatment,' he said, his eyes scrutinising the little girl as she lay on the examination couch. Then he removed his checked trilby, leaving stray wisps of unruly hair poking out at odd angles. 'How is she doing, Nurse Flynn?' he asked gently, with a nod to Ed.

'As well as she possibly can be,' Lara replied. 'She rallied after we used suction to clear her throat. She still has a high fever and a rapid pulse, but her breathing and colour have improved markedly.'

'That's good to know,' he breathed, seeming to release some of the tension in his shoulders. 'Mrs Hewitt said she'd called an ambulance, but I've just got back from the Infirmary and all hell's been let loose there with the spread of this. The ambulance service is overwhelmed. I've asked her to ring back and tell them I'll drive the little lass to the cottage hospital myself. Angus is running the fever ward with Nurse Greenwood and I've already telephoned and spoken to Matron Sharples. They still have capacity to take more children.'

Lara felt so much better knowing Sue would be handed over to staff she knew and trusted. 'That's excellent; Nurse Greenwood is very competent and it's so good she's working with Angus.'

Bingham was nodding, then ruffling his hair, but he still had a deep line between his brows. He shot a glance to Ed. 'Do you want to come with me and hold your little lass in the back of the car?'

'Yep.' He nodded. 'I'm up for that, Doc.'

'You won't be able to go onto the isolation ward, though; it's out of bounds to family and visitors to help reduce the spread of infection.'

'No problem,' Ed said gently. 'I just want to see my little lass safely delivered to the hospital, that's all.'

Bingham turned to Lara. 'Right, Nurse Flynn, I'll take it from here. I've already ordered Nurse Wright into the kitchen for a cup of tea and a bite to eat and you've had an extremely busy morning, so I suggest you go and join her, take a break before you're called out again.'

'Yes, but I was just setting out on my first routine visit.'

Bingham scrunched his brow. 'We're in new territory now until the diphtheria burns itself out. Do the routine visits if you've got capacity but this outbreak is whipping up and it'll be all-consuming for a while. So unless there's a life-threateningly urgent non-diphtheria case, the rest of the local populace will have to wait. And our patients, even the grumpy ones, will fully understand the reasoning for that.'

Lara offered a nod and as she made to leave, Ed reached out to her. 'Thank you, Nurse Flynn, for what you've done today and last year when Sue was scalded. And of course you delivered our William so I'm thinking you might be our guardian angel.'

'Well, I wouldn't go so far as that,' she replied. 'We nurses are definitely earthbound and not heavenly. But thanks, Ed. It means a lot to know we're appreciated.'

As Lara walked towards the kitchen, she stopped briefly to update Lizzie on what would happen now with Sue.

The young mother listened carefully to every word with baby William still sleeping in her arms. 'Can I just nip in to see her before she goes to the hospital?'

'I'm afraid not, Lizzie. Once the diagnosis is made, we must isolate the child from other babies and children who aren't symptomatic to cut down the spread.'

Lizzie's shoulders dropped but she glanced up with a nod. 'Yes, of course. And Ed's in there with her.' She stood up then with the sleeping baby in her arms. 'Thanks for what you've done, Nurse Flynn. And for letting Ed go to the hospital.' Then with tears shining in her eyes, she said, 'I've no idea how he even found out, but the news got to the sawmill somehow. And I'm glad he's able to go with her. She's a real daddy's girl these days, our Sue.'

'Yes, I saw that,' Lara replied with a gentle smile. 'And he's such a big softie with her.'

'I'm glad of it and since William was born, he's even been helping around the house. And he's often out with Sue down the street to his mum's... Having said that, I need to go to Betty's, let her know what's going on. She'll be worried sick.'

'Yes, of course, Lizzie. And just so you know, our Dr Fitzwilliam will be looking after Sue at the cottage hospital. He's currently in charge of the fever ward.'

'That's good.' Lizzie sighed. And as she made to move, Lara

reached out gently to touch the sleeping baby's cheek. 'He's a good little thing, isn't he? Every time I see him, he's settled.'

'Yes,' Lizzie said, then she frowned and shook her head. 'It's always our Sue who's getting into bother or being ill.'

Lara smiled. 'Well, maybe when she's older, things will settle down.'

'I hope so, Nurse Flynn,' Lizzie replied as she walked away, then called over her shoulder, 'because if they don't, I'm going to be a grey-haired old woman way before my time.'

Marion was already at the kitchen table and she glanced up enquiringly as Lara walked back in. She felt wrung out but instantly, she was updating her colleague. 'Sue's very much holding her own, and Ed is taking her with Dr Bingham to the fever ward at Ridgetown Hospital.'

'That's good news,' Mrs Hewitt called from the kitchen counter as she vigorously chopped carrots.

'Phew, thank goodness,' Marion breathed. 'It didn't look that way when we first clapped eyes on her.'

'No, it did not,' Lara replied with a groan as she slumped onto her chair, suddenly exhausted and feeling the dull throb of a headache gathering behind her eyes. For the first time since the outbreak had begun, she wasn't sure how she could keep going with the ever-increasing burden of cases and the stress of treating seriously ill children. She gulped, then swallowed hard to stop herself from sobbing out loud; if she began to crack now then Marion and Mrs Hewitt would also be caught up in it.

Marion, clearly sensing she was struggling, leaned across the table to hold her hand. 'Let's just take a breather now, hey? While we can.'

'Wise words,' Mrs Hewitt called from the Aga as she settled her pan of carrots with a firm clunk on the hotplate.

Lara drew a slow breath and as she felt the steady pressure

of Marion's hand, she began to feel the weight of what she'd been carrying begin to ease.

Marion was nodding now and speaking gently. 'Let it out, Lara. I've been crying into my pillow every night for those poorly children.'

Lara gulped, then she was swiping away tears with her free hand as Marion held on to her, anchored her.

'Any better?' Marion asked gently.

'Yes, I think so,' she replied, her voice husky with tears. 'But I might need a couple of aspirin.'

'Coming up,' Mrs Hewitt called. Then she added, 'And I'll cut you some cake; you definitely need cake.'

In moments, the housekeeper was placing some tablets and a still warm from the oven slice of Victoria sponge in front of her.

Marion giggled then and said, 'Me and Angus have a theory that if the end of the world does come, Mrs H will be there with freshly baked cake to ease the pain.'

'I will indeed,' the housekeeper laughed as she leaned on the table. 'Speaking of Angus, I heard from Dr Bingham that he's heading up the fever ward at Ridgetown Hospital with that nurse who came to help out when you were in hospital, Marion.'

'Yes, I heard that too,' Lara said. 'Nurse Greenwood is lovely.'

Mrs Hewitt was nodding, 'Yes, she is... and I'm hoping those two might get close, if you know what I mean.'

'Inevitably, they will. It's the nature of the work... And I know what you're thinking, Mrs H, because I thought the same back in the summer.'

'What? What are you both thinking?' Marion asked as she reached for another slice of cake.

'Angus and Nurse Greenwood would make a wonderful couple,' Mrs Hewitt said firmly.

Marion looked a little startled, then she was beaming. 'Yes, of course. They would be very nice together.'

'All we can do is wait and see,' Lara murmured as she took another delicate bite of her cake.

'Blow that.' Marion grinned, a cake crumb stuck to the corner of her mouth. 'I'm already going over all the ways we could possibly bring them together outside of work.'

And as Lara and Mrs Hewitt began to laugh, Marion tucked into her cake even more enthusiastically.

9

The next morning, as Lara walked down the empty village street to visit Daniel Makepeace, an elderly patient with advanced heart failure she'd attended since her first week at the surgery, she glanced to the cottages at either side and saw warning notices for infectious disease in each of the affected dwellings. The Cronshaws' cottage bore a sign just in case baby William was carrying the infection. Lara also noted a warning in the cottage directly opposite – a new family who'd recently moved to the village: a young mother, Sophie Lampton, with three-year-old identical twin girls. Lara had never met them, but Marion had told her how she'd found the two red-haired, poorly little girls snuggled together in bed. Then, in the window of the house next door to the Old Oak pub, a warning had been placed yesterday by the Taylor family after young Robin's diagnosis had been confirmed. It was of course necessary to have these signs, but their lettering seemed to loom out at Lara causing a tightness in her chest.

Aware that Daniel hadn't received a visit for some days due

to the ongoing medical emergency, Lara felt more than her usual level of concern for him. But as she tapped on his door then walked into a kitchen warmed by a well-fuelled stove, she was relieved to find him bright-eyed as he rested back against his pillows. He was so thin, he appeared lost in his bed, but he was wearing the blue woolly hat and mittens knitted by his niece, Esther. And as he turned his head to smile a greeting, his dark eyes twinkled and his expression was decidedly jaunty.

'Morning, Mr Makepeace,' she called, placing her medical bag down by the side of his bed.

'Morning, Nurse Flynn,' he replied, but he was frowning deeply. And when he spoke again, his voice was raw with emotion. 'I hope you're holding up with all those poorly children. This is one too many outbreaks of horrible childhood fever for an old fella like me to take.'

Lara heaved a sigh. 'Well, as you know, it's a very grim time for the affected families. But we're working hard to treat as many children as we can.'

She heard him draw a raspy breath, then he was slowly shaking his head. 'Well, I suppose there's better medicine now than when I was a lad. But we lost three children – two boys and a girl – to diphtheria when I was at Ingleside School.'

Lara felt her heart thud dully in her chest. 'That must have been awful.'

He swallowed hard. 'Aye, it was. And when I could still get up to the church, I used to visit their graves and spend time thinking about those lively little children – always full of fun. And I'd gaze up to the sky and give thanks for me and my Martha having come through when some of our school mates didn't.'

'Oh, so you and Martha were in the same class,' she said,

needing to distract him from grim, upsetting memories of diphtheria at a time when the mortality rate was way higher than anything they saw now.

Daniel smiled, displaying his single tooth. 'Martha was a year younger. But as you know, the village school teaches all ages together.'

'Yes, I was there recently to see the new headmaster, Mr Armistead. It's a lovely old building, isn't it?'

'It is indeed... and it's a great deal older than me. In fact, some folks say it was built at the beginning of the eighteenth century.'

'Well, it's certainly standing the test of time. And it's lovely with its golden-yellow stone and mullion windows.'

'That stone came from Ridgetown Quarry; at least that's what my father used to say. And he was a pupil there as well.'

'Your family must have a heck of a legacy here in the village, Mr Makepeace. Something to be proud of.'

He nodded, then pushed his blue knitted hat further back on his head so more of a tuft of white hair escaped. 'Aye, but I'll be the last with the Makepeace name... My niece, she's married so she's a Robinson. And like I've told you before, me and Martha never had any children... so that's it: the end of the line.'

'I suppose so, Mr Makepeace. But Esther's children are still your family even if they don't have the same surname.'

He seemed to ponder what she'd said for a few moments. 'I've never really thought about it like that, Nurse Flynn.' He smiled. 'Those two girls of Esther's – Joan and Sarah – they're lovely lasses. And her youngest is a lad and she called him Daniel, after me.'

'So there you go... that's your family line continuing through Esther.'

He nodded and tried to smile but his eyelids were already drooping, then he yawned and within moments, he was fast asleep. She'd observed some weeks ago that his bursts of energy were getting shorter, probably due to his worsening heart failure. And it made her sad to think that maybe she'd soon be saying goodbye to him. But the nature of her work meant that inevitably, she'd get close to her long-term patients and in this tight-knit rural community, she'd feel the loss when the time came.

She slowly shook her head as she focused back to her work. 'I'm just going to check your pulse, Mr Makepeace,' she said gently, even though he was still sleeping. Then she was palpating his wrist with the tips of her fingers to feel for the delicate, irregular thread of his pulse. He stayed asleep even as she checked his blood pressure and as she packed her bag and murmured a gentle goodbye, he still didn't stir. She hoped he'd hold his own until the better weather came and he'd be able to return to the back room with the shuttered window open to the air, looking out over the field where Leo's cattle grazed.

As she walked back up the deserted street, she saw Miss Shaw, the postmistress, waving at her through the Post Office window. It startled her; the steel-haired woman had always seemed stern and had been unflinching in her standoffishness to Lara as a newcomer to the village. Shocked, Lara raised a hand to return the greeting and the postmistress smiled, which surprised her even more. Then hearing voices up ahead, she spotted Ada the barmaid descending the steps of the Fleece, closely followed by Mr Armistead. They were chatting as they walked, and Ada raised a hand, called out a greeting. 'Hello, Nurse Flynn. How are you doing?'

'Very busy with the work. But keeping going like everyone else.'

Mr Armistead pressed his lips together, nodded, then he said, 'It's just so strange with the school closed and the village street so empty.'

'Yes, indeed, especially since Ingleside exists, in fact thrives, on gossip and conversation.'

'You've hit the nail on the head there, Nurse Flynn.' Mr Armistead laughed. Then slightly awkwardly, he added, 'Well, me and Ada are working on a plan to deliver food parcels to the families who are isolating.'

'Good thinking,' Lara said, and it wasn't what he'd just said that made her feel warm inside, but the adoring way he glanced to Ada. Lara knew right then, even if Ada was oblivious, that the new headmaster was well and truly besotted.

'That's so nice,' Lara breathed, not realising she'd made the comment out loud until Ada asked, 'What? Sorry?'

Lara opened her mouth to make something up but she picked up the sound of a commotion down the street: loud voices and a dog barking. Shocked, she switched around. Her heart skipping a beat when she saw Vic Taylor with a large, brindled lurcher at his side, approaching Alice's door. He was knocking fiercely then rattling at the locked door, trying to force his way into his estranged wife's new home.

She felt something click deep inside and in seconds, she was walking briskly back down the street. 'You can't go in there, Mr Taylor; the house is under quarantine.'

He switched round, his eyes boring into her, his straggly, brown hair poking from beneath a flat cap pulled low over his forehead. 'Ah, if it isn't Nurse Fancy-Pants,' he growled. Then his features seemed to soften and when he spoke again, his voice had an edge of sorrow. 'You'll be pleased to know I'm inclined to let bygones be bygones. Especially since I've just found out Robin has gone down with a bad dose of diphtheria.'

Vic's dog whimpered and pulled on its lead.

Lara stepped closer, sensing the man's distress. In that moment, her concern overrode the difficulties she'd had with him since she'd first taken up her post as a country nurse. Right from the start, he'd badmouthed her and once, he'd physically attacked her. She dropped her voice. 'I'm sorry, Mr Taylor. I know how badly you want to see Robin, but the quarantine measures are strict.'

Instantly, he was shouting brokenly, almost sobbing. 'I need to go in there! I have to see my son.' His voice sounded harsh, but Lara saw tears shining in his eyes. And despite the threat he'd posed previously, she felt her heart soften towards this ragged, desperate man.

'I'm so sorry, Mr Taylor, but the families in quarantine can't be visited.'

He doubled over as if punched in the gut. He was weeping and stamping his feet and appeared to be breaking down. 'Please let me go in; I have to see Robin,' he begged.

Lara never thought she'd ever see Vic in this state, and all thought of his violence and aggression was now thrust aside. With her next breath, she said, 'Well, I'm part of the medical team looking after Robin and I'm allowed to go into the house. Your son is being nursed downstairs in the sitting room, so how about I see if he's well enough to come to the window for a few moments? How does that sound?'

He growled a little, couldn't meet her eye as the dog whimpered and whined at his side, its ears flat to its head. Then he glanced up sharply, his eyes blazing as he seemed to hold back a sob. 'It sounds like I've no choice. So I have to say yes, don't I?'

'All right, just let me go in first. If Robin is well enough, I'll bring him to the window.'

'We'll wait with you, Vic,' Ada said gently, and Lara saw the protective way Mr Armistead stepped closer to her.

Lara nipped quickly to the back of the house and once Alice had the door unlocked, she slipped into the kitchen. Alice was white-faced, with two bright-red anger spots on her cheeks, the set of her mouth indicating she wouldn't be pushed around by anyone. 'So, what's going on out there, Nurse Flynn? What does that so-called husband of mine want?'

'Well, he's worrying about his son and if Robin's well enough, I was wondering if Vic could see him through the window, just for a few moments. Obviously, I'll ask Robin if that's what he wants to do.'

Alice narrowed her eyes, and she was shaking her head. 'I'm not sure about this, Lara.' Then she sighed heavily and spoke again, 'But Robin does ask about his dad so if that's what he wants to do... providing it's just for a few minutes...'

'What's going on?' a deep voice asked as Alice's uncle, Josh, strode into the kitchen, his muscular frame and strong presence giving a clear indication of his past life as a prize fighter. His eyes blazed with anger as he ran a hand through his close-cropped, grey hair and Lara caught a glimpse of the snake tattoo on his forearm. He turned to her, fixing her with his bright gaze. 'Is what I've just overheard correct... Vic's outside and he wants to see Robin?'

'Yes. But it'll just be for a few moments through the window.'

Josh clenched his fists, emitting a low growl. 'Given you're in charge of this, Nurse Flynn, I'll keep my nose out of it. But if he so much as gestures at coming inside, I'll have him good and proper.'

'I don't think it'll come to that,' Lara said, praying she was right because all the responsibility for this rested on her shoulders. 'So, are we ready to proceed?' she asked, glancing to Alice.

Alice lifted her chin, seemed to rally. 'Yes, let's get on with it then. Or he'll be standing out there all day.'

Robin did seem better than the last time Lara had visited him, and he listened carefully to what she had to say as he lay resting in bed. Then his blue eyes flashed interest and he nodded his head. 'Yes, I'll see Dad,' he croaked, his voice barely above a whisper.

As Lara helped him to the window, she had to swallow hard to hold back tears when she saw the heartfelt concern on Vic's face. 'Hello, matey,' he called, pressing the flat of his hand to the glass. 'How are you doing?'

'As well as I can be,' Robin croaked, mustering a weak smile.

The look of anguish on Vic's face was enough to confirm he understood how poorly his son was. As Lara mouthed, 'I need to get him back to bed,' Vic nodded, tears shining in his eyes.

Then, with one final press of his hand to the glass, Robin called, 'Bye, Dad,' and Lara led him away. In seconds, the lad was wheezing and coughing violently and as Lara glanced back through the window, she saw Vic walking away with his head down and shoulders hunched.

'Come on, son. Let's get you back into bed,' Alice said briskly as she came to the other side of him.

'I'm glad Dad came,' Robin whispered hoarsely as they settled him between the covers.

Alice glanced to Lara with a quick smile. Then, once Lara had checked Robin's pulse and temperature and written everything up on the observation sheets they now kept by the side of each diphtheria patient's bed, she scrubbed her hands with plenty of soap and water and said her goodbyes.

As she clicked the door shut behind her, a gust of freezing-cold January wind whipped up and came straight at her. She clamped a hand over her nurse's hat and began to stride up the street. But then a sharp voice called from behind and she stopped in her tracks. It was Vic again, raising a hand and shouting a thank you… Then a taller man with much broader shoulders stepped out from a side alley and, the hairs at the back of Lara's neck prickled as she recognised the shape of him. He'd been with Vic that night they'd broken down on their way back from Ingleside Hall.

'This here's my mate, Jimmy Diamond,' Vic offered.

Before she could speak the man replied roughly, 'Hello there, Nurse Flynn. Vic's told me all about you.'

Lara didn't like the man's assured tone, and she felt unsettled by the confident thrust of his chin. So, she merely raised a hand, called a goodbye, then continued up the street.

'Hope to meet you again soon,' Mr Diamond called, and a shiver flashed through her.

She didn't turn around; she tightened her grip on her medical bag and kept going. And as more gusts of freezing-cold wind came at her, she set her mouth and increased her pace. As she walked, she focused on getting back to the surgery, only turning to glance over her shoulder when the street had quietened and there was no sign of Vic or his mate Jimmy.

Shaking her head, making herself leave it behind, she focused on her next visit – the Haworth family. It had been a relief to hear from Bingham that little Daisy was making a good recovery and might soon be transferred from the Infirmary to the isolation ward at Ridgetown Hospital. She knew it would be comforting for the family to know their baby girl was closer by.

Thinking of the role Angus was currently fulfilling at the cottage hospital, she felt proud of their young doctor. She'd also been surprised at how much she missed his jocular presence around the kitchen table. Each evening, as they sat with Bingham at the head, it felt as if a piece of a puzzle was missing.

Angus would be back soon enough though... Already, she could feel the rate of new cases beginning to ease. She held that thought as she nipped down the side of the surgery to collect her bicycle, and in moments, she was pushing off towards Brock Farm.

Cycling hard to make up for lost time, she arrived breathless, then she was pulling her leather bag from the bicycle basket and walking over the yard to the farmhouse door.

She knocked, waited, listened to the sound of brisk footsteps. Mrs Haworth opened the door, her hair dishevelled, her eyes red-rimmed with exhaustion. 'Come in. I'm so glad to see you,' she said quietly. 'We had a rough time last night with the two boys coughing and wheezing. But now this morning, it seems to be clearing.'

'I'm so glad to hear that.' Lara smiled, as she wiped her feet on the mat just inside the door. 'Let's hope they're through the worst of it now, hey... And I'm thinking you'll have had a call from Dr Bingham to report on Daisy's progress?'

'Yes, and he told us she's holding her own,' Mrs Haworth said. But with her next breath, the farmer's wife looked wretched and she had tears glinting in her eyes. She pressed the flat of a hand to the centre of her chest and sobbed. 'I can't even find the words to describe what an empty place I have here in my heart with my baby girl away. Not being able to see her and with more time to come at Ridgetown Hospital, she'll have grown and changed so much when she comes home, and I'll have missed it all. And maybe she won't even know me any more.'

Lara felt for the woman. 'I'm so sorry, Mrs Haworth. My heart goes out to you.'

The woman nodded, swallowed hard.

'And I know this will offer little consolation, and I've never worked at the Infirmary in Preston, but I did visit the children's ward one day with Dr Bingham and it's so lovely. Some of the walls are tiled with nursery-rhyme displays and they have toys for the children, and the nurses were very attentive.'

Mrs Haworth gulped, nodded. 'Even having that bit of information helps me. I can picture her now... Will she be in a cot?'

'Yes, the hospital cots have cast-iron bars, and they're painted white, and there's a special isolation area for the babies. Everything is spotlessly clean.'

The farmer's wife cleared her throat. 'Thank you, Nurse Flynn. I have a feel for it now and it's eased me a little.'

'Daisy will be back soon, Mrs Haworth.'

The woman nodded, wiped a hand around her face. 'We'll just keep going, looking after our two boys. And hopefully, by next month, when Shrove Tuesday comes around, we'll all be around the table eating our pancakes together.'

'I truly hope so, Mrs Haworth,' Lara said gently.

Once she'd completed her assessment of Gordon and Bobby, it felt satisfying to be able to assure Mrs Haworth that the boys were definitely improving. Their older brother, Frank chuckled. 'I know they are, Nurse Flynn, because they're up to mischief again. Last night, Bobby hid Gordon's toy truck under the bed and for the first time since they got sick, they were rolling about laughing and play-fighting.'

'That's good to hear... and did Bobby give him back his truck?'

'Yes, but the little blighter was laughing so much, he set himself off with a fit of coughing.'

Lara smiled and it felt good to feel the tension she'd carried beginning to unwind. 'Well, Frank, I hope they're not going to drive you mad before school reopens. But what a good job you've done here looking after your brothers.'

'He has, hasn't he?' Mrs Haworth said, her eyes shining with pride.

Frank ran a hand through his hair, ruffling it. 'Well, they're a darned nuisance, but they're my baby brothers.'

Lara reached out to him. 'You ought to be proud of yourself.'

Frank's cheeks flushed and he was shaking his head. But Lara could tell he was pleased by the compliment, and quite rightly so.

As Lara followed Mrs Haworth down the stairs, then out through the kitchen to the back door, that feeling of turning a corner with the outbreak of infection remained with her and it gave her a warm glow.

'It'll be me or Nurse Wright for the next visit in a few days' time... and I'm hoping we might be able to discharge your boys then.'

'Good, that's good.' Mrs Haworth gulped. 'And thanks for listening to my concerns over Daisy... It's helped me, Nurse Flynn. I'll keep my chin up, keep going till she's back home.'

Lara nodded, said her goodbyes, and as she walked across the yard through the clucking hens to her bicycle, she felt the weight of all she'd been carrying these past weeks begin to ease just a little.

'Cock-a-doodle-do,' a large, glossy, coppery-brown cockerel offered ear-splittingly loudly as if in celebration.

Lara didn't flinch; she'd got used to the farmyard noises now. But it made her recall how startled she'd been when she'd first heard that loud crowing in the barn where she'd delivered Mrs Haworth's daughter. She savoured the memory of that special day when she'd knelt among the straw to deliver Daisy. And she told herself she'd known as soon as the baby had given her first lusty cry that she'd be strong.

As she pulled her bicycle from the wall, a certain slant of

light from the watery, winter sun glimmered on the rough, pot-holed track that led out to the road. And for some reason, it offered hope, as if indicating the beginnings of a way out from a difficult time. It made Lara smile properly for the first time in ages and as she pushed off on her bicycle with her breath steaming in the air, she felt as light as air.

10

A few weeks later, as the gusty, cold and wet weather turned to clearer skies with brighter, freezing-cold air, there had been no new cases of diphtheria for a while. Children were continuing to be discharged from hospital, the village school had reopened and Angus had returned from his secondment to the cottage hospital. And it all felt as if the old order was being restored. It was good to have the junior doctor back at the kitchen table, but he'd been almost silent at first and seemed to have turned in on himself. Marion had managed to get through to him and he'd loosened up enough to tell her of the harrowing cases he'd had to deal with on the fever ward. With tears streaming down his cheeks, he'd spoken of the deaths of two tiny children he'd fought hard to save. It was only then as they picked up on Angus's grief that the reality of their own experience became clear. Bingham had been solemn but immensely supportive that first evening the young doctor had been back at the table. But seeing Angus pale and quiet with dark smudges beneath his eyes had unsettled all the team.

At least no Ingleside children had been lost but some were

still recovering in Ridgetown Hospital, including Daisy Haworth, who'd only just been transferred from Preston Royal. She'd been set to come home sooner but there'd been a tense few days when she'd relapsed. Lara had barely slept the night they'd heard the news and the next day, she'd ridden out to check on Mrs Haworth, arriving at the farm just as the woman was beginning to fold in on herself.

Lara knew the Ingleside children had come through by the skin of their teeth, and they would still be nursing the more severely affected ones for a while longer. There'd need to be strict monitoring of those who'd been most poorly: Daisy Haworth of course, once she was home from hospital, but also Poppy Douglas, Robin Taylor and little Freddy Lennox, who had been under Angus's care at the cottage hospital. It made Lara's heart twist when Angus had told her how sick Freddy had been and how he'd needed a tracheotomy. The thought of the smiley, mischievous little lad being so very poorly still made her breath catch... He'd been through so much already after his mother had been acutely unwell with a mental breakdown and he and his brother and sister had gone missing, hiding out to stay safe. She thought back to that moment when, as part of the search party, she'd seen Freddy run out from their hiding place, straight into her arms. The joy of it lifted her now, brought her back to the present. And, realising she'd been standing outside the back door of the surgery on her way to her first set of routine visits for a while, she carried on walking to the shed to retrieve her bicycle.

'You all right? You must have been out here for ages,' Marion's voice called from behind.

'Yes, I'm OK,' she replied, fixing a smile as she turned to her colleague. 'Just getting my head around my visits. It's all a bit odd being plunged back to normal.'

'Oh, yeah. Feels weird,' Marion groaned. Beside Lara now, her colleague was linking her arm and pulling her close. Dressed in two pairs of wool trousers and sturdy leather boots, Marion was all set to go out on her motorcycle.

It worried Lara how things might be out on the country lanes. 'Is it safe for you to go out on Gloria? Mrs H said it's going to be icy.'

'Yeah, don't worry. I've managed worse, and I can always leave the motorbike behind and make my way on foot.'

Lara felt heartened by Marion's straightforward approach to most things in life.

Then her colleague pulled her close and said, 'Oh, and tomorrow night, me and Angus are planning to go out round the pubs with the rest of the village to celebrate the end of isolation. What do you think? Do you want to come?'

Lara felt her breath catch; it somehow felt too soon. But when Marion growled softly, 'Come on, Lara. It'll be a lively night full of local colour and it's time to get back out there,' Lara knew she couldn't say no.

'In that case, how can I refuse.' She smiled, and Marion offered a whoop of joy.

For a fleeing moment, Lara wondered if she'd be able to leave the pub early. But she knew she couldn't desert Marion because no doubt Angus would be fully in there with his drinking buddies Ed Cronshaw and of course Leo. She told herself she hadn't thought of Leo for ages. But even as she tried to make it real, her cheeks flushed with heat. Then she made herself cast back to that awkward evening at Ingleside Hall when she'd witnessed whatever it was that seemed to be going on between Leo and Philippa. Usually, when she strayed to this, it made her dismiss Leo's attentions. But right away, she flashed back to the kiss they'd shared in the vet's surgery, and her stomach did a flip.

'Oh for goodness' sake,' she muttered under her breath.

'For goodness' sake what?' Marion called cheerily as she wrestled her motorcycle out of the shed.

Lara pasted on a smile and, never quick to think up an excuse, she said, 'Oh, that it's very cold and it might be slippery on the roads.'

Marion frowned and they were in such close proximity that Lara could tell her friend wasn't taken in by her mention of the weather conditions they faced most days in winter. But Marion didn't challenge her; she simply said, 'Well, whatever the weather, off we go. Out into the fray.'

'Indeed we do,' Lara replied with a grin.

Right then, as she grabbed her bicycle by the handlebars, for the first time in ages, it felt like business as usual. Especially when Angus came running full pelt out of the back door, still with a piece of toast and jam in his hand. 'Morning, nurses,' he called, then slipped on ice and almost fell flat on his backside. 'Ha, always forget it's winter. Need to be careful,' he called as he slid around the corner en route to the little blue Austin which was parked skew-whiff down the side of the surgery.

In moments, he was back. 'Oops, windscreen's full of ice. I need some warm water and a scraper.'

Then, as he pushed the final corner of toast into his mouth and ran back inside the surgery, Lara and Marion began to laugh.

'How many winters has he worked here?' Lara asked.

'Ah, well, let me see... this will probably be his third... so no wonder he's not used to the icy conditions.'

Lara was still chuckling as Marion began to move her motorcycle.

In the next second, Angus ran past with a bucket of steaming water and one of Mrs Hewitt's wooden spatulas. He slipped again in the same place, then righted himself, laughing as he went back to the car.

As Lara wheeled her bicycle out to the street, she began to focus on her list of morning visits. First up was Freddy Lennox at Foxglove Cottage; the family had moved back there so they could be at home for his discharge from hospital. The mother of the family, Lydia was still in the local mental institution following her diagnosis of puerperal psychosis. Bingham had visited her, and he'd said it had been heartbreaking to see her in the regulation striped dress of a mental institution – silent, glassy-eyed, her hair greasy and unkempt. The doctors weren't optimistic for her recovery, and they were already thinking of her as a long-term patient. Lara struggled with that, and it made her even more protective of the Lennox children. At least though, the eldest boy, Michael, had been able to get back to school.

With her breath steaming in the air, she felt her feet slip on ice, so she wheeled her bicycle up to the turning which led down to the sawmill. Seeing grit on the road, she mounted and got a feel for the slippery conditions as she rode slowly by the mill workers' cottages. As soon as the gradient steepened, her front wheel began to slide, so she dismounted and proceeded on foot, the mechanical whir and thump of the mill engine and the screech of the big circular saw growing ever louder.

As she passed by the mill, she glanced to the yard for the familiar faces of Ed Cronshaw or Danny Ryan, but there was just a young lad muffled in a woolly hat and thick scarf sweeping the yard and another fella up in the crane with a huge tree trunk lashed by a chain. She tried not to look but her eyes couldn't help but be drawn to the place by the mill wall where she'd discovered a fire that had been set one night in autumn when she'd been returning from the Lennoxes'. It still niggled her that no one had been charged with it. Ed had always been convinced the perpetrator was Vic Taylor, but there'd been rumours that her former boyfriend from Liverpool, Patrick, had also been involved after he'd met Vic in the Fleece when he'd come to Ingleside looking for her. None of it seemed to fit together and the case had now been closed by the young detective from Ridgetown Police Station: Adam Stirling.

Lara drew a slow breath. With the time that had passed and the recent rigours of the diphtheria outbreak, what had happened at the mill didn't feel quite so pressing. But even as she tried to push it out of her head, it came back a little too strongly for her liking. That's when she remounted her bicycle and pushed hard against the pedals, hoping the exertion required to get up the gritted incline beyond the mill would help refresh her. It seemed to do the trick and once she reached the mill pond, she was already feeling better.

She dismounted her bicycle, wheeled it to the stone wall that surrounded the pond and for a few moments, she gazed out over the almost black, perfectly still water. Ice was forming at the edges and seeing it made a cold shiver run through her. Time to move on, get to her visit. But before she remounted, she glanced back across the flat expanse of water. Even with the noise of the mill in the background, it felt peaceful.

As Lara remounted her bicycle and pushed on towards Foxglove Cottage, she began to feel free, as she often did out here. Even though the trees were bare, the wildflowers had died back, and the grass was brown and withered, she remembered that she loved being out here close to the fells with the big sky above. Marion had told her to keep an eye out for the first snowdrops, because once the tiny, white flowers made their appearance, spring would be just around the corner.

Her first glimpse of the cottage took her back to that first ante-natal visit to Lydia Lennox in the autumn. Seeing it again now, after all that had happened, it somehow looked different. In fact, as she pulled up on her bicycle, she understood why. Previously, the cottage had been in a state of disrepair with broken roof tiles, peeling paint, and desperately in need of a new front door. But now, all those issues seemed to have been addressed and as she propped her bicycle against the newly whitewashed wall and tapped on the brand-new door, she could smell fresh paint.

As she waited for admission, all seemed quiet, then a small child was shouting, 'Door, door!' and she recognised little Ava's voice.

Steven opened up with his daughter clinging to his leg.

'Nurse Flynn,' he called with a bright smile as Ava squealed with excitement and reached up with both arms for her daddy to pick her up. Ava was chuckling and bouncing up and down on Steven's hip, her blonde curls jiggling. Then she was pointing to Lara and saying, 'Nurse Fin, Nurse Fin.'

'Nurse Flynn,' Steven gently corrected as Lara said hello to the little girl. Then he led the way into the cottage. And as Lara closed the door behind her, Steven walked with his baby girl to the truckle bed against the wall and placed her gently down amid a pile of toys. Most of which Lara remembered having been donated by local people after the children had gone missing.

He was at the stove then and calling over his shoulder, 'Won't be a minute, Nurse Flynn... I'm just getting to grips with this ancient contraption. It's blowing either too hot or stone cold at present.'

'I'm afraid I have no advice to offer,' Lara replied as she felt the first waft of overly heated air. 'But at least you've got it plenty warm enough in here.'

He turned to her and she noted his flushed cheeks and sweat-stained brow. 'I'm afraid it's a bit too hot now.' He chuckled. 'In fact, it's probably a good job I'm starting my new job at the mill on Monday morning, and Betty Cronshaw will be taking over here because for the life of me, I can't work out how this blasted stove works.'

'Yes, it's probably for the best you're going back to work,' Lara replied. Then, she glanced around approvingly. 'The cottage is looking very pristine with its new door and fresh paint and all the redecoration inside as well. You must have been busy.'

'No, that wasn't me,' he replied, his voice thickening with emotion. 'The fellas from the sawmill, they came here secretly to fix up the cottage and redecorate for us coming home.'

'That was such a nice gesture.'

He gulped, nodded. 'I mean, if they hadn't done enough already, turning out like that to search for the children when they went missing last year.'

'They're a good lot, those sawmill fellas,' Lara offered, and Steven nodded. Then he wiped a hand across his brow to clear the sweat from his overheated face.

'Where's my patient, Freddy?' Lara asked. As soon as the words were out of her mouth, she heard a rattling cough and the door to the bedroom burst open and the boy came running, his eyes alive with excitement when he saw her.

'Have you brought some chocolate like Nurse Marion?' he asked brightly, then began to hack with a cough.

What he'd just said made Lara smile, but his cough sounded awful. She was straight to him with a gentle arm around his shoulders. Once he'd recovered from the cough, she said, 'I'm sorry, Freddy, I forgot the chocolate. But I'll bring some next time if I'm down for your visit.'

'That's OK.' He shrugged, then he was coughing again but already over to the truckle bed with Ava and the toys. It nearly brought tears to Lara's eyes when she saw the little girl pat her brother on the back.

'You all right, Freddy?' she asked in her baby voice.

'Yes, just barking like a dog,' the little boy replied, then he was on all fours, pretending to wag his tail, and Ava was giggling.

Lara couldn't help but be moved by the little lad's resilience. He'd lost quite a bit of weight when he'd been in hospital, so his chin was sharp and his eyes seemed overly large and even more expressive in his thin face. He'd always been a lively one but given he was so poorly, his energy surprised her. If anything, he'd gained in spirit.

When Steven saw her smiling, he said, 'He's a little trooper, isn't he, our Freddy? I'm the one who's mithering about his cough, so that's why I rang the surgery.'

'Don't you worry,' Lara said with a smile. 'That's what we're here for: to check things out and reassure. Particularly when the patient is a child.'

Steven nodded and she could see tears shining in his eyes. Then he said, 'I suppose I worry more because I'm a single parent now, with Lydia still away in hospital.'

'You're doing a good job,' Lara said firmly. 'Better than any man I've ever seen left in charge of small children.'

Steven flashed a smile and she could see how pleased he was with her remark. And it was true, every word.

She shifted her attention to her patient, who was still pretending to be a dog, but he sounded as if he was choking with that hacking cough. Once it had settled again, she called to him, 'Come on, doggy, come to me.' He came, still pretending to wag his tail. 'Now sit,' she said and he sat back on his haunches and brought up his arms like a begging dog. 'Now, little doggy, will you let me listen to your chest and take your temperature?'

He nodded, pretending to pant, but hacking with a cough in between.

She placed her thermometer under his arm, then whipped her stethoscope out of her bag and listened to his chest back and front in moments. 'Good boy,' she said, then gave him a pat. 'Now, just stay still please for a little while longer till I find out how warm you are.'

Freddy sat, still panting.

'Good doggy,' Lara said once more, patting him gently and stroking his hair as he lifted his chin and she noted the well-healed tracheotomy scar on his neck – still bright red but it would fade.

'How is his temperature?' Steven asked anxiously from the stove as she read the thermometer.

'It's in normal range, so no worries there. And when I listened to his chest, there's a bit of a rattle higher up, probably something left over from the diphtheria. But lower down is clear and as we can see he's active and very much himself. We need to keep an eye on things but so far so good.'

Steven's shoulders dropped and he turned fully to her with a broad smile. 'That's such good news... I thought maybe I hadn't been looking after him properly and that's why his cough sounded worse again.'

Lara offered Freddy a smile, then walked to Steven and placed a hand on his arm. 'You're doing sterling work here. Your little boy had a bad dose of the infection so he's taking longer to recover. But he's coming on in leaps and bounds – literally.' She chuckled as she glanced back to see him jumping on all fours.

He heaved a sigh. 'Well, that's good to know.'

'All down to your attentive care,' Lara replied as she slipped her stethoscope into her medical bag and prepared to leave. Then Freddy and Ava both came running at her and she crouched down to give them a hug. 'Now you two be good for your daddy,' she said gently and Ava was running to Steven, shouting, 'Daddy, daddy.'

And as he swept her up into his arms, he murmured, 'Hello sweetie pie,' and snuggled her close.

'What about me; am I sweetie pie?' Freddy called from the truckle bed, then coughed as he jumped up and ran at Steven with such energy, Lara was even more sure he was well on the way to recovery.

Turning as she reached the door, Lara called, 'I'll be off now and as I've already said, I'm pleased with Freddy's progress. You'll need another visit in a few days to check he's continuing to improve and it'll be me or Nurse Wright depending on our schedules. But in the meantime, if you have any concerns, go straight to your neighbour, Nora Hurst, who I believe is still looking after baby Jamie, and use her phone to call the surgery.'

'Will do,' Steven called, cradling Ava on his hip with one arm while Freddy clung to his leg. 'I know it's good for Michael to be going to school, but my goodness do I miss him. I didn't realise just how much he was doing with looking after these two. I don't know what I'll do when the baby comes back from Nora's.'

'You'll manage. And you'll have Betty coming every day to look after the children and I'm sure Nora will be bobbing in. It will work; you'll have to make it work.'

He nodded, his face still flushed with heat from the stove, his red hair dishevelled as he stood laden with two of his children.

'See you in a few days, if I'm down to visit,' she called with a smile and a raise of her hand as she exited the cottage.

She paused for a moment after she'd clicked the door shut behind her. Out in the air, she noted the stillness of the outdoors in stark contrast to the muffled noises of Steven and the children inside the cottage. Then as the lone cry of a curlew broke the spell as it soared high above, she walked to pull her bicycle away from the whitewashed wall to continue her visits. As she wheeled away, a sense of completeness settled over her and she felt glad that she'd been given this visit today.

11

'It's Saturday night and we are going to have a right good knees-up,' Marion called down the stairs as Lara dashed up to get changed for the celebration marking the end of the diphtheria outbreak. But even as she reached the top step, she heard the surgery door burst open and a ragged voice shouted for help. Right away, she recognised Lizzie Cronshaw, so she ran back down with Marion, calling after her, 'Do you want me to take this one?'

'No, I've got it!' she shouted back.

Lizzie was wide-eyed, panicking, with little Sue in her arms breathing noisily, then wracked with a choking cough. 'I think it's the diphtheria come back, Nurse Flynn. Just listen to her.'

Lara had begun assessing Sue as she ran down the stairs and the timbre of that cough was different to diphtheria. Also, once a child recovered, they didn't pick it up again, so that was another reason she was ready to stand by her assessment. 'I think she's got croup, Lizzie. It's a similar cough, but not diphtheria.'

'Are you sure, Nurse Flynn?' Lizzie sobbed. 'It sounds like the diphtheria to me.'

'I'm certain,' Lara said firmly, confident in her diagnosis especially since all she'd heard for weeks was the tight cough of diphtheria.

'Thank goodness,' Lizzie groaned as Sue writhed in her arms, then the little girl was coughing, croaking, and crying.

'She needs steam to loosen her cough,' Lara said. 'Let's go back across the road and put a big pan of water on the stove.'

Lizzie nodded, already leading the way.

'Are you sure you don't need assistance, Nurse Flynn?' Mrs Hewitt shouted from the kitchen doorway.

'Certain,' she replied. 'The only thing I do need is a good, strong cup of tea and a bite to eat when I get back.'

'Right you are,' the housekeeper called, the note of concern in her voice following Lara out through the door.

The Cronshaws' cottage was just across the street, so they soon had a big pan of water heating on the stove. And as steam filled the small kitchen, even as Sue began to hack again with the cough, like magic, it eased. Lara felt relief flood through her. Even though she'd been sure it wasn't diphtheria, it was always wise to maintain flexibility with any diagnosis. But croup had now been confirmed so she felt safe to leave.

'She's settling now, Lizzie. Just keep going with the steam and if you've any further concerns, pop over to the surgery. It'll be Dr Bingham on call because the rest of the medical team are out tonight.'

'Yes, that's good to know,' Lizzie replied, only half-listening, still distracted by Sue's hacking cough.

Then, even as Lara was saying her goodbyes, the cottage door burst open and Ed ran in, his eyes wide, his breath coming quick. He was full of anxiety. 'I've just seen Leo in the pub, and he said he'd seen you running across the street with your medical bag. What's wrong? Is it Sue? Is it William? And why is there so much steam in here?'

'Everything's fine, Ed. Your Sue's got a touch of croup, that's all.'

'Are you sure it's not more diphtheria?'

'Yes, I'm certain. She might need more steam to settle her croupy cough, but these cases usually resolve in twenty-four to forty-eight hours.'

Ed was nodding vigorously, his eyes darting from Sue to baby William, who was still sleeping peacefully in his crib in the corner of the kitchen. 'Do you think the baby will catch it as well?'

'Maybe but given he's still being breast fed, he'll have more resistance, so it's less likely. But if you or Lizzie are worried, run across to the surgery. Dr Bingham will be holding the fort tonight and he'll be straight there if you need anything.'

Ed ran a hand around his face and heaved a heavy sigh.

Lizzie reached out to him then. 'But, Ed, I thought you were going to be out tonight with the rest of the crew to celebrate the end of diphtheria?'

He was shaking his head. 'Not now, I'm staying right here,' he grunted, already removing his jacket. 'My kids are what matters and besides, it'll be so packed out in the pubs, you'll hardly be able to get served. I'll go out next weekend, when things have settled down.'

Lizzie nodded. 'All right, if you're sure.'

'Course I'm sure,' he replied, grinning then and putting an arm around Lizzie's shoulders, pulling her close as she held onto Sue.

'I'll leave you to it, then,' Lara said, making to the door.

Ed called after her, 'If you are going out tonight, Nurse Flynn, it's already feeling like it's going to be one of those wild nights that go down in local history – so you take care out there.'

'I'll be fine, Ed,' she replied, smiling as she opened the cottage door.

* * *

Marion was at the kitchen table, already dressed in her going-out clothes, when Lara made it back to the kitchen to claim her cup of tea and bite to eat.

'Everything in order?' her colleague asked, bright-eyed, gazing directly at Lara while attempting to eat a piece of chocolate cake without disrupting her red lipstick.

'Yes, all fine. A case of croup that instantly responded to steam.'

'Excellent news,' Marion replied with gusto, as she gestured to the slices of cake in the middle of the table. 'Take one before I eat the lot.'

'Oi,' Mrs Hewitt called from the kitchen counter. 'I've got a bowl of vegetable soup and a ham sandwich here for Nurse Flynn before she starts on the cake.'

Marion was giggling and shaking her head. 'Well, she'd better hurry up or all of this cake will be gone.'

'What cake?' Angus growled as he came through the door, his unruly, blond hair neatly coiffed. He was dressed smartly in a blue shirt and red-striped tie, carrying his thick tweed jacket over his arm.

'Ooh, look at you, man about town,' Marion teased.

'Well, it's worth making the effort. Just like you, dear Marion, with your red, cake-crumbed lipstick.'

'Oh no, is it?' She frowned, then she was pulling out her handkerchief, dabbing at her mouth. 'Sod it,' she said, as her lipstick smeared on the hankie. 'I don't care if I need to reapply my lippy. This chocolate cake is so delicious, I'd sacrifice all my make-up and my new blue blouse as well.'

'Oh, so you're also wearing blue.' Angus grinned between mouthfuls of cake. 'In case you haven't noticed, we're matching tonight, and my new blue shirt is almost the exact same shade as your blouse.'

'Oh yes, I didn't realise,' Marion said with a sticky, chocolatey smile. 'Maybe we could call it our new going-out-to-the-pub uniform.' Then she cleared her throat and when she spoke again, her voice was husky with emotion. 'And just so you know, Dr Angus Fitzwilliam, we missed you terribly around this table when you were away at the cottage hospital.'

Angus swallowed hard; he seemed to be fighting back a sob. 'I missed you all too.'

Mrs Hewitt cleared her throat, bustling from the kitchen counter with a plate of sandwiches. 'Help yourselves,' she called raggedly.

'Oh dear,' Lara sighed. 'I'm not sure if I can go out tonight after all. It feels like we haven't paid enough attention as a team to how hard it's been these last few weeks. And now we're back together, maybe we should stay in and spend some time around the table.'

'If only I could, Nurse Flynn.' Angus chuckled, the first flash of mischief in his eyes since he'd returned. 'But I have already promised my brothers in arms – Mr Leo Sullivan and Mr Ed Cronshaw – that tonight, we will lead the race to the bar.'

'I think it might be just you and Leo,' Lara said through a mouthful of the ham sandwich she was now eating hungrily between spoonfuls of soup.

'Oh, how so, Nurse Flynn? Do tell.'

'I've just come back from the Cronshaws'. Sue's got the croup and Ed heard in the pub that I was visiting so he rushed back home, and he was all worried. So he said he'd be staying in to look after the children.'

'Ah, so one man down,' Angus breathed as he leaned back in his chair. 'Good for Ed, though.' He nodded. 'He'll be sorely missed, but that's just how it is. Mr Sullivan and I will have to take the blow on the chin and continue our quest without him.'

'Hark at you, Dr Fitzwilliam. You sound all posh when you talk like that,' Mrs Hewitt offered.

'He is posh,' Marion cackled. 'We've just got used to it, that's all.'

'I can get by in the land of the yokels, especially when a big night out is coming up,' Angus said with a dramatic flourish of his hand. Then he reached for a sandwich from the plate Mrs Hewitt had just brought to the table.

As Lara sat quietly eating her soup, taking in the delicious banter between Angus and Marion, Mrs Hewitt settled at the table with her cup of tea and was soon joining in, alternately laughing then mock-scolding. It made Lara feel calm, grounded. After all the disruption of their usual pattern of work, this felt like a regrouping, a show of strength as they bounced back. Bingham was notable by his absence but even though he wasn't physically present, his place at the head of the table seemed to emanate power. When the brown and orange striped tabby cat, Tiddles, strolled in from the hallway en route to the warmth of the Aga where he'd stretch out his white-tipped paws, he brushed his silken back against Lara's leg, and she tapped into an even more luxurious moment of contentment.

Then as Angus pushed back his chair, slipped on his jacket and called, 'Once more unto the breach,' he was gone from the kitchen and the dynamic shifted again. And that's when Lara realised she wasn't even washed or changed for her night out.

'Oh no, I still need to get ready,' she cried as she jumped up from her seat and ran out of the kitchen to the sound of Marion's full-throated laughter.

Fifteen minutes later, she was trotting back down the stairs and into the kitchen – washed, dressed, and with her make-up expertly applied.

'How on earth do you do that so fast?' Marion asked.

'I leave everything ready and waiting beforehand, then just get on with it.'

'You look lovely, Nurse Flynn.' Mrs Hewitt smiled. 'As do you, Nurse Wright.'

'Thank you, Mrs H,' the two nurses called together as Marion jumped up from the table and walked around to link Lara's arm.

'You two have a good time. You deserve it after how hard you've worked.'

'Exactly, of course they deserve it,' Bingham cried, as he strode abruptly into the kitchen with a folded newspaper under his arm, his hair poking untidily from beneath his checked trilby, which bizarrely, he'd taken to wearing indoors.

His sudden and eccentric appearance triggered Lara back to the morning she'd been called to assist Mrs Hewitt with the removal of a mouse from the kitchen, and Bingham had turned up with his bare legs poking out from a striped nightshirt.

'We will have a good time, I'm sure we will,' Lara called, her breath catching as she struggled to hold back a giggle.

Then as they bustled into the hall to grab their thick wool coats, with Lara rapidly explaining the reason for her amusement, Marion was also giggling.

They were quickly down the corridor and as Marion opened the front door, loud laughter and shouted conversation from the Fleece across the road met them head-on.

'Sounds packed out,' Marion murmured.

By the time they'd climbed the stone steps to find the doorway fully blocked with folk squashed into the smoke-filled pub, Lara was already shaking her head.

'Let's go down to the Old Oak – should be quieter there,' Marion offered, pulling on Lara's arm to lead her away.

The street was busy with revellers and this early in the evening, it all felt very light-hearted with banter and laughter passing between folks. A group of sawmill fellas, still with sawdust in their hair from their Saturday-morning shift, were outside the pub door with their pints, their breath steaming in the cold air. Lara recognised Danny Ryan, the father of a baby she'd delivered back in the summer. Immediately, he was all smiles, then he raised his glass. 'Here's to you nurses for all you've done to look after our bairns.'

The fullness of his tone, the meaningful way all the sawmill men raised their pint glasses, brought tears to Lara's eyes.

Then, with a catch in her voice, Marion said, 'Thanks for that, fellas… It's been a tough time for everyone.'

'It has that.' Danny smiled. 'But we're out tonight to mark the end of it. So you get yourselves in there and raise a glass to all that's gone. It's a bit packed out, but you should be able to get to the bar. That young doctor of yours, he's already there with his mate the vet, and they're having a fine time.'

'I bet they are.' Marion grinned.

Even as they walked into the smoke-filled pub, they saw Angus, already swaying, with his arm around Leo's shoulders. They were about to squeeze through when Leo glanced over his shoulder and his face lit up with a smile when his eyes met Lara's.

She felt it then, in the pit of her stomach: that stronger connection they had since they'd kissed.

'You OK?' Marion shouted above the noise of the pub.

'Yes, I'm fine. It's, er, just a bit crowded in here,' she replied as her tummy did another flip.

Clearly sensing Lara's hesitation, Marion expertly pulled her through the crush of pub-goers. 'We'll get there. I'll make sure of that,' Marion called over her shoulder.

When a space opened at the bar, Marion slipped right in and pulled Lara next to her. She was away from Leo, but she could still feel his eyes on her and it gave her goosebumps.

'Come up here, come to us,' she heard Angus shouting slurrily.

'In a minute. We'll get served first,' Marion called. Then she turned to Lara. 'Pint of bitter?'

'Yes, please,' Lara murmured, and in that moment, when Leo leaned forward on the bar and grinned directly at her, she felt a jolt of pleasure as she recalled the intimacy they'd shared before all the stress of the diphtheria.

Once they had their drinks, a fraction more space opened up and they were able to shuffle along to the end of the bar and take their places close to Angus and Leo. Lara ended up at the edge of the group next to Marion, with Leo at the far side, but as his eyes snagged hers, he smiled deliciously.

'It's good to be out,' Leo called. 'Let's raise our glasses to that.'

When Marion linked Lara's arm and they shouted a cheers together, Lara felt happy, joyful even, and she knew she'd remember this moment.

After another glass of ale, she was beginning to feel even more relaxed, but when Marion switched to drinking shorts, she shook her head and declined a double whisky and soda.

'Just a half of bitter for me,' she told Leo when it was his turn to buy the round.

'You sure?' he called.

'I'm certain.' She laughed, and with the loosening effect of the alcohol, as their eyes connected, she felt an even stronger buzz of excitement through to the pit of her stomach.

'You're very shmiley, Nurse Lara,' Marion slurred.

'Yes, and so are you, Nurse Marion,' Lara replied, grinning back at her.

Once their glasses were empty, Angus called, swaying a little, 'It's time to move. Let's go up to the Fleesh.'

'Yes,' Marion replied, grabbing his arm as he lurched to the side.

Lara felt as if she and Leo had become the responsible ones as they steered their friends out of the pub. It was pitch-dark outside now but lights from the cottages at either side of the street gave enough light to see.

'It still sounds busy up there,' Lara said, as she pulled Marion close, making sure she was steady enough to walk.

Leo was walking behind with Angus, who'd begun to slurrily sing 'Show Me the Way to Go Home'. His choice of song seemed appropriate, and they were all laughing at his determination to walk in a straight line as he wove his way up the hill.

'Whoa, hang on a minute there, matey.' Leo laughed as he grabbed Angus and righted him.

'Yeah, you steady on there, mate,' a sharp, mocking voice mimicking Leo's called from behind. Lara's skin crawled as she recognised that friend of Vic Taylor's, Jimmy Diamond.

'What? Who's that?' Leo called back over his shoulder, his brow furrowing.

'Just keep walking,' Lara said firmly. But it was too late; Leo had stopped in his tracks and he wouldn't budge. So she had no choice but to confront Jimmy as he walked up the street with a brindled lurcher at one side and a very drunk Vic Taylor at the other.

'Can we help you with something, Mr Diamond?' Lara called, her voice suddenly taut with nerves.

Marion slurred, 'Don't shpeak to him, Lara. He's not a nice man.'

Jimmy glinted a malevolent smile. 'I think you'll find, Nurse Wright, that I'm a very nice man.'

Instantly wondering how this man knew Marion's surname, Lara urged again, 'Come on, just keep walking.' She pulled on Marion's arm, but her friend was frowning and she wouldn't budge.

Jimmy seemed stone-cold sober, and he was glaring at them, the brindled lurcher by his side with its ears back offering a sorrowful whine. 'Less of that,' he growled, yanking the dog's chain unnecessarily hard. Then he fixed Lara again with his sharp eyes and with a nasty, lopsided smirk, he said, 'I was just going to tap on Alice Taylor's door. After all she's still the wife of my friend Vic here. So surely, he should be allowed access to her and the children.'

Lara felt a jolt of anger. She stepped forward, right up to him. 'Don't you dare disturb Alice and the children; Robin is still very poorly.'

Jimmy narrowed his eyes. 'Well, he's still Vic's son though, isn't he? And from what my friend has said about you, Nurse Lara, you're the one that made up a bunch of lies to separate him from his family in the first place.'

Even Vic was calling out, 'No, it wasn't her... It was my fault.'

Leo, staggering slightly, was right beside Lara now, shouting for Marion to grab Angus and steer him up to the Fleece.

'Oh, here he is, the brave young vet,' Jimmy called peevishly. Then he narrowed his eyes, spat, 'I've heard you've recently acquired a little dog, a Jack Russell terrier that exactly fits the description of the one I lost a while back.'

Leo was shaking his head. 'Nah, you've heard wrong. The dog I found would never associate with someone like you.'

Jimmy's eyes flashed with anger and Lara knew she had to step in to defuse the situation. But in the next split second, Jimmy growled, 'That dog's mine and I'm taking him back.'

Leo shouted, 'You bloody well stay away from my dog,' and tried to swing a punch, which Jimmy expertly dodged. Then with a heavy, deadening sound, Jimmy landed his own punch right there, hard, straight in Leo's face. And as a spray of bright-red blood arced away, the young vet slumped hard to his knees on the cobbled street. His face already a mass of blood, he was groaning, then wailing, and his head began to loll.

Jimmy cackled loudly as he strode away, pulling Vic with him. He called menacingly over his shoulder, 'I'll be back for my dog, Sullivan.'

Lara was straight there beside Leo, the shock of what had just happened clutching at her chest, squeezing the air from her lungs. But she grabbed hold to support him, pulling a handkerchief from her pocket. His face crumpled, he was shouting out with pain. His nose was pouring blood and it looked broken, so there was nothing she could do right now but press her neatly folded white handkerchief to the gaping wound above his left eye. He yelped with pain, then he was drunkenly sobbing, 'Lara. I'm so sorry, Lara.'

Marion was beside her now. 'What's he ranting on about?' she slurred, then she shook Leo's shoulder. 'Shut up, you eejit. This isn't about Lara and it's not your fault. It's that Jimmy who should be sorry.' Marion was swaying a little but out in the cold air, she seemed to be rapidly sobering up.

'We need to get him up to the surgery,' Lara said firmly.

She glanced to Angus, who stood swaying and grinning

further up the street. Clearly, he wouldn't have the capacity to help her move anything. Marion was probably her best bet.

'Right, come on, let's get him up off the road.'

In the next second, Danny Ryan was staggering up the street and Ed threw open his cottage door and was running down. 'Lizzie's just told me she heard shouting. What's going on? Leo! Are you all right, mate?' he called, coming to an abrupt halt in his stockinged feet. Ed was visibly upset at the sight of Leo, but he soon had him up on his feet. 'Who did this to you, mate? Just give me the word and I'll give 'em what for.'

Leo couldn't answer; he looked awful with blood still pouring from his nose and the cut above his eye. Lara held her blood-soaked handkerchief in her balled fist; there was nothing more she could do right now to staunch the bleeding.

Ed looked stunned as he supported Leo, then he was growling and shouting, 'Whoever did this needs to look forward to a good hiding.'

Lara was sure she caught a ripple of faraway laughter, but she couldn't be certain because her heart was pounding so loud in her ears.

Marion and Angus were rapidly sobering up, but Lara was the only one who was clear-headed enough to take charge. 'Bring him straight to the surgery so we can get him patched up.'

Danny had had a fair bit to drink, so Ed took most of Leo's weight as they supported him, almost dragged him up the street, shouting out in pain.

Lara's heart was still hammering in her chest; tears stung her eyes at the injustice of it all. They'd been having a lovely night out, a celebration of all they'd come through. And now it had been cut short by a nasty, violent man.

'Whatever's going on?' Mrs Hewitt cried as she met them at the door. 'Oh dear, poor Leo, what's happened to him?'

'He's been punched in the face by an associate of Vic Taylor's,' Lara hissed through gritted teeth.

Bingham was shouting, sounding very agitated as he strode out of his room on the ground floor. 'What the blazes is going on? Leo's not a fighter; he's our local vet. Something needs to be done about those blasted hooligans.'

'I agree,' Lara groaned. 'But right now, we need to get Leo patched up. He almost passed out, it was such a hard punch. And I think his nose might be broken.'

'Poor Leo,' Mrs Hewitt wailed, her eyes shining with tears as she tried but failed to hold back a sob.

'He's going to be fine, Edith,' Bingham soothed. 'I'll just pop a few sutures in that cut above his eye and straighten his nose. And once the bruising has faded, he'll be as good as new.'

The doctor reached out to put an arm briefly around Mrs Hewitt's shoulders. Despite all the drama, Lara couldn't help but be moved by his gentleness, even though it was overshadowed by the impact of him using the housekeeper's first name. Even Marion, still sobering up, didn't miss a beat. In the next second, she whispered, 'Edith?' with a ripple of amusement in her voice. Lara needed to swallow hard to stop herself from giggling – probably a nervous reaction to what had just happened out on the street. But she also knew that Leo's injuries were relatively mild; he'd soon be recovering. And this thing with Mrs Hewitt and Bingham had helped to take the edge off and bring the whole episode back down to something far less fraught.

12

Next morning, first thing, Lara's thoughts were for Leo and his busted nose. She was reasonably sure the strong painkiller Bingham had prescribed would have helped him get some sleep but still she felt anxious over him. Recognising this was beyond the ordinary level of concern she had for a regular patient, she muttered to herself under her breath, 'Come on, he's just a good friend, that's all.' But even as her steaming breath hung in the bitingly cold air, she knew she wasn't being exactly honest with herself. She growled under her breath and in what felt like an act of defiance, she swung her bare legs straight out of bed and planted her feet squarely on the cold floor.

'Urgh,' she shuddered, as her teeth began to chatter.

Already, she was grabbing her clothes from the barely warm radiator, shivering as she pulled on her woollen vest, thick blouse and hand-knitted jumper. She couldn't shake the violence of Jimmy Diamond's attack and knew she needed to get down to the vet's to check on Leo.

As she stole quietly down the stairs in the Sunday-morning stillness of the surgery, she heard the gentle rattle of crockery from the kitchen and knew Mrs Hewitt was up first as usual and going about her duties.

'Morning, Nurse Flynn,' the housekeeper called cheerily as Lara entered the kitchen. 'I've just brewed a pot of tea, so you're exactly on time.'

'Thanks, Mrs H.' Lara smiled, walking to the kitchen counter to collect the steaming pot swaddled in its red-crocheted tea cosy.

'Did you sleep after all the goings-on last night?' Mrs Hewitt asked as she approached the table with a plate of hot, buttered toast.

'Yes, kind of. But I woke with a jolt feeling as if I hadn't slept at all.'

Mrs Hewitt was shaking her head as she poured the tea. 'Poor Leo. I hope he's all right. It was like the Wild West out there last night.'

'Well it was all fine till Vic and that Jimmy Diamond showed up,' Lara sighed. 'And we were having such a nice time.'

'Those men are mindless hooligans. If I had my way, I'd clear them off the streets and lock them up for good.'

Lara felt a little startled by the housekeeper's strength of feeling. But it was heartening to have her support.

'It's horrible when any human is attacked like young Leo last night,' the housekeeper continued. 'We know him so well, and I've probably told you this before, but I've always had a soft spot for the young vet. Maybe because his mother died so young and he was brought up by his father – who's a good sort, but he went through the same troubles as our Dr Bingham during the war, so he has his own demons.'

'Yes, that's true... And maybe, Mrs H, you have this thing about Leo because of what happened with your own son.'

A shadow seemed to fall over the housekeeper's face and

Lara wished she'd kept her mouth shut about the son, Ben, whom Mrs Hewitt hadn't seen or heard from since the end of the war.

'I'm sorry, Mrs H. I shouldn't have said that. I hope it hasn't upset you.'

Mrs Hewitt visibly shook herself. 'No, it's not you. Ben is with me anyway, during the day and at night in my dreams. And I'm lucky to have found someone like you who I can confide in. I learned many years ago that the sharing of a sorrow can help to lighten it.'

'I hope that's true,' Lara said gently.

They sat quietly together then with the spit of the Aga fire in the background. And when they heard the tolling of the church bell through the thick walls of the surgery, Tiddles came to rub his silken fur against Lara's leg, purring loudly, arching his back and flicking his tail as she stroked him.

'You're such a softie with that lazy, good for nothing cat.' Mrs Hewitt smiled as she got up from the table and collected the crockery.

Lara raised her head, beaming a smile. 'I can't help it; he's just so sweet.'

'He is with you and me. But he gives short shrift to the rest of the household, especially Dr Bingham.'

'Yes, I've seen how he jumps up and runs off the second Bingham raises his voice.'

'Sometimes, I envy that cat, being able to escape like that.' Mrs Hewitt chuckled as she walked to the sink with her crockery.

Tiddles pricked up his ears as if he'd been listening to every word the housekeeper had just uttered. Then he glanced to Lara and trotted away. It gave her the spur to move on. 'Well I know it's freezing cold out there this morning but I'm thinking of taking a walk. And on my way back, I'll tap on Leo's door, see how he's doing.'

'Yes, that's an excellent idea,' Mrs Hewitt called from the sink as she vigorously washed the dishes. 'Give him my regards. Tell him if he needs anything at all to let me know. Him and his dad, they don't eat properly. So I'd be happy to plate up some Sunday roast dinners if that's what they want.'

'I'll be sure to ask. And I'll see you later.'

'Enjoy your walk,' the housekeeper called over her shoulder, already beginning to hum, then sing, the Al Bowlly classic they'd recently listened to on the radiogram, 'Love is the Sweetest Thing'.

As Lara walked out to the corridor and pulled her thick coat and knitted hat from the brass hooks, she picked up on the song. She was humming the tune under her breath as she walked down the tiled corridor to the front door. Usually, a melody like that with its simple sentiment would make her feel relaxed but this time, it made her breath catch. Must be that strong cup of tea, she thought as she pushed open the front door and walked out into the bright, cold morning air.

The street was deserted, the cobbles shiny with ice. Glad of her thick-soled walking shoes, she pulled on the knitted gloves she always kept in her pocket and marched determinedly down towards the humpbacked bridge. As her breath steamed in the air, she was soon out on the country lanes where the dead grass and bare branches sparkled with frost. The lanes were empty and as she reached the place where she could look out over the splendour of the frost-covered fells, she leaned on a field gate and drew solace from the view. Then, walking back to the village, nicely warm inside her thick coat, she felt renewed. But as she approached the village, her worries over Leo resurfaced and she felt the urge even more strongly now to call by the vet's surgery.

Walking briskly to the door, she hesitated a second before knocking, just in case Leo was sleeping. There was no reply and as she was about to try again a voice from up the street called a cheery good morning. It was Ed, smiling and waving as he stood in his stockinged feet at his door.

'Morning,' she shouted up to him. And remembering the key role he'd played in getting Leo to the surgery, she added, 'Thanks for your help last night.'

'All part of the service.' He grinned as he struck a match to light up a cigarette.

Then Lara turned to knock again but just as she raised her hand, the door swung open, and Leo's dad was there, his deeply lined face pale and heavy with exhaustion.

'Morning, Mr Sullivan,' she offered pleasantly. 'I'm just calling by to check on Leo. But if he's still sleeping, I can come back later.'

Just as the senior vet opened his mouth to speak, Leo called from behind, 'It's all right, Dad, let her in.'

Arthur smiled, then stepped back. As she walked by him, he reached out to pat her arm. 'Thanks for what you did for my son last night, Nurse Flynn. You and your surgery colleagues made an excellent job of patching him up.'

She nodded and smiled. 'Well, you know what it's like when any creature is injured. We medically inclined folks get going and crack on with a response.'

'We do; it's in our blood,' Arthur replied.

'Are you saying I'm the same as an injured animal?' Leo called light-heartedly.

'Oh no, nothing like that,' she replied. 'Those creatures are far superior.'

Leo was laughing, then he was wincing with pain.

'Oh, sorry. I didn't mean to make you laugh. It must hurt terribly.'

'No, I'm fine. Just fine,' Leo groaned.

'He'll soon mend up,' Arthur offered as he walked past Lara.

'How are you doing?' Lara asked gently, as soon as Arthur had closed the door.

'Oh, never better,' Leo replied jokily, trying to offer his lopsided grin but wincing with pain.

Lara was already up close, scrutinising the black silk sutures Bingham had applied above Leo's eye. 'The stitches are good but there's a lot of swelling and bruising around your eye and your nose. It all seems to be in order, but we won't know if your nose will be straight till the swelling goes down.'

He was staring intently at her with his one good eye, and she could sense the emotion in him.

'You're entitled to feel bad, Leo,' she said gently. 'As you know, these injuries are superficial and they'll heal but the shock of this, especially when it's been a deliberate attack, well, that might take some time to ease.'

He seemed to gulp a breath, his one good eye looked shiny with tears. 'Thank you, Lara. Yes, I am still shocked, but it's not just that, I need to tell you that I—'

The little Jack Russell came running through from the back then, effusively wagging his tail.

Lara was immediately distracted. 'Hello there, little fella,' she called, stroking the dog, giving him a gentle scratch behind the ears.

'Looks like Lucky loves you too,' Leo said wistfully.

Lara felt what he'd just said with a jolt and knew she needed to respond before her cheeks flushed pink. 'Well, we nurses, vets, doctors, we look after all of our patients, don't we?'

Leo was trying to smile but the movement of his face made him wince with pain. He croaked, 'Yes, we do look after all. But some are more—'

Right then, a loud hammering came to the surgery door.

'What the...? Must be an emergency,' Leo muttered as he staggered to open up.

But Lara had a bad feeling about the aggressive knock and in the next second, when she heard Jimmy Diamond's voice, her instinct was proved right. Straight away, she stooped down to scoop up Lucky. Held him close against her chest with her heart pounding.

'I've come for my dog,' she heard Jimmy growl.

'He's not your dog,' Leo replied firmly.

'Well, he matches the description of the ratter I lost some weeks ago.'

'You have no proof. And even if you have a claim, why wait till now? The dog I found had been abandoned. He was dangerously thin and on the point of collapse.'

'Point of collapse,' Jimmy mimicked aggressively. 'You don't know what you're talking about. Call yourself a vet.'

'There's no more to be said,' Leo grunted, trying to close the door.

But Jimmy had his booted foot right there and he pushed back hard against the door, then grabbed Leo and hauled him outside.

Lara didn't hesitate; she marched straight there to stand beside Leo with the dog whining in her arms.

Jimmy wasn't alone. He had a timid-looking young man with him, a grey lurcher by his side. Thankfully, there was no sign of Vic Taylor.

Jimmy shot a glance in Lara's direction and his eyes burned

into her. 'Oh, so here we have the dog snatcher's accomplice, our very own Nurse Flynn.'

Lara held his gaze firmly, lifted her chin, grateful to hear doors opening up and down the street, as one or two villagers nosed out of their cottages. She eased even more when she heard Ed's voice calling, 'You all right there, Leo?'

'Yeah, so far so good, mate. And Mr Diamond is just about to leave.'

Ed was beside Leo now. 'All the same, I'm staying right here. Just in case Mr Diamond needs some assistance with his leaving.'

Jimmy shot Ed a fierce glance, then with a sarcastic grin, he grunted, 'Well, well, if it isn't our man about town, Mr Edward Cronshaw... Me and you go back a long way, don't we, Ed?'

'It's all in the past now, Jimmy. You know that.'

'Not sure if I do,' Jimmy mused for a moment. Then he switched his attention back to Leo. 'The dog is mine, Sullivan. You know that. And I'll be back every day if required till you hand him over to me.'

Lucky whined miserably and Lara stroked him and whispered soothing words to settle him.

The tension seemed to break. But just as Jimmy flashed an aggressive glance towards his timid, scared-looking young companion and gestured for him to get moving, a ragged figure staggered out from the shadow of a building at the bottom of the street and began to march up the hill. It was Vic Taylor.

Jimmy shot Leo a triumphant glance. 'Well, it looks like we have reinforcements. So maybe we can take the dog after all.'

Instinctively, Lara clutched Lucky tighter. Then, as Leo gestured for her to take the little dog inside, Ed emitted a blood-curdling yell and ran at Vic.

In a heartbeat, Vic froze, then he began to laugh maniacally. 'You're no match for me, Cronshaw, you never were.'

'Stop this now!' Leo yelled, but it was too late. Ed had thrown his first punch and it had hit the mark, busting Vic's nose.

But Vic was still laughing, his face alive with hatred. And in the split second Ed was distracted by Lizzie screaming down the street for him to stop fighting, Vic came back strong with a punch to Ed's gut.

Something snapped inside Lara and she handed the dog to Leo, marched over to the two men. 'If you have scores to settle, do it somewhere else. That's enough now. Stop it. Both of you.' Then quietly but very firmly to Ed: 'Lizzie's up the street with your children; you need to stop this right now.'

Ed gasped, straightened up, before staggering away, calling back over his shoulder, 'I'm done for now, Taylor. But we're not finished yet... We'll be settling this score in due course.'

'I'm ready, Cronshaw. And next time, you won't be able to walk away.'

Lara was incensed. 'Enough! Your children are just there, in that house across the street.'

Vic glanced to Alice's new home and a fleeting sadness crossed his face. But with the next breath, he seemed to bury his emotion with a harsh grin. Then he wiped a hand across his face, smearing blood from his busted nose.

Jimmy Diamond had been standing quietly aside, and Lara sensed how much he'd been enjoying the disruption. 'Come on, Vic. That's enough for now,' Jimmy called, his voice abrupt, authoritative, and Vic turned to follow him. The young lad shot a sorrowful glance towards Lara before trailing after them, his lurcher dog whining pitifully.

'That young man needs to be rescued,' Lara murmured quietly.

'Yes, I agree,' Leo replied. 'But right now, Nurse Flynn the peacemaker, let's get back inside for a good, strong cup of tea.'

'I won't say no to that.' She grinned.

As soon as they were back in through the door, Leo placed the little dog down on the flagged floor. He shook himself before trotting away.

'My dad will've left him a treat in his food bowl. The little fella's already spoiled rotten,' Leo said, trying to smile but wincing with pain. He drew a slow breath to steady himself. 'Right, so first things first,' he groaned, 'let's get the kettle on—'

Immediately, the telephone began to ring, the noise jangling Lara's stretched nerves.

As Leo answered, she motioned to him to say she'd go. But he shook his head, held up a delaying hand as he listened to the voice at the other end of the line. 'Right, so the bull is limping badly now. Yes, I see. Well, I'll let my dad know and one of us will be up there as soon as we can. All right, yes. Bye.'

'I'll let you get on with your work,' Lara said as he replaced the receiver.

'Yes, but no. I mean, why don't you stay for that cup of tea?'

Just as she opened her mouth to reply, another loud knock came to the door, then it burst open.

'Leo,' a woman's voice called, full of concern.

It was Philippa Harrington and as Lara turned to offer a polite smile, she noted the woman's bright gaze and narrowed eyes. It was on the tip of her tongue to explain the reason why she was in the vet's surgery but she knew she didn't have to do that.

'Ah, Philippa,' Leo croaked, then coughed. 'Are you OK?'

'Yes, *I* am. But I heard you were injured last night in some punch-up. So how are you?' As Philippa narrowed her eyes to scrutinise the extent of his injuries, Lara saw her face blanch. In moments she began to recover, but when she spoke her voice was seething with anger. 'Who did this to you, Leo?'

'Oh, just some local fella who's taken a dislike to me.'

'I need his name and address. My father knows people who can sort things like this.'

'No, no. It's fine. Just some drunken brawl, that's all.'

Philippa shot a glance to Lara. 'Did you see it? Were you a witness?'

'Yes, I was there. But this is Leo's issue, not mine... So I'll say goodbye for now and leave you to it.'

Leo shot her a forlorn glance. 'Thanks for your help, Lara. I'll see you around.'

She raised a hand, called a goodbye.

Then as she made to move, she felt the heat of Miss Harrington's gaze. And given there was nothing for Philippa to be jealous of here, bar that one brief kiss that she'd only told Marion about, Lara was happy to leave whatever it was Miss Harrington had brought with her to the vet's surgery well and truly behind.

As she walked to the door, she heard the little dog yap, and he trotted after her for a final stroke and a scratch behind his ears.

'Come on, Lucky. Come to me,' Philippa called, but her voice sounded tight, and it made the dog whine and press even closer to Lara. She had no choice but to gently prise him away and tell him to stay. But even as she exited the surgery, he was trying to push his nose through the crack in the door.

'It's just because I helped the little fella in his time of need,' she murmured to herself as she finally got out through the door and closed it behind her. But as she walked up towards the surgery, she couldn't hold back the broad smile that curled at her lips now she was walking freely, out in the open air.

13

A few days later, Lara was pulling her bicycle from the shed to attend her first call of the day: a return visit to Freddy Lennox at Foxglove Cottage. She shivered in the icy cold as she placed her medical bag in the bicycle basket, and as she wheeled her bicycle down the side of the surgery, a watery feeling of anxiety spread up from her stomach. She couldn't account for it, but once or twice during her nursing career, she'd had intuitive feelings about a patient's condition. Surely though, Steven would have telephoned if Freddy's condition had deteriorated. There'd been heavy frost overnight and already she could see patches of ice on the cobbles. Thankfully though, someone, probably Mrs Hewitt, had spread ash down the side of the building and in a track out to the road, so her feet had at least some grip. Lara hoped Angus would take more care this very icy morning as he careered haphazardly away in the little Austin. The thought of him revving the engine and setting off at speed made her breath catch. But he'd driven previous winters out here so surely, he would be fine. Even as she thought it, her foot slipped on shot ice, and she almost fell flat on her back. 'Aargh!' she cried as she righted herself, feeling her face flush even in the biting cold. She felt riled but the burst of adrenaline boosted her and made her even more vigilant for more black ice.

Step by careful step, she wheeled her bicycle up to the turning which led down to the sawmill and relief flooded her when she saw that the road had been gritted. Nevertheless, she still felt the need to test the conditions, so she continued to wheel her bicycle, walking briskly now but still scanning the ground for ice.

'Morning, Nurse Lara,' a bright voice called as she walked by the mill cottages. It was Danny Ryan's wife, Rose, with the baby girl Lara had delivered back in the summer on her hip. It brightened her to return the cheery greeting and with the smiles that were exchanged, Lara felt almost as if she were part of a white-frosted, picture-postcard village scene.

Then, as she continued down the hill with the bare branches of the leafless trees arching starkly above her, she got into a rhythm with her walking, her feet instinctively feeling for slush and grit and avoiding shot ice. But as the thud of the mill engine grew louder, she heard shouting, agitated voices from the mill yard and it made her stomach twist. She quickened her pace to see what was going on. Maybe there'd been an accident, and someone needed attention. As she drew closer, she saw two men arguing in the yard and she recognised the taller one instantly. It was Ed Cronshaw, and he was swearing and pointing up to the crane where his mate, Danny Ryan, sat with breath steaming in the bitterly cold air.

'He needs to come down; he's freezing up there!' Ed shouted as he squared up to the shorter man, whom Lara recognised as the mill manager who stood in a thick overcoat and cap, his gloved hands holding a clipboard.

Lara saw the manager tap his pen against the clipboard and

she could tell he wasn't backing down. She was right there now, passing by the yard as other men emerged from the mill building to stand with Ed.

'Come on, Mr McAllister, give Danny a break; he'll freeze to death up there,' called a tall, thin man swaddled in a wool coat cinched at the waist by a leather belt.

The man with the clipboard sighed a heavy breath that hung in the air like a tiny cloud. Then he offered a tight nod, gazed up to Danny and gestured with his pen for him to climb down.

All the men in the yard cheered and the manager huffed and puffed as he briskly strode away.

Lara felt glad Danny had been released and she enjoyed watching the camaraderie of the men as they clapped him on the back as soon as he was down in the yard. She almost called out to them, but she didn't want to disrupt the moment they all seemed to be revelling in. So she passed quietly by.

Knowing the road would be gritted almost all the way up to Foxglove Cottage, Lara mounted her bicycle and pushed hard to make a start on the uphill climb that led to the mill pond. It was hard going and still quite slippery in parts but at least the exertion warmed her up. As she approached the iced-up pond, she noted silver frosted trees and bushes at the far side. Drawing closer, she pulled up for a few seconds to view the ice that had frozen the mill pond solid overnight. It looked flat and icy white, and she wondered if it would be thick enough for skating. As her eyes shifted and flitted around the whole perimeter, she noted what looked like a boulder peeking out of the ice at the far side. Something didn't look quite right about it though, so she leaned over the wall to get a closer look.

With her next breath, she felt a plunging in her stomach as if she were dropping in freefall. She needed to hold back a scream. But she was sure now; there was no mistake about it. What she had seen at the far side of the pond, poking out of the ice, was a human head, with icicles for hair.

'No,' she groaned as what felt like a shock of electricity went through her body. She squared her shoulders, quickly slipped over the wall to walk around the frozen pond and take a closer look.

After a few strides, she was sure of what she'd seen, and it made her breath stick in her throat. Even though she was used to dealing with all manner of injuries and she'd seen many dead bodies, to happen upon this so casually as she went about her routine duties already felt stranger and more challenging than anything she'd ever witnessed. She stopped for a few moments to steady herself as she made out the detail of the body – it was an adult male with longish, dark hair frozen into strands. As she walked the final distance, she was aware of the bold marks her footsteps left in the frost and her breath seemed to steam even more. Careful not to slip, she moved steadily until she was right beside the poor, dead man. The head and face were rimed with frost but there was something about the shape of the head and that straggly brown, icy hair that triggered recognition. With what felt like a punch to the gut, she knew this was Vic Taylor.

Even though she had never liked the man, this was a lonely, tragic way for any human to die. And what about Alice and the children? She thought of how Robin had been so pleased to see his dad through the window. She couldn't bear to think of the impact this would have on the family. Then instantly piling on top of that, something screamed in her head telling her that this was no accidental death. Her mind recoiled from the thought; maybe Vic had been drunk – he was often drunk – and he'd slipped. But why had he come all the way out here and climbed over a wall? Then she thought of the bad company he'd been keeping and knew in her gut that Jimmy Diamond had a hand in this.

As the shock of what she'd found began to ease, she crouched down beside Vic and felt immense sorrow – not so much for him but for Alice and the children. Then, with her next steaming breath, her brain began to click over next steps: she'd need to call the police, contact the surgery. Maybe she'd have to cancel her morning visits because she'd be a witness.

The thought of little Freddy Lennox and the family waiting for her visit galvanised her into action. She was up now, walking quickly back around the pond and climbing over the wall. She mounted her bicycle and freewheeled back down to the mill where she could make a telephone call.

Even before she reached the sawmill, she'd made up her mind to keep quiet about Vic's body. It would be a natural instinct for some of the men to go straight out to the pond and take a look. And given her gut instinct that Vic's death was not an accident, she didn't want any vital clues to be trampled underfoot. So, once she got to the mill, she headed straight to the foreman's cottage where she knew they had a telephone and knocked briskly on the door.

In moments, a middle-aged woman with a kindly face opened up. 'Can I help you?' she asked.

'Hello, yes. I'm one of the local district nurses. Please can I use your telephone?'

'Yes, of course,' the woman replied, smiling and indicating for Lara to follow her through to the back room of the beamed cottage, warm and cosy with the delicious smell of baking. The contrast with the scene she'd left at the mill pond couldn't have been starker. And as the woman pointed to the telephone table, she leaned in to say gently, 'It's always good to help some poor soul suffering illness or injury.'

Too late for that, Lara thought as the woman clicked the door shut behind her. She picked up the receiver, feeling her heart jump with the urgency of the situation. First, she rang Ridgetown Police Station to report the finding of Vic's body to what sounded like a young police constable who was so shocked, he could barely get his words out. Next she contacted the surgery to inform Mrs Hewitt. The housekeeper was speechless for a few moments, then she sounded angry. 'That poor family. Just when Alice and the children are settling in the village and things are improving. But I can't say I'm surprised that's how Vic ended up... However, he's still a father to those children and goodness knows how they'll be after this.'

Lara felt the shock clutch at her chest again, squeezing the air from her lungs. But she managed to steady her voice so she could ease Mrs Hewitt. 'So, I'm thinking it's best to keep this to ourselves for now. Obviously, let Bingham and the rest of the team know. I need to go back to the mill pond and wait for the police. They've already said I'll have to give a statement. So if you could rearrange my morning visits, I'd be very grateful.'

'Yes, of course I can do that,' Mrs Hewitt replied, her usual businesslike tone still frayed around the edges. But she rapidly seemed to be pulling herself together.

As Lara replaced the telephone receiver with a heavy clunk, she took a moment to compose herself before walking back through to the kitchen where the foreman's wife was rolling out pastry.

'Thank you for that,' she called, knowing that as soon as the news broke, it would spread through the village and outlying areas like wildfire, and the woman would perhaps think, *Oh, so that was why the nurse needed to use the telephone.*

As she walked back outside and wheeled her bicycle by the mill, she felt relieved that the yard was deserted. But just as she thought it, a familiar voice called out, 'Nurse Flynn. How are you doing this cold and frosty morning?' and Ed waved jovially then blew a kiss.

'Morning to you too, and I'm absolutely fine,' Lara replied, feeling the wrench of not being able to express her true feelings. When the news did break, she wondered how Ed would take it given he'd had a bad falling out with Vic, a man who'd previously been a drinking buddy. And the rift had happened because Ed had come to her rescue after Vic had violently attacked her. The thought of it now made her shudder.

Back at the mill pond, she felt relieved to find the body still there at the edge of the ice where she'd left it. As if, absurdly, while she'd been away, someone might have come and dislodged it. She parked up her bicycle and clambered over the wall to take up what now felt like a vigil. As she walked back to the body, her leather boots brushed through the frost-covered grass and the bright, glistening sparkle of it was in such stark contrast to the tragic remains of a human life that lay in the frozen pond, it made her feel even more emotional.

As she waited for the police to arrive, she checked and rechecked her identification of the body to make sure she'd got it right. Of course she had, but all of this seemed so strange, so beyond any experience she'd ever had that she felt heightened and anxious. She stepped carefully back and forth, looking for clues as to how long the body had been there and what might have happened. There were no footprints, so he had either slipped accidentally into the pond or been pushed in there before the hard frost in the coldest reaches of the night. But what had Vic been doing out here by the mill pond anyway? It triggered her back to the autumn when she'd been riding out to the Lennoxes and she'd discovered those fires in the mill yard. Maybe her assumption that it had been Vic Taylor had been correct. But why was he back here now? She recalled a theory of Mrs Hewitt when they'd been trying to unravel the mystery of the fires. The housekeeper had thought Vic was a suspect because he'd been ostracised from the local community. And he'd slunk off embittered and hitting back at the villagers maybe by setting the fires to put men out of work. It still struck Lara as plausible but right now, out here in the frozen landscape, her body was so cold, she couldn't be sure her mind was working properly.

Stamping her feet to try and warm herself up, she continued to walk back and forth over the same short distance. Then she removed her leather gloves and blew warm breath onto her bitterly cold hands.

Just when she thought she was going to freeze to death, she heard the putter of a vehicle out on the lane and relief flooded through her. Then, as a police car pulled up and a man's voice called her name, she noted the unmistakeable Scottish accent of the inspector she'd dealt with previously. 'Hello, Inspector Stirling. I'm over here,' she shouted and raised her hand.

She watched as he neatly vaulted the wall, then walked towards her, muffled in a thick overcoat and tartan scarf. His dark hair poking from beneath his black Fedora hat.

'We meet again, Nurse Flynn,' he called in greeting, then slipped, then picked himself up and continued to walk towards her.

'I wish it was under better circumstances,' she said, feeling the dull weight of what she'd found. 'But as you can see...'

'Yes, indeed.' He frowned, his breath steaming heavily in the air as he scrutinised the scene.

He squatted down next to Vic.

'I didn't tell the person who answered the call at the police station but I'm very sure that this is Vic Taylor, a local man who might also have been a suspect for setting those fires at the mill.'

'Ah, yes. Of course,' he said, glancing up, bright-eyed from his close inspection.

Other police officers had now pulled up and were scrambling over the wall. He shouted across to them, 'We'll need spades and pickaxes to release him from this ice. Go down to the mill and ask if they can supply.'

'Right you are,' one of the officers called before jumping back over the wall.

'It looks like he slipped into the water by accident,' the detective murmured almost under his breath.

'I wouldn't be so sure of that,' Lara offered. 'Not that I'm remotely qualified in detective work, but this man has recently developed a close association with a local gang, and he's been ostracised from the village. So the picture is complex.'

'Mmm, I suppose we'll know more after the post-mortem,' Stirling offered by way of reply as he pulled a penknife from his jacket pocket, opened it up and began to chip at the ice around Vic's neck.

Lara squatted down beside him to watch closely as more of Vic's neck was exposed.

'Doesn't seem to be any sign of bruising around the neck, which might rule out strangulation,' Stirling said with a quick glance to her.

Lara leaned forward to scrutinise it. 'That might be the case, Inspector... but there is a thin, red line around his throat. It looks like a ligature mark to me.'

Stirling sucked a breath, peering closely to where she was pointing. 'Well spotted, Nurse Flynn. You've a better eye than most of my officers.'

He was examining again as Lara sat back on her heels, still

reeling with what felt like confirmation that this local man, father to Robin and Lucy, had been murdered in cold blood. Her mind flitted over her most recent encounter with Vic and thoughts of Jimmy Diamond came right at her. But why would Jimmy do away with one of his own gang members? She thought back to the last time she'd seen Vic in the village when he'd had that scrap with Ed. There'd been no hint of a rift with Jimmy then, but it worried her now to think over how angry and aggressive Vic and Ed had been towards each other. But no, surely it couldn't have been Ed who'd done this.

Stirling sat back on his heels, a faraway look in his eyes as he ran a hand over his angular jaw. Then at the sound of the police constables returning with spades and picks, he motioned for Lara to stand back so the team could hack at the ice to release Vic's body. To see his tragic remains pulled from the water sent a deep shudder through her. At least though, he seemed unharmed elsewhere. So maybe the death he'd met with had been clean and quick. But she couldn't bear the thought of the police going to Alice and the children to relay this terrible news.

'I'll come with you, to his wife's house,' Lara said firmly. 'He was estranged from the family, but he came into the village recently to see his son who is still recovering from a nasty dose of diphtheria.'

'So Vic wasn't all bad, then?' Stirling offered.

Lara sighed. 'I suppose people rarely are. It's just a question of degree. But the man who runs the gang Vic was part of, Jimmy Diamond, I think I can say with confidence that he is thoroughly bad.'

'Ah yes, I've encountered Mr Diamond several times. He's a very slippery character and no doubt will have all bases covered when it comes to telling us who he was with and where he was last night.'

'No doubt. But I feel sure he must have played a part in this.'

At the sound of an ambulance approaching, Inspector Stirling blew out a breath. 'Stick by me, Nurse Flynn,' he ordered. 'Once the body has been removed to the mortuary, we'll go to the village to let his family know. I'm taking it that you're sure of the identification?'

'Yes, without doubt, that is... was... Vic Taylor,' she replied, then almost as if the whole tragic event caught up with her in one go, she emitted a deep sob and covered her face with both hands.

Stirling placed a gentle hand on her arm. 'Just let it out,' he murmured. 'It's always the best way.'

'Yes, I know.' Lara sniffed. 'It's not so much for Vic, but for his family.'

The inspector nodded, patted her arm. 'I can go alone to the Taylors' house if you want.'

'No, I'm coming with you. I want to be there to support the family,' she said firmly as she swiped tears from her eyes with gloved fingers. Then she was straightening up, readying herself to see this through.

14

Arriving back to Ingleside in Inspector Stirling's car with the weight of all she'd witnessed weighing heavily upon her, Lara felt wrung out as the detective parked his car outside Daniel Makepeace's cottage and they got out together to cross the road to the Taylors' house. Ignoring the enquiring glances from villagers out on the street made her feel the weight of the news they were carrying even more acutely.

Lara walked ahead of the detective to knock on Alice's door, in the same way she'd done with Vic when he'd been desperate to see Robin during the diphtheria outbreak. She swallowed hard, drew the slow breaths she'd used all the way through her nursing career when tragic news needed to be broken.

She felt the inspector hesitate behind her and when she glanced over her shoulder, his features clouded for a moment. 'I'm just thinking, Nurse Flynn, it might be best if I take the lead with delivering the news. Alice knows you well so maybe if you follow up to support and answer any questions.'

'I'll go with that,' Lara breathed. But her gut tightened at the prospect of handing over the delivery of such important news. She hoped Stirling would be up to it.

As she tapped on the door, she sensed or probably imagined a quietening in the street, as if the village were holding its breath. Then, as she heard someone bustling to answer, she steeled herself. Alice opened up with a bright smile, then instantly frowned when she clocked Inspector Stirling.

'Is something up? Lucy's at school; is she all right?' Alice croaked, sounding panicked.

Lara reached out to her. 'Yes, Lucy's fine. We're here on a different matter. Can we come in, Alice? Inspector Stirling has some news about Vic.'

'What the heck has he been up to now?' Alice groaned. But in the next breath, the weight of whatever news was coming also seemed to hit her. 'Come on, let's go through to the kitchen.'

The inspector removed his black Fedora hat and followed Alice with Lara behind. Once they were in the warm kitchen, he asked gently, 'Who have you got here at home with you right now, Mrs Taylor?'

'Just me and my son Robin – he's in bed in the front room still recovering from diphtheria. My daughter Lucy is at school and my uncle, Josh MacDonald, who also lives here, is out at present.'

'That's OK, we don't need the rest of your family to be part of this just yet. But the reason we are here is to deliver some sad news about your ex-husband.'

Alice pressed her lips into a firm line, seemed to hold her breath. And as Lara saw Stirling hesitate, she wondered for a split second if she'd need to step in. Then Alice spoke again, her voice jangling in the quiet of the kitchen. 'Go on, give it to me. What's Vic been up to now?'

'I'm sorry to have to tell you, Mrs Taylor. But your ex-husband was found dead in the mill pond this morning. He may have drowned, we're not sure yet.'

'What?' Alice gulped. Then she let out an agonising groan. 'No. Are you sure?' She switched her gaze to Lara. 'Is this right? Have you seen Vic's body?'

'Yes, I was the one who found him… I'm so sorry, Alice, but there's no question about it.'

Alice clutched her head with both hands. She just stood there, completely stunned.

'I'm so sorry, Alice,' Lara said, her heart twisting as she walked to place a steadying hand on her arm.

Alice sucked in a tight breath. 'Well, we weren't close, as you know. And in these last few years, he hasn't been a good husband or father to his children. But to hear that he's dead…' Her body was shaking now and when she spoke again, her voice was strangled in her throat. 'However am I going to tell the children?'

'You will, Alice, you'll find a way,' Lara said gently but firmly.

Alice swallowed hard, nodding, her attention drifting for a few moments. Then she swiped a hand around her face, straightening up. 'I'm so glad you're here, Nurse Flynn. I don't know what I'd have done without you.'

'I know, it's a terrible shock,' Lara offered gently.

Alice seemed to be rapidly collecting herself. 'So, Inspector. Do you know what Vic was doing at the mill pond?'

Stirling cleared his throat. 'As yet, we don't have the answer to that question… but Nurse Flynn saw his body when she was passing by to visit one of her patients.'

Alice was nodding, seeming distracted, her cheeks flushed bright pink. Then she began to cry – deep, gut-wrenching sobs.

Lara put an arm around her shoulders. 'I'm here with you,

Alice, for as long as you need. And if you want, we can send up to the school for Lucy right now?'

Alice was shaking her head vigorously. 'No, it'd be too upsetting for her to be brought back here till I've properly got my act together. And she'd be worried and fearful... It's taken her till now to get her confidence back after what happened up at the farm. Let her have the rest of her day at school without knowing. I'll break the news as soon as she's back.'

'That's up to you, Alice. And of course, we'll support you with that.'

Alice pulled her flour-dusted apron straight and when she spoke again, her voice was strained but it had some energy. 'So, Uncle Josh has nipped up to the Fleece to see the landlord, Sid Lightfoot, about something or other and he said he wouldn't be long. I'll wait for him to come back, give him the news. Then we'll both go upstairs to Robin and tell him together.'

'Sounds like a good plan,' Lara breathed. 'And I can stay with you as well, if you want?'

Alice was already shaking her head. 'No, Lara, you're busy enough with the living. There's no need for you to be spending more time than required on those that have passed on.'

'Are you sure? I'm happy to stay, at least for a while?'

'No, you get on.' Then she glanced to the inspector. 'And thank you for coming here in person, Inspector Stirling. It means a lot that you did that.'

'All part of the service,' Stirling replied gently. 'But there is one more thing I'd like to share with you, if that's all right. It might be upsetting so I can hold on to it for later if that's what you want.'

'No, fire away,' Alice replied sternly, squaring her shoulders as she appeared to physically brace herself.

The inspector cleared his throat. 'It's just that I need you to know that we'll be investigating your husband's case further because it's possible he died under suspicious circumstances.'

'What do you mean, suspicious circumstances?' Alice growled. Then her face blanched and for a split second, she looked bewildered. When she spoke again, her voice was barely above a whisper. 'I was going to say I hadn't been expecting that... but Vic's been away for a while now and he's fallen in with a bad crowd. So maybe I shouldn't feel as shocked as I do...'

Inspector Stirling was slowly nodding his head. 'I'm so sorry, Mrs Taylor. I know this gives another highly unpleasant dimension to your husband's death. But it didn't feel right to hold it back because it won't be long before I need to ask some questions as part of the investigation.'

Alice was frowning and her voice was still weak but strengthening now. 'I'll help as much as I can. But there's probably not much I can tell you because we've lived apart for over six months now. And even before that, Vic was a law unto himself, always off out somewhere or getting drunk and causing bother. We didn't have a good marriage and things got much worse before we broke up. He could be violent and threatening, even sometimes towards the children. I've felt better than I ever did living apart from him here in the village...'

Alice gazed to the floor and Lara could only imagine the thoughts firing through her head. She heaved a sigh and glanced up with a piercing gaze. 'Well, when it comes down to it, Vic is, was, the father of my children. So, yes, I'll give you as much help as I can to make sure all of this is dealt with in the proper manner.'

'Thank you for that, Mrs Taylor,' the inspector said. 'Unless you have any more questions, we'll leave you to it for now.' He shot a meaningful glance to Lara and placed the hat he'd been gripping with both hands back on his head.

As Lara turned to follow Stirling to the door, she called over her shoulder, 'Remember, Alice, I'm only up the road. So if you need anything at all or just want to talk things through, shout as loud as you need.'

'I will, Lara. I promise.'

As soon as they were back outside, it felt as if all the village had stopped in their tracks to gaze at them. Stirling cleared his throat, moved swiftly to the car. 'Get in,' he ordered. 'I'll drive you back to the mill pond to collect your bicycle. I need to visit the crime scene again anyway.'

'Right, yes. Of course,' Lara replied, feeling thrown out by all the frowns and questioning glances of the villagers out on the street.

Just as they were about to get in the car, Lara spotted Josh walking down towards them. His face clouded and his eyes narrowed when he saw the detective, but he picked up his pace and began to walk towards them.

'That's Alice's uncle, Josh MacDonald,' Lara murmured.

'Oh, right. So why don't you tell him what's happened, and I'll gauge his reaction?'

'Josh is a gentle giant. I'm sure he's got nothing to do with what happened to Vic,' Lara hissed.

The inspector twisted his mouth, clearly not convinced.

Lara felt a slow burn of anger on Josh's behalf. Yes, he had tattoos up his arms, he'd done some prison time and in his younger days, he'd earned a living as a prize fighter. But all of that was way back in the past and it certainly didn't make him a murderer. She was glad she would be the one to deliver the news about Vic and as she beckoned for Josh to approach, she noted the deep line between his brows. Clearly, he knew something was up.

'Josh, I'm so sorry but we've just been in to see Alice to deliver some distressing news about Vic.'

Josh narrowed his eyes. 'What's he been up to now?' he asked, his voice deadpan. Then he shot a glance to Inspector Stirling. 'I'm thinking it's not good, given the plain-clothes police are onto it.'

'It isn't good, I'm afraid. I'm sorry to have to tell you but Vic was found dead in the mill pond this morning.'

Josh stood rock solid, clenching and unclenching his fist, and his expression barely flinched as Lara told him the detail. Once there was no more to be said, she reached out to place a gentle hand on his muscular arm. 'I'm so sorry to have to bring this news to you. And we've already been in to tell Alice. Is there anything you need to ask?'

He was already shaking his head. 'No, Nurse Flynn. I just need to get into the house to be with Alice and Robin.'

'Yes, of course,' she said.

Once Josh had turned to walk away, Inspector Stirling beckoned for her to get in the car. As he fired up the engine, she slipped into the passenger seat, her mind still processing Josh's reaction. Then as they drove up through the village with local folk staring at the car, she needed to work hard to maintain a neutral expression. Fleetingly, she saw Leo emerge from the door of the vet's. He frowned when he saw her in the police car, but she knew he'd find out soon enough what had happened because once it got out, the news would rip through the village like wildfire.

'Can I take another look at where I found the body?' she asked as Stirling prepared to turn right down the road to the sawmill.

'Yes, of course you can,' he replied. 'It might help you deal with the shock.'

Lara dismissed that theory. But once they were pulling up by the mill pond where her bicycle had been left propped against the wall, she felt her breath snag. And as she followed Stirling back around the pond, seeing the hole in the ice where Vic had been pulled out, it made the whole thing startlingly real, and she needed to ball her hand into a fist to keep herself steady.

'Are you coping?' Stirling asked gently.

'Yes. But it feels so sad now, seeing the place where I found him.'

The inspector nodded. 'Yes, it's an empty space... a mystery...'

'No wonder you're a detective,' she replied, beginning to feel some release. 'You have a whole other way of seeing things.'

He twisted his mouth, shrugged. 'Sometimes, it helps, other times it doesn't. It all depends on the case.'

'What are your initial thoughts on this case then?'

He fixed her with his bright gaze. 'Mostly, people are murdered by those they know. So that's where we'll be starting, particularly with that gang Vic had fallen in with. And of course his family members.'

The mention of family troubled Lara because clearly, Alice and the children weren't suspects, so that left Uncle Josh.

'I know some of the gang who Vic's been hanging around with. As does Leo Sullivan, the vet. We'll give you as much information as we can.'

'Good. Right. So I could do with beginning that process as soon as possible.'

'Well, why don't you come to the surgery when you're done here? I'm heading back now for a bite to eat. So please, join us for lunch.'

'Would that be all right? I don't need any food; I can just bob in to ask some questions.'

'No, sorry, you won't be able to do that. Our housekeeper, Mrs Hewitt, would never forgive me if I treated you like that. She loves to feed people, so you'll have to eat.'

He smiled then, his eyes crinkling at the corners, and she saw a flash of warmth that undercut the well-honed professional demeanour she recalled from when he'd attended the surgery to ask questions about some fires that had been set at the mill. Although nothing had been proved back then, Vic had been a suspect. And now he was gone, snuffed out, just like that. And despite the threat he'd always posed, she felt broken into bits by the suddenness of it. Especially when she thought of Alice and the children... But Vic had always been on the wrong side of things and when he'd fallen in with Jimmy's gang, his situation had only got worse.

* * *

As soon as she arrived back to the surgery, after removing her thick, winter coat and nurse's hat and kicking off her sturdy boots, she bobbed into the kitchen to ask Mrs Hewitt to set another place at the table. Then she was straight up to her room to wash her face and scrub her hands with warm, soapy water to refresh herself but also remove the taint of what she'd witnessed. She took a few moments to steady her breathing, and knowing she'd have to give a full account of it all to her team, she realised how desperately she needed a cup of hot, sweet tea.

All, bar Dr Bingham, were seated around the table when she entered the kitchen. Marion jumped up from her seat with a sandwich in her hand. 'Well done, Lara,' she called, then stepped around the table and almost crushed Lara's ribs in a strong bear hug. 'I don't know how I'd have managed if I'd found a murder victim. I'd probably have run off screaming.'

'I don't think you would, Marion, given what we nurses have to deal with on a daily basis... But I must admit, it was a shock.'

Mrs Hewitt was slowly shaking her head. 'It must have been terrible for you, Lara. Finding him that way.'

Angus cleared his throat, spoke gruffly. 'Well, I think I'd have managed. I mean, we had to perform post-mortems as medical students, and some of the bodies were the mortal remains of those with questionable morals.'

'Ha, you mean criminals?' Marion called across to him.

'Yes,' Angus replied with a single nod.

Then Mrs Hewitt quietly pointed out that those bodies he'd dissected during post-mortems hadn't been village folk who were well known to him.

'True, Mrs H. True.' Angus nodded as he reached for two more ham and pickle sandwiches.

Bingham bustled in to take his place at the head of the table. 'What's this about post-mortems?'

Mrs Hewitt's eyes shot wide, and she called out to him, 'Oh, Dr Bingham. You've been out on visits all morning, so you don't know.'

'What the blazes don't I know?' he replied with an irritable edge to his voice. Then he slumped onto his chair at the head of the table, still wearing his battered trilby hat.

'It's Vic Taylor. He's been found dead in the mill pond.'

'Probably murdered,' Marion called, her eyes like saucers.

'Hmph,' Bingham replied, as if murders were being reported every other day. Then he frowned deeply, let go a heavy sigh. 'What a terrible thing... I hope Alice and the children are all right. They've had enough on their plates recently.'

He reached for the teapot, as the rest of the team sat quietly assessing which way the senior doctor might blow.

'So, is anybody going to tell me the detail of the case?' he grunted.

'Lara, I think that's up to you,' Marion offered as she reached for another sandwich.

Mrs Hewitt sighed heavily. 'Well if we're going to get into the nitty-gritty, I'll bring the cake out early because we'll definitely need it.'

They sat quietly for a few moments as the housekeeper cut some hefty slices of the large chocolate cake and set one aside with the plated sandwiches she'd already prepared for Inspector Stirling.

Once she was back at her place, she propped both elbows on the table and leaned in. 'Nurse Flynn is a key witness in the investigation because she found the body. So, Lara, tell us what happened.'

Lara felt all eyes on her as Marion gave an encouraging nod. Then as she began to tell the story from the moment she'd stopped to gaze over the frozen pond on her way to the Lennoxes, she felt the detail cohere. And she even remembered some extra information that might be useful to Inspector Stirling.

The whole table sat listening intently with no interruptions, not even from Angus. Once she was done, the group sat quietly for a few moments, then Bingham cleared his throat and spoke up. 'Well, Nurse Flynn, you've had quite a morning... I don't recall anything like this in all the time I've lived and worked here. And given we know the deceased and his family, it makes it all so personal. But I think we need to put that aside if we're going to help with the investigation.' He glanced to Lara with bright eyes, 'And of course it's you, Nurse Flynn, at the heart of all this. And I agree with what you said about the ligature mark around his neck; it might well be the cause of death. But at this time of year, the ponds and rivers are freezing cold so that alone could have killed him.'

'Yes, good point,' Angus said solemnly as he reached for another slice of chocolate cake. Then as he took his first bite, he spoke again as he chewed and swallowed. 'But why would anyone bother to put a ligature around his neck if the cold or maybe drowning had already done the job?'

'I take your point, Dr Fitzwilliam,' Bingham mused. 'So maybe he was already deceased and whoever pushed him in there was merely disposing of a body.' The senior doctor fell silent for a few moments as he gazed down to his plate. When he looked up, he heaved a sigh. 'Whatever's happened, it's a tragic loss of a man's life. Things never seemed to run smooth for Vic and he's not conducted himself well at times, especially in the last few years. But he's still Alice's husband and a father to two children so that needs to be at the forefront of everybody's mind.'

'Quite right, well said, Dr Bingham,' Mrs Hewitt called as she reached to pat his arm.

Bingham cleared his throat. 'So why don't we propose a toast to Vic Taylor? He wasn't always the best person he could be, but he was a husband and a father, and he was born and bred in this village. And no one except a nasty, murderous thug deserves to lose their life so tragically.'

'To Vic,' Mrs Hewitt called, and they all solemnly raised their cups.

Then Angus added, 'And let's hope it doesn't turn out that he was a horrible, murderous thug.'

Bingham glanced sharply to him and opened his mouth to speak but Mrs Hewitt was there first. 'Well, Dr Fitzwilliam, I suppose we do need to bear that in mind. But given we've got Alice and the children to consider, let's pray that isn't the case.'

'Hear, hear to that, Mrs H,' Bingham called and raised his cup. He glanced down the table then to Lara. 'And please, let's recognise the part Nurse Flynn played in all this. She often seems to be in the line of fire when it comes to unusual events or emergencies and yet again, she's been called to withstand all that's been thrown at her. So well done to you, Nurse Flynn.'

They all lifted their cups again and Lara felt her cheeks flush. Then she was shaking her head and saying, 'Well, I know for sure that any one of us around this table would have done the same.'

Marion reached out to her then. 'Not me, I wouldn't. I'd have run away screaming and shouting, I know I would.'

Lara was about to reply when a voice called from the corridor. 'Hello. It's Inspector Stirling. Am I all right to come in?'

'Yes, of course,' Mrs Hewitt replied, rising from her seat and heading to the kitchen door to guide him in.

In that split second, Lara saw Marion's eyes flash wide and her cheeks flush pink, and she remembered how taken her friend had been with the detective when he'd visited in the autumn to ask questions about those mill fires. As the inspector removed his hat and Mrs Hewitt offered him her chair next to Marion, then placed the food she'd plated up in front of him, Marion continued to sit wide-eyed, taking in every detail as Stirling settled himself at the table. And while he sipped his tea and ate his sandwiches, he offered a round-up of the morning's events and Lara could see how his bright, quick mind had absorbed every detail. Mrs Hewitt had pulled up a stool to sit by him and, along with the rest of the team, she appeared fascinated by what he was saying. Then, after he'd asked a few questions and chatted some more to Angus and Bingham, he politely offered his thanks and left to continue the investigation.

As Marion followed Lara out through the kitchen door, she

whispered under her breath, 'How amazing is Inspector Stirling? I like him even more now I've seen how he can take charge. And he's so bright and quick and—'

'Enough now, Marion.' Lara smiled. 'Let's see how he gets on with the investigation before we go overboard.'

'Oh, Lara,' Marion mock-growled, linking her arm and pulling her close. 'As you well know, going overboard is my specialty.'

Lara picked up the mischief in her friend's voice and as they walked together to gather their thick wool coats and district nurse's hats from the hooks in the corridor, she felt the tension she'd carried since she'd found Vic begin to loosen a little around the edges.

15

In the days following the discovery of Vic's body, there had been fervent gossip rippling around and about the village. But Lara had begun to feel in the dark because there'd been no more questions from the police, no new information, so she had no real idea of how the investigation was going. In the meantime, she'd had to steel herself to cycle by the mill pond on another follow-up visit to little Freddy Lennox. Even though she'd tried hard not to look, she couldn't help but gaze to where Vic's body had been found. It had sent a cold shiver through her and tears had stung her eyes. But thankfully, the warmth of her reception at Foxglove Cottage, with Freddy even cheekier and barely coughing, had felt like balm to the soul.

On her return to the village, though, she'd seen Stirling's car outside the Taylors' yet again. And given she'd been the one to find the body, it had all begun to feel exasperating. It was a police enquiry, she understood that. But it didn't stop her from feeling frustrated.

The last time she'd called by to check on Alice and the children, Alice had seemed strong, as had Lucy. But Robin, still in bed and making a slow recovery from diphtheria, had been hit very hard by his father's death. The last time Lara had bobbed in to check on him, he hadn't been showing much interest in anything. What felt worse was the police still hadn't released Vic's body for burial. Often, a funeral was a marking point, a way of loosening grief, but this was a murder enquiry, so nothing followed a familiar course.

So, as Lara walked down the hill on a routine visit to Daniel Makepeace and saw the inspector's car parked up yet again outside the Taylors', she had to fight to hold back her frustration. The last time she'd spoken to Alice, she'd said that the stress of repeat visits from the police, asking what felt like the same questions over and over again, was taking its toll on the whole family. Lucy was missing school, Robin was listless and seemed to be losing the will to live and Uncle Josh had become a silent, pent-up ghost of his former self. Lara felt like knocking on Alice's door and going right in there to challenge Inspector Stirling. Because from what was being reported back to her, she didn't recognise the man who'd supported her after she'd found Vic's body.

Lara fixed her eyes on Daniel's cottage as she tried to blot out the inspector's car. In her attempt to shift focus, she almost collided with Lizzie Cronshaw, who was coming up the hill with baby William on her hip.

'What's going on down there? Do you have any idea, Nurse Flynn?' Lizzie asked, gesturing with her head to the police car.

'I've no idea,' Lara replied, striving to distract Lizzie by reaching out to say hello to the baby. 'This little fella looks like he's doing well,' she offered, as Lizzie shifted the weight of him on her hip.

'Yes, and I'm beginning to feel how heavy he's getting. I think he's going to be tall and broad-shouldered, just like his daddy.'

Lara opened her mouth to reply but shouting voices came at her from down the street. The commotion seemed to be coming from the door of the Taylors' house and all those out on the street stopped in their tracks and turned to view what was going on. Lara's stomach lurched as she saw Josh being dragged from the house by two uniformed police, with Alice shouting and screaming, 'It's not him; he wouldn't hurt a fly!' as she struggled to pull the officers away. Instinctively, Lara set off at a run, her district nurse's bag clutched in her hand.

'What's going on?' she fired at Inspector Stirling, who was waiting by his car.

He was already shaking his head. 'Sorry, Nurse Flynn. This is a police enquiry. I can't give any information at this stage.'

'Nurse Flynn!' Josh wailed, as he was dragged out through the door towards a waiting police van.

'What's going on, Josh?' Lara called after him, her voice breaking.

Josh's eyes blazed in her direction then he stopped struggling. It almost brought tears to her eyes when she noted the blood streaming from his nose and a cut beneath his eye where he must have resisted arrest. 'I didn't do it, Nurse Flynn. They're taking me in because they've got nobody else.'

'I hear what you're saying, Josh. You stay strong,' she called after him, sensing the heat of the inspector's gaze she turned to him. He was stern-faced and barely offered a nod before slipping into his car and setting off to follow the police van up the street. No doubt heading for Ridgetown Police Station where they'd put Josh in a cell.

Most of the villagers out on the street stood silently as the police vehicles passed by but a couple of ragged-looking women who worked at Ridgetown Mill were booing and shouting, 'Go on, Josh MacDonald. Once a criminal, always a criminal.'

Lara heard a gentle voice from behind her and turned to see Miss Shaw. 'Those women don't know what they're talking about,' the postmistress said sternly. 'I know that man better than most. Ever since he moved here, he's been coming into the shop buying stuff for the poorer families in the village. That new woman over the road, the one with the twin girls who were poorly with diphtheria – Josh MacDonald's been buying food for them for weeks.'

Lara felt her throat tighten with emotion. 'Well, that doesn't surprise me one bit. Let's hope he's cleared and back home soon.'

Miss Shaw looked sceptical. 'It won't be straightforward, given he has a criminal record for assault. But I'd be willing to defend him any day of the week because from what I've seen of him, the man's a saint.'

The street had filled up quickly with plenty of village folk out of their cottages, all of them gossiping about Vic and Josh. Lara raised a hand to Miss Shaw before turning to head down to Daniel's. But then a familiar voice called urgently from behind, 'Lara, what's going on? Are you all right?'

It was Leo and she was so pleased to see him. He was smiling deliciously despite the still-fading bruises on his face and the ever so slight crookedness of his broken nose – a brutal reminder of the attack by Jimmy Valentine. And after she'd filled him in with what had just happened on the street he muttered under his breath about wrongful arrest and police incompetence. Then his eyes glowed with warmth as he asked, 'Do you have time to nip in for a cup of tea?'

'No, sorry. I'm running behind. I need to get on with my visits.'

'Right, yes, of course. But call by soon, will you, Lara? To see

Lucky, if nothing else. He's often by the door whining and I feel sure it's for you.'

Lara smiled and it helped her relax. 'I need to go now. But yes, I'll call by soon.'

'Good, that's good,' he replied breathily. Then he reached to brush his fingers against her hand. She felt a gentle shiver run through her body, and it stayed with her as she walked away.

Daniel was sleeping when Lara finally got in to see him. The deep lines on his thin face were relaxed, his snow-white hair neatly combed. He looked peaceful, content with the world, and as she moved quietly and gently to record his pulse and blood pressure, she hardly disturbed him at all. When he did blink open his eyes, he murmured, 'I thought I heard shouting out on the street, Nurse Flynn. Is everything all right?'

'Everything's fine, Mr Makepeace,' she replied, knowing how sensitive he was and not wanting to burden him with news he didn't need.

He had already slipped back to sleep, and she knew it was a sign that this patient, one of the first she'd visited as a country nurse, was slowly losing ground. She needed to swallow hard to hold back tears when she thought of the little robin that used to perch on the sill and come for the cake crumbs Daniel left. There was a sweetness to this elderly man, something almost otherworldly. Right now, here with him in the cottage, it made her feel peaceful even though she sensed the tension and the gossip still rippling through the village.

As she stepped out and clicked Daniel's door shut behind her, she glanced across to the Taylors' and knew she had to nip in to check on Alice and the family. She knocked, waited, but there was no sound from within. Then just as she was about to head back up to the surgery, the door swung open abruptly and

Alice was there, breathless, her hair dishevelled, her eyes blotched red with crying.

'Come in,' she croaked.

Lara's heart twisted with concern. As she followed Alice to the kitchen, she felt the silence of the house close around her like a heavy blanket. And as Alice gestured for her to take a seat at the kitchen table, she waited quietly as her friend poured two cups of tea from the pot and added two good spoonfuls of sugar to each.

'I'm so sorry for what you're going through,' Lara said gently as Alice slumped onto the seat opposite.

'It certainly isn't your fault, Lara. But that police inspector will have a lot to answer for if he doesn't release Josh soon.'

Lara felt the sting of the words, and she had to struggle to keep her voice steady. 'What grounds do they have to keep him locked up anyway?'

Alice was shaking her head. 'Very shaky grounds. But the major one is that Josh doesn't have an alibi for the night before Vic's body was found.'

'Well, where was he?'

'Out. He just said he was out, but he wouldn't say where.'

The information niggled Lara and for a split second, she felt unsure of Josh's innocence. Then she recalled what Miss Shaw had said about him buying food for the poorer families in the village, and it didn't tally with someone who could commit murder... even if the victim was a violent, dangerous man in his own right.

She took another sip of tea, spoke gently. 'There must be a reason why he wouldn't say where he was. All he'd need would be for someone to vouch for him. It doesn't make any sense.'

Alice shrugged, then she was shaking her head. 'He was out

that night, that's all I know. I even told him I'd lie for him and tell the police he was here.'

'Yes, but if they found out, you'd be arrested as well.'

Alice sighed. 'Yep. So that's why I changed my mind.' She ran both hands through her dishevelled hair then brushed it away from her face. 'It's so frustrating because I know there'll be a simple answer to this. It feels as if it's at the tips of my fingers, almost within reach.'

'Josh can't have done it. That's what I know,' Lara said, her mind clicking through the reasons she was sure even though there was no proof. One image that came to her was the first time she'd met Alice's uncle, when he'd walked up the village street carrying Lucy in his arms when she was recovering from a badly infected wound on her leg. He'd seemed like a knight in shining armour come to rescue Alice and the children after the terrible time they'd been having with Vic. But then, even the best of people can act on impulse. Could Josh be one of them?

'No, it's not Josh,' Alice said, almost as if she'd read Lara's thoughts.

'He's good, through and through. So this will get sorted one way or—'

A loud hammering came from the door and Alice jumped up from her seat, the flat of her hand pressed to her chest. 'Who the heck is that?' she growled as Robin called from the sitting room, his voice panicked, 'Mum, who's that? What's going on?'

Lara followed Alice, needing to find out who was at the door.

It was Betty Cronshaw, her cheeks flushed bright red, and she was sobbing.

'What is it, Betty?' Alice asked, her voice full of concern, already with an arm around the older woman's shoulders as she led her into the house.

Betty was gasping for breath, trying to speak. But the words wouldn't come.

Lara used her most soothing of voices. 'It's all right, Betty, I can see you've had a shock. Just take a deep breath. That's it, yes. Just breathe.'

Betty sucked in air as if she were surfacing from drowning. Then she dabbed at her eyes. When her voice came, it was barely above a whisper. 'I'm so glad I'm on a day off from the Lennoxes'. It feels as if it was meant to be.' She slumped then sucked in more air. 'Alice, it's about your Uncle Josh. The thing is, I know exactly where he was that night Vic was killed.'

'Where? Where was he?' Alice urged.

Betty gulped, dabbed at her eyes with the flat of her hand, then she croaked, 'It's my fault. I told him not to say anything to anybody in the village because I didn't want any backlash from my deceased husband's family in Ridgetown.'

None of this made any sense and Lara was on the verge of speaking more firmly to Betty just to get the story out of her when the older woman swallowed hard, looked directly at Alice and said, 'I know where Josh was because he was with me. In my cottage and in my bed.'

Alice gasped out loud, doubled over for a few seconds. 'He should have said. Why didn't he say?'

'Because I told him not to. My family are strict Methodists and any rumours of having relations outside of wedlock, even if you're a mature woman who's been widowed like me, it would be taken very hard.' Then Betty sobbed. 'And Josh is such a good, kind, honest man, he wouldn't ever break a promise.'

Lara felt relief flood through her. She knew right away that if Betty would speak out for Josh and give him an alibi, the police would have to release him.

Alice was smiling and crying all at the same time, she

grabbed hold of Betty and smacked a kiss on her cheek. 'Thank you so much, Betty. If you'll go to the police with this, we can get Josh out.'

Betty gulped, nodded. 'I know, that's why I'm here. Blow what the rest of the village and my deceased husband's family or even Reverend Hartley think. Josh is the kindest man, and I love the heart and soul of him. So he's not staying in that police station one second longer than need be.'

A triumphant glance passed between Lara and Alice, and as Betty dabbed at her eyes, Lara reached for Alice's hand and gave it a squeeze.

Betty sniffed loudly, then she croaked, 'I hope Josh will manage. I can't bear the thought of him being locked up. He had such a terrible time as a young man when he was in prison.'

'Josh will be fine, Betty,' Lara said firmly, reaching out to put an arm around her shoulders.

Later, after all the necessary calls had been made to the police and Bingham had given Betty a lift to Ridgetown Police Station, where her statement to prove Josh's alibi could be taken, Lara received a call from Inspector Stirling to say that Josh and Betty would be brought back to the village in a police car.

Lara still felt annoyed with Stirling, but she could hear the contrition in his voice and knew he was genuinely sorry for the distress he had caused. And she supposed that, given Josh had no alibi and was a known antagonist of Vic's, there was probably no choice but to arrest him.

'So the case is ongoing,' Lara said. 'And I'm thinking you're still no nearer finding Vic's killer.'

The detective sighed into the phone. 'That just about sums it up. But we might have some more leads. Ones I can't disclose.'

'Well, I'm thinking you should look into that associate of Vic's – Jimmy Diamond.'

'We already have. And he has an alibi.'

'Or so he says,' Lara replied. 'Jimmy Diamond has been threatening and aggressive in the village. And if you want proof, just ask Leo Sullivan, the vet.'

'I'll take all you've said into account. But there is some evidence emerging of antagonism between Vic Taylor and a man who works at the mill. I can't give the detail right now, but it's related to an ongoing dispute.'

Lara knew that the new suspect was probably Ed Cronshaw, and this felt like a punch to the gut because the open hostility between him and Vic had stemmed from the grudge Vic had borne towards her simply for being a city girl. Vic had attacked her when she'd attended the delivery of Ed's baby son. Up until that point, Ed and Vic had been drinking buddies but after the assault, Ed and many others from the village had ostracised him. And that's how he'd ended up with Jimmy Diamond.

'I need to tell you something, Inspector. I'm thinking your new suspect is Ed Cronshaw and if I'm right about that, you need to listen carefully to what I have to say.' As she went through the detail of what had happened to her at Vic's hands and how Ed had defended her, she heard the inspector draw a slow breath.

'Do you have any witnesses to this attack on you?' he asked.

'Yes, Ed of course. And his wife, Lizzie, who was upstairs with her newly delivered baby.'

Lara could tell Stirling was thinking it through, but when he spoke again, his voice was brisk. 'So, I have no reason to doubt the testimony of a professional person such as yourself. But I'm just wondering why you didn't report this attack by Vic Taylor to the police?'

'I thought about doing it but Vic had already been ostracised from the village so to some extent, it felt dealt with.'

'I'm assuming you have witnesses to your injury?'

'Yes, of course. Dr Bingham will corroborate my story.'

Stirling sighed out a breath. 'The more I look into this case, the more muddied the waters become…' Lara thought he was about to end the call but then he added, 'Oh, and there is one more thing you might be able to help me with. Those cigarette stubs with the gold band we found when you reported the fires that were set at the mill in the autumn. I don't think I ever got around to asking you because it was all overshadowed by the Lennox children going missing. But do you have any clue as to who might have smoked them?'

Lara sighed. She didn't really want to go into it because it meant raking up her past with Patrick. They were the brand he'd smoked but she'd also seen Lord Harrington with them as well.

'Do you have a reason for asking this now?' she said, hoping to dodge the question.

'Yes, in fact I do. We found a pack of those same cigarettes in Vic Taylor's pocket.'

'Oh, right. I see.'

Still, she toyed with deflecting but of course, now a man had died under suspicious circumstances, this had gone way beyond some petty arson attacks on the sawmill.

'Yes, I do have a couple of leads… One of them can probably be ruled out immediately, because it's Lord Harrington from Ingleside Hall. The other is my ex-boyfriend, Patrick Kavanagh, a solicitor from Liverpool. He travelled up to Ingleside on the night of the Harvest Ball to harass me about an emerald necklace he'd gifted when we were in a relationship. I'd been on the verge of returning it to him but he turned up at the ball in an aggressive state. So I gave it straight back to him. However, I learned later from Ada Lightfoot, the barmaid at the Fleece, that Patrick had been seen chatting to Vic Taylor that night before he came up to Ingleside Hall. Then he came back to the village unexpectedly a few weeks later driving a brand-new sports car. I bumped into him, we spoke briefly, but I did wonder why he'd returned. I'm just thinking that maybe Patrick was the source of those cigarettes.'

She could hear by Stirling's silence that he was mulling it over. Then he said, 'Well, is it possible that Vic Taylor stayed in touch with Patrick Kavanagh?'

'It's possible, but why would he do that?'

'I've no idea, Nurse Flynn. But in my line of work, it pays to have all questions answered.'

'Yes, I suppose it's like forming a diagnosis,' Lara replied, keeping her voice light but already niggled by the thought of Patrick being triggered by this and drawn back into her life.

'Exactly so,' the inspector replied, and she knew by his change of tone he was about to say goodbye. 'So, Nurse Flynn, thank you for answering my questions. I need to go now but I'll be back in touch as required.'

'OK, goodbye,' she called as Stirling ended the call and put down the receiver.

She stood for a moment with the phone in her hand, the conversation she'd just had running through her head. She wondered if she'd done the right thing by mentioning Patrick, but she'd had no choice because it was relevant to the case. She tried not to set too much store by it but as she strove to push it back, she found it sticking because she knew in her heart that Patrick was a volatile man who couldn't be trusted and she regretted once more that she'd had anything to do with him.

16

'Come on, Lara,' Marion called up the stairs as soon as Lara had stepped out of her bedroom. 'It's Saturday, Bingham's on call and we are going out... and not to the pubs in Ingleside either. I've seen a good weepy film with an afternoon showing at the Palace in Ridgetown. I can't quite remember the name of it, but I watched it a couple of years ago and it was good. So it should do the trick.'

'What trick?' Lara asked as she trotted down the stairs. 'What are you talking about?'

'We've both been mooching around since we came through the diphtheria outbreak. And now you've had all that business with the police and finding Vic's body. It's grim, far too grim for two young ladies like us... We should be wining and dining, going out to the pictures or a dance, not straggling about the village with Angus and Leo.'

Lara began to giggle. 'You make us sound like social butterflies, not two district nurses.'

'Exactly. And quite right too, Miss Flynn.'

Then she pulled Lara into an embrace and began to dance her all the way down the green-tiled corridor.

Abruptly, the surgery door opened and Bingham bustled in. 'What the blazes are you two doing? Have you no dressings to prepare, no poultices to make? No patients to see?'

Lara knew he was joking by the glint of amusement in his eye. If they'd caught him at another time, on a different day, they might have got a telling-off instead. But as Bingham put down his battered, leather medical bag and shrugged off his thick overcoat and the stripy, woollen scarf he'd taken to wearing during the winter months, he seemed to pick up on their lightness of being.

Marion called to him as they danced all the way back up the corridor, 'We're off out to the pictures this afternoon, Dr Bingham, if that's all right with you. Are you able to cover any calls that come in?'

'Yes, of course I can do that. It's time you two girls had some time off. Cooped up in these four walls or out on the cold, dark country lanes... You bright young things need to see something different.'

'We can be back to cover this evening if you want,' Marion offered, both eyebrows raised.

'I wouldn't hear of it; you stay out as long as you need. It's Saturday night, for goodness' sake. Tell young Angus to take time off as well.'

'What's that?' Angus called from the kitchen.

'Dr Bingham is saying you can take the rest of the day off. Do you want to come with me and Lara to the pictures in Ridgetown?'

'Not my thing, but I have a new pal from the cottage hospital. He's a very rare person indeed – a male nurse. And he's not from around here and I keep promising I'll take him out to one of the local pubs in Ridgetown. So I could go and see him.'

Marion narrowed her eyes. 'A male nurse, you say. Sounds novel. I've never heard of such a thing.'

'Oh, we had one at the Liverpool Royal. I didn't ever work with him so I can't say whether he was any good or not, but he was quite a novelty. I think he worked in theatre.'

'Well I'm already looking forward to meeting this rare beast,' Marion announced.

Lara shouted through to the kitchen, 'Oh, and Angus? I'll drive back from Ridgetown if you like. So you don't have to take care over how much you drink.'

'Doesn't usually stop me.' He laughed. 'But it might save us from ending up in a ditch.'

'Right, so that's a deal,' Marion purred as she grabbed Lara for another turn of the green-tiled corridor.

Later, as she snuggled up to Marion in a red velvet balcony seat in the packed-out Palace Cinema and the curtains slowly opened to reveal the screen, Lara felt a tickle of expectation and pulled her friend closer. 'I can't remember the last time I went to the pictures. I'd forgotten how much I love it,' she whispered, as someone shushed her abruptly from the row behind.

It made Marion stifle a giggle and she whispered back, 'Uh-oh, it's the cinema police.'

Lara needed to muffle her laughter with a hand across her mouth and as she did so, she realised how out of character it was for her to be so giggly in a public place. Maybe it was the stress of the diphtheria outbreak and all those poorly children, closely followed by finding Vic's body, that had tipped the balance. Whatever it was, she pushed it right back now as she snuggled next to Marion, who had begun to rustle in her pocket for the bag of Liquorice Allsorts they'd bought from the Ridgetown sweet shop. A sharp voice behind shushed them again. Then a harsh-sounding woman further back hissed, 'Stop shushing; it's worse than the rustling.'

Lara was trying so hard to contain her laughter, she felt as if she couldn't breathe. But as the projector began to whirr behind them and the beam of light picked out a haze of cigarette smoke, the crackly music of the opening credits began to roll, and her skin prickled with expectation. Then, apart from one or two audience members with tickly coughs and the occasional strike of a match or click of a cigarette lighter, there was barely a sound as the first half of the film played. At intervals, a sturdy usherette walked up and down the aisle to shine her light.

'She's on surveillance,' Marion whispered. 'Just in case some couples go as far as a kiss.'

'It's less strict in Liverpool,' Lara offered, as the beam of the torch instantly swept to her face and she was directly shushed. She needed to swallow hard not to laugh, and she could feel Marion's body shaking with silent giggles.

Somehow, they got through the first half of the film without making too much noise. Then they had a cup of tea and an ice cream during the interval and were back for the second half. The film was overblown in its portrayal of star-crossed lovers, but Lara enjoyed the escape it gave her. And when the fictional couple finally found each other as the end of the film approached, she joined the rippling cheers of the audience as they kissed in the flickering light of the projector. Lara swiped at her eyes with her fingertips, and she had to root in her pocket for her handkerchief. But Marion was properly sobbing with tears streaming down her face.

'I'm so glad they found each other,' Marion croaked then blinked in the stark electric light that had just clicked on. Lara helped her up from the velvet seat that now looked far less luxurious as all the scuffs and cigarette burns were exposed.

'Come on, out you go. We need to tidy up before the next showing,' the sturdy usherette with a cigarette clamped in the corner of her mouth called.

Marion wiped her eyes with the sleeve of her coat and grinned at Lara. 'Right, so let's get into that pub across the road and see what Angus is up to.'

'I don't think it'll be much of a surprise.' Lara grinned as she linked Marion's arm. 'He's been in there a good few hours, so I think we know how he'll be.'

Many of the cinemagoers were also heading into the pub so Lara had to pull Marion briskly along so they could squash in before it got too crowded.

'There he is,' Lara cried as she spotted Angus at a small table in the corner of the pub with that new friend of his from the cottage hospital. She turned back to Marion, who had been distracted by a tall, broad-shouldered man with a thatch of blond hair who was standing at the bar with a glint in his eye.

Angus had seen them now and he was standing up from his seat, calling out and beckoning to them.

'All right, we can see you,' Marion replied as Lara guided her away from the blond man, who seemed rather drunk.

'Marion. Lara. Let me get you a drink,' Angus called as he stood up from the table, slightly slurry but not too drunk.

'Just a lemonade for me,' Lara replied, diligent as always when it came to her driving responsibilities.

'A whisky and soda for me please, Angus. And if you're paying, make it a double.'

The dark-haired young friend of Angus's from Ridgetown Hospital stood up then to shake their hands. 'Hello, I'm Ralph.

Angus's colleague.' He seemed a little shy and it made Lara warm to him.

'Hello, I'm Nurse Flynn, one of Dr Fitzwilliam's colleagues from the surgery.'

'Why so formal, Lara?' Marion grinned, reaching out to shake Ralph's hand. 'Hello, I'm Marion and I know you'll understand this, but I have to put up with Angus's strange sense of humour on a daily basis.'

The young man chuckled and as he glanced to Lara, she noted his bright-blue eyes.

Marion slipped in beside Ralph. 'So, come on, Ralph, spill the beans. What's Angus like when he's out on loan to another team?'

Ralph's cheeks flushed a little. 'He's probably one of the best doctors I've ever worked with.'

'Come on,' Marion growled.

Ralph seemed to startle. 'No, really. Your colleague is good at what he does. And we first worked together on the diphtheria ward, so it was a very challenging time.'

'See, Nurse Marion? I have my admirers.' Angus announced as he arrived back to the table with the drinks.

'Of course you do, Fitz. It's just that they are few and far between, that's all.' Marion grinned, instantly turning to a straight-faced Ralph to add, 'I am of course, only joking. As you may have figured out, me and Dr Fitzwilliam have a playful but scathing relationship. And it pains me to say this... but yes, Angus is increasingly making his mark as a... not sure how to put it...'

'As a competent young doctor,' Lara chipped in.

Marion raised her glass. 'Yes, here's to Dr Angus Fitzwilliam, a competent and occasionally charming young doctor.'

'To Fitz,' they all cried, clinking their glasses.

Marion narrowed her eyes and leaned playfully towards Ralph. 'So, come on... what's Angus really like at the cottage hospital?'

Ralph had a twinkle in his eye when he spoke again. 'There's nothing more to say. He's excellent. He does of course have competent support from the nursing staff, including myself.'

'Yes. Of course I do.' Angus grinned as he took a slurp of his beer, leaving a line of froth on his top lip. He wiped it away with his sleeve, then leaned in and dropped his voice. 'There is of course still an issue with Matron Sharples. I think she has the bones of many former young doctors buried in the garden behind the hospital.'

Marion began to chuckle. 'How do you know you won't be next?'

'I don't. That's the thing and that's how she retains her power.'

Lara remembered the day Angus had shown her around Ridgetown Hospital when she'd first started and she'd picked up right away what a formidable woman Matron was. She leaned in to say, 'Don't be afraid, Angus. Senior nurses like that are trained to smell fear. You need to stand up to her.'

Angus groaned theatrically. 'She'll have my head for sure, if I do that.'

Marion turned to Ralph. 'How is she with you?'

He glanced to Angus. 'Sorry, mate... but you bear the brunt of it. She's nice as pie with me. She seemed to take to me right away like I was her long-lost son or something.'

Angus sighed, twisting his mouth. 'There you go. I rest my case... I am the tormented one.'

Lara was trying to figure it out but there was no logical train of thought to follow. 'She must have sympathy for the lone example... I mean, I've only ever met one female doctor and you,

Ralph, are the first male nurse I've spoken to. So maybe she feels protective of you?'

'Maybe,' Ralph said.

Angus was nodding. 'Yes, that kind of makes sense. You're like a protected species.'

Ralph chuckled. 'That's a good way of putting it. I mean, it's the same for female doctors but I'm not sure their male colleagues would be as generous towards them as many of the nurses are to me.'

'Trust me. Most of the doctors don't have a shred of generosity,' Angus said.

'Well, Angus,' Marion replied, 'it's a good job you're mostly working with us. We look after each other no matter what.'

Angus was grinning and he raised his glass. 'Here's to the Ingleside team and of course to you, Ralph, my ally at Ridgetown Hospital.'

'Oh, but don't forget Nurse Greenwood,' Lara added quickly.

'Oh, yes. Sally's lovely,' Marion cried.

'Yes, she is,' Ralph replied.

Angus put an arm around Ralph's neck and pulled him close. 'We men need to stick together, Ralphy... It's like a war zone out there sometimes, working with all those women.'

Ralph grinned.

'And it's good that Matron Sharples likes you because she scares the bejesus out of me,' Angus groaned softly. 'As does Dr Bingham.'

'Oh, Bingham's all bluster. He loves you really,' Marion called as she put an arm around his shoulders.

From there, the rest of the evening flowed seamlessly, and inevitably, by the time they were leaving the pub, Angus and Marion were a little unsteady on their feet.

'It's been absolutely, blithering... good night,' Angus slurred, as he leaned in to say something quietly to his new friend.

Moments later, Ralph glanced to Lara and murmured, 'I've no idea what he just said but it sounded positive. And it has been a very good night.'

Lara smiled, reaching out to him. 'Yes, your friend Angus is just like Marion. They both enjoy letting off a bit of steam in the pub. Whereas I'm thinking, Ralph, you are more like me.'

'Yes, most definitely.' He chuckled. 'I like a couple of pints, but that's it. Mainly because I can't stand being tipsy and then there's the horrible hangover the next day.'

'Me too. I can't bear to waste a full day like that. Although, thinking back, when I've had to do just that, well, it seemed as if I benefitted from it in an odd kind of way. Maybe like blowing away the cobwebs or something.'

Ralph tipped his head to the side as if weighing what she'd just said.

Then Lara suddenly shouted, 'Whoa!' as Angus swayed heavily to the side and Ralph had to jump forward to grab him.

As they hit the cold air outside, Marion appeared to sober up, but Angus seemed worse.

'I can assist you to the car with them, if you like,' Ralph offered.

'Thank you, that would be such a good help,' Lara replied.

As she steered Marion to the car, Ralph grappled with Angus, and they soon had the two drunken ones loaded into the back. Then, as Lara called, 'Wish me luck,' she slipped into the driver's seat and raised a hand to Ralph as she revved the engine and slowly pulled away.

'I like your friend Ralphy. He's a good egg,' Marion slurred from the back seat.

'Yeah, yeah, Ralph is the best,' Angus replied.

And as Lara headed out on the road to Ingleside, Angus shouted, 'Tally ho, driver! Put your foot down.'

To which Marion replied, 'Shush up, you nitwit. She's the only one who's shafe to drive.'

It made Lara smile and as the two of them in the back began to sing 'Show Me the Way to Go Home', she felt strangely content. And apart from a bright-red fox, with eyes that flashed yellow in the headlamps, slipping across the road directly in front of the car as they approached Ingleside, it was an uneventful journey.

Slowing now to negotiate the sharp bend into the village, she felt the back wheels slide on ice and she countered it with her steering. Then she caught the twinkle of lights from the village cottages and felt glad they were almost home.

Just before they reached the surgery, she felt sure she saw the flash of a torch beam down the street, and it made her wonder who could be out at this time of night in such freezing-cold weather. The first name that flashed in her head was Vic Taylor and it sent a shiver of guilt right through her. Vic was gone, forever. So of course it couldn't be him. But even as she parked up the little blue Austin and assisted Marion and Leo out of the back, that feeling of being watched stayed with her, raising the tiny hairs at the back of her neck.

Back in the warmth of the surgery, with Angus swaying unsteadily and laughing noisily as he tried to tell a funny story, Mrs Hewitt came out of the sitting room to help him off with his jacket. And as she pulled his woolly hat from his head, his tousled blond hair almost stood up on end. 'It's time you got your hair cut, Dr Fitzpatrick,' she said firmly.

'But Misses Haish, I only had it done lash week.'

'Well if last week was just before Christmas, you might be right.' The housekeeper grinned as she steered him along the corridor to his room. 'Now shh,' she said firmly. 'Dr Bingham's having an early night, and he won't be best pleased if he gets woken by you.'

'Yes, Fitz. You quieten down,' Marion called loudly down the corridor as Mrs Hewitt and Lara both shushed her.

Then Mrs Hewitt said gently, 'Come on, now, Angus. This is your room. In you go.'

'Thank you, Mrs Haish,' he replied.

Lara already had Marion in hand and as she steered her into the kitchen for a glass of water and a cup of cocoa, her friend leaned in with a delicious smile. 'You are my best friend ever, Lara. The very best. And I never, ever, want to work with any other nurse. If Florence Nightingale came through that door right now... I'd say, no. Not you. I want Nursh Flynn.'

It made Lara chuckle. 'Well, that's reassuring because right now, I've no intention of working anywhere else, ever.'

And even though what she'd just said had been to settle Marion, it seemed to strike a chord. Could she, would she, stay on as a nurse at Ingleside Surgery for the rest of her career?

'Come on, Nurse Flynn,' Mrs Hewitt called as she bustled back up the corridor and into the kitchen. 'Let's get the kettle on and I'm sure you'll both need a slice of hot, buttered toast before bedtime.'

'Most definitely, Mrs H,' Lara replied as she assisted Marion into her chair.

Mrs Hewitt smiled. 'It's good for Marion and Angus to let off steam. I'm just glad it's not every weekend or I don't know how we'd manage.' She paused then with the kettle in her hand and gazed directly at Lara. 'I do worry about you though, Nurse Flynn. What do you do to unwind and relax?'

Lara was about to say, *I like to read, go on long walks... look at trees and flowers...* But as she thought it, it didn't seem to be enough.

Marion, who'd been slumped at the table, straightened up and swayed her shoulders from side to side. Then she grinned and said, 'Most of all, Nurse Flynn likes to boogie woogie. You should have seen her at the Harvest Ball.'

Lara and Mrs Hewitt cracked up laughing. Then Lara was shaking her head, about to deny it when she realised Marion had been spot on; she loved to dance. But right now, her favourite thing ever was sitting at this table with Marion and Mrs Hewitt and the warm smell of toast in the air.

17

A bright, colder than ever, Sunday morning greeted Lara as the pale morning light crept in through a chink in her curtains. Her first thought was the pre-breakfast walk out to the country lanes that had now become her Sunday ritual, unless any emergency calls came in, of course. So, quickly, her teeth chattering, her breath steaming, she dashed out of her room to the freezing-cold reaches of the bathroom. Then dodged straight back to slip into her walking clothes. Once she was fully dressed, she ran down the stairs, almost colliding with Mrs Hewitt as she bobbed out of the kitchen carrying Bingham's egg and bacon breakfast tray.

'Strewth, I thought I was going to lose the lot,' the housekeeper muttered good-naturedly. Then, as she strode briskly down to Bingham's room, she called over her shoulder, 'It's colder than ever this morning. I nearly slipped flat on my back when I went out to get some coal for the Aga. So you watch your step out there, Nurse Flynn.'

'Will do, Mrs H,' Lara called as she grabbed her thick wool

coat, hat and gloves from the brass hooks, her body yearning to be outside in the clear, bright air.

She loved Sunday mornings because they were so quiet with the post office and the butcher's shop closed. As she walked down the deserted street, she glanced to the still-drawn curtains of the Taylors' house and knew they would remain like that, out of respect, until after Vic's funeral. She held back a shudder at a flashback to finding the man's body. Still no one had been charged with the crime but from what Inspector Stirling had last said, a strong suspect was beginning to emerge. She knew it'd be around the village in a flash if someone had been arrested so clearly, there was no news yet. She'd gone over it many times and come back to the same conclusion: it had to be linked to Jimmy Diamond and his gang and the word around the village was that Jimmy could wheedle his way out of anything. But Vic had been part of that gang, so it didn't really make sense. One thing she was sure of though was that timid, young man she'd seen with Jimmy was not the type to be a gang member, never mind a murderer.

She huffed out a breath, making herself leave behind her swirling thoughts. Then as she walked over the humpbacked bridge, she paused for a few moments to view the thick ice at the edges of the brook. It made her shiver, and she pulled her woolly hat down more firmly as she marched away with her breath steaming. The lanes were deserted, and it made her feel free and delighted to see the white, icy frosting on the bare branches of the trees and hedges. And she felt charmed by the glossy, green leaves of the holly still showing their bright-red berries. A stark contrast to the bare branches of the oak and birch rimed with frost. The more she walked, the warmer she became, and gazing out to the fields empty of livestock, the clear, quiet landscape offered peace, the occasional fluttering of birds in the hedges and the beauty of a red-breasted robin on an icy branch singing so sweetly, it stopped her in her tracks and almost brought tears to her eyes.

Sighing a contented breath, she leaned on a frosted farm gate and gazed out to the spare expanse of fields with the whitened fells rising magnificently in the background. She drew a slow, steady breath of icy air, huddled against the gate and smiled. It felt as if right now, just in this moment, this place belonged to her alone and nothing could touch her.

'What you doing out here on a Sunday morning?' a rough voice called from behind.

It shocked her and set her heart beating so fast, it felt like it was coming up into her throat. Instantly, she knew it was Jimmy Diamond and as she turned to face him, she felt her stomach clench at the two dead, bloodied rabbits tied with string that he carried in his left hand.

She swallowed hard, determined to stand her ground. 'I'm not doing anything apart from enjoying a walk,' she said firmly.

He smirked, then made a low noise at the back of his throat. 'Well, it would be nice if we all had the luxury of doing nothing on a Sunday morning. Most of us round here need to work every day.'

She didn't take him up on what he'd just said, and she was feeling increasingly exposed out here alone with him. 'Well, I was just heading back to the village to check if there are any emergency calls. So I'll leave you to it, Mr Diamond.'

'I'll leave you to it, Mr Diamond,' he mimicked, making her words seem petty.

She stepped away and began to walk quickly. But all the while, she could feel his eyes on her and it gave her an uncomfortable feeling at the back of her neck. She was also angry, very angry that he'd spoiled her Sunday-morning solace.

Walking faster now, almost marching, she was soon back to the outskirts of the village and as she crossed the bridge, she slipped on shot ice and almost fell flat on her back.

'Whoa, Nurse Flynn. Go easy there,' a voice called good-naturedly. It was Leo, out down the street with the little dog on a lead.

Lucky came running, pulling to get to her with his tail wagging furiously. After the threatening encounter out on the lane, it lifted her spirits.

She squatted down to pet the little dog, and he was revelling in it, panting, wagging his tail and licking her face.

'Steady on,' she laughed, 'I've already had a wash this morning, thank you very much.'

'Wow, he really loves you, doesn't he?' Leo said quietly, with almost a tinge of jealousy.

She straightened up, smiled. 'Well, I'm sure he likes you too.'

'Mmm,' Leo replied with a waggle of his head from side to side. Then he grinned. 'So, where've you been, all alone on the country roads so early in the morning?'

'Just my usual Sunday walk.'

Lucky was shivering now so Leo stooped down to pick him up, then cradled him like a baby.

'Well, it's always good to see you,' he said gently, his voice full of warmth.

'And you too,' Lara replied. Then she narrowed her eyes and leaned in to examine his face. 'You've still got a shadow of a bruise around your eye but that cut has healed very nicely. Who took the stitches out for you?'

'Oh, I did.'

'Yes of course.' She laughed. 'I forgot you're medically qualified.'

'Well, maybe not to a human-patient level but I know how to

deal with all sorts of living creatures, including myself.' His smile had broadened now and when he spoke again, his voice thickened. 'I just need to say, Lara. I don't know what spell you've cast on me but every time I see you, I just—'

'Ooh, very nice to see you two young things all lovey-dovey on a Sunday morning,' a harsh voice called from behind.

It made Lara gasp, and Leo was already shaking his head, his eyes blazing. 'Good morning, Mr Diamond. What business do you have here on a Sunday morning?'

Jimmy brushed by Lara, catching her deliberately with the dead rabbits he carried. 'Oops, sorry about that, Nurse Flynn. Might be a bit of blood on your nice clean trousers there.'

'No worries,' she replied, 'given you're just passing through.'

'Ooh, young vet, she's sure of herself, isn't she? You need to watch your step there.'

Lara exchanged a firm glance with Leo, one that said, *Let's not engage with him*. But Jimmy had already stopped in his tracks, and he seemed perfectly at ease.

Leo beckoned for her to follow him towards the surgery.

'Sorry, am I disturbing you two lovebirds?' Jimmy called after them with mock-sweetness. 'I didn't mean to interrupt your Sunday morning.' Then his voice switched to a growl. 'But until you return my property, my dog, I think I'm entitled to turn up as often as I like.'

The little dog whined miserably, as if he'd understood every word that Jimmy had said. Lara glared at Jimmy.

'She's a sparky one, your little nurse... I'm beginning to see the attraction.' Jimmy smirked.

Lara saw Leo square his shoulders and knew he was riled by Jimmy's taunting. 'Don't react; it's what he wants,' she hissed.

'Mmm,' Jimmy murmured, 'looks like the little lady is calling the shots here. That's a shame; I thought you had more spunk than that, Sullivan.'

Leo muttered under his breath and if it hadn't been for Lara blocking him, he would have swung a punch.

'Come on, Sullivan, if you want to fight it out, we can do it here, right now. The winner keeps the dog.'

Lara felt something snap inside of her and she grabbed Leo's arm. 'Come on, we're going inside. There's nothing to be gained by brawling in the street.'

'Quite right, Nurse Flynn. But this will be settled in due course and then you'll find out how much there is to lose.' Jimmy twisted his head to leer at them before continuing up the street.

Lara stood beside Leo as they both watched him go.

'I'm so sorry,' Leo said, once Jimmy had turned at the top of the hill to walk towards Ridgetown. 'I didn't want you to get snarled up in that.'

Lara was already shaking her head. 'Well, before you get carried away with all your manly, chivalrous talk, let me remind you that I live and work here in Ingleside. So inevitably, I'm snarled up in whatever comes my way.'

'Yes, I realise that. But you know what I mean. He's a dangerous man, Jimmy Diamond; everybody knows that. And he's top of the list of suspects for Vic's death.'

'Yes, I suppose he is. But do you know what, Leo? I'm damned if I'm going to let the likes of him intimidate me, you, or any of the good folks in this village.'

'Whoa!' Leo cried, as if he'd been stung. Then he grinned. 'Well, Jimmy's right about one thing. You are sparky. And I certainly wouldn't want to get on the wrong side of you.'

She laughed and linked his arm. 'Come on, scaredy cat...

how about making me a nice cup of coffee? It'll fuel me up and keep me on edge, so I'll be ready to rise to your defence.'

'Sounds like a deal.' He grinned. And as they walked towards the door of the vet's, the little dog trotted beside them, vigorously wagging his tail.

They were barely through the door before Leo reached for her, and maybe it was the adrenalin still coursing through their bodies from their encounter with Jimmy, but when he pulled her close, they were falling on each other and kissing. Leo winced, his broken nose still tender, but it only made him pull her closer. Breathless, they drew back for a moment and as he gazed to her with his crooked smile, Lara's heart did a little flip.

'Is that you, Leo?' Arthur called as the door to the living quarters clicked open.

They both startled and sprang apart.

'Yes, Dad, it's me. I'm with Nurse Flynn. She's come in for coffee.'

'Oh, that's nice. Good morning, Nurse Flynn,' Arthur called, stepping through to greet her properly. After Lara had returned the greeting, he added, 'Just wanted to say hello but I'll leave you both to it and get back to my newspaper.'

'All right, see you later,' Leo called after him.

The moment had been broken so with a pat of Leo's arm, Lara settled on the chair beside his cluttered desk. And as they chatted back and forth, Lucky jumped up to snuggle on her knee.

Then, after Leo had finally brewed the coffee and it had been consumed, she rose to leave and the little dog trotted after her, happily wagging his tail.

'Oi, traitor.' Leo laughed, sweeping him up in his arms just as he tried to squeeze out through the door with her.

Lucky emitted a low whine but as Leo scratched him behind the ears he seemed to settle. Lara leaned in, spoke softly to the little dog. 'Look, you be a good boy and I'll see you again very soon.'

Leo was chuckling as he stood with the dog in his arms to wave goodbye. It pleased her to see him so relaxed after the shaky start to the day they'd both had. And as she briefly placed a gentle hand against his cheek, she felt a moment of completeness.

All seemed quiet as she walked back up the street but even as she pushed open the surgery door and walked along the corridor, shrugging off her coat, she caught the sound of raised voices in the kitchen: Bingham and Angus.

'Lara,' Marion's voice hissed from up the stairs, 'don't go in there just yet.'

At that, Bingham's voice rose in a crescendo. 'How many times have I told you about this? What the bloody hell?'

She couldn't hear what Angus was saying but his voice was shaky.

Marion's eyes were like saucers as she gestured for Lara to climb the stairs.

'What is it? What has he done?'

'Oh, I've no idea,' Marion replied. 'Perhaps he's misplaced some piece of medical equipment or other. Maybe one of those sphygmomanometers Bingham loves so much.'

'Ah, right, that could well be it. I had a blood pressure monitor issue with him in my first week; he lent me his best and I accidentally dropped it in the street. But Mrs H cleaned it up and I'm not sure if he noticed or not, but he didn't say anything.'

Marion began to chuckle. 'Oh, he will have noticed all right; he has an eagle eye for that kind of thing. It's what makes him a good doctor, I suppose. But sometimes, when he gets caught up in some relatively trivial issue, he goes overboard.'

Lara shrugged. 'I suppose we all get like that sometimes. I mean, I can be absolutely ridiculous.'

Marion snorted to hold back a laugh. 'So, go on. If you're ridiculous, what have you done recently that's so outrageous?'

'Well, the other day, I forgot to wear my woolly vest when I was going out on visits, and you know how cold it is now.'

Marion twisted her mouth. 'Nah, that doesn't really qualify. I once forgot to wear my navy-blue bloomers.'

'You what?'

'Yes, I was distracted by something, can't remember what. But I went out on my motorcycle knickerless. It was freezing cold.'

Lara began to chuckle and it set Marion off. They just couldn't stop giggling.

'Whatever's going on up there with you two nurses?' Mrs Hewitt called from the corridor.

'Just telling stories, Mrs H,' Marion replied, then she gestured for the housekeeper to come and join them. 'What's happening in the kitchen, Mrs H? Is Angus going to come out alive?'

'Yes, he will live. But he might be required to ease off going to the pub for a little while.'

It felt for a moment that Mrs Hewitt wasn't going to give them any more detail but with a glint in her eye, she leaned in to whisper, 'Our Dr Fitzwilliam got up out of bed last night, came out of his room and he must have still been drunk because he got lost on the way back and Bingham woke to find him sleeping in the armchair next to his bed.'

'Oh my,' Lara said, then she pressed her lips together hard to stop herself from laughing out loud.

But Marion had already doubled over as if she'd been winded and she just couldn't control her giggles.

'Come on, you two. Let's go into the sitting room, put the radiogram on to drown out the sound of those two in the kitchen.'

'Good thinking, Mrs H,' Marion said.

So, led by the housekeeper, they snuck down the stairs like two naughty children and slipped into the front room. And as Mrs Hewitt clicked the door shut, they all began to giggle like a bunch of schoolgirls. Mrs Hewitt cleared her throat, stifled her laughter and shushed them as she tipped her head to one side to listen. 'Sounds like the altercation might have drawn to a close.'

Then Bingham's voice roared once more, and Lara clamped a hand over her mouth in surprise as he called up the corridor, 'Mrs Hewitt, please come and rescue me from this blithering idiot of a young doctor.'

The housekeeper pressed a finger to her lips and motioned for the two nurses to stay put as she slipped out of the sitting room, leaving Lara and Marion holding their breath.

'Poor Angus, though,' Lara said.

'Yes, poor thing,' Marion said, trying not to laugh.

'No, come on. Let's get along to the kitchen and give him some support.'

'You're right.' Marion sighed. 'He's already got a bad hangover and with this as well...'

'I know, it's a shame. And we had such a good night out.'

As they exited the sitting room, Bingham burst out of the kitchen and stamped his way towards them, his face flushed, his hair sticking out wildly from beneath his checked trilby. 'See if you two nurses can knock some sense into our young doctor, will you, please?' he grumbled in passing.

'We'll see what we can do,' Marion called after him as he stomped into his room and banged the door shut.

Angus was in his place at the table when they nosed into the kitchen. He glanced up sheepishly, then groaned, 'I suppose you heard most of that?'

'Yes, it was loud, so we heard quite a bit,' Marion said, walking over to put a gentle arm around his shoulders. 'But we don't think any the worse of you for it. We had a good night out and it was lovely to meet your friend Ralph. But maybe if you want to keep on the better side of Bingham... don't drink quite so much.'

'I'll try,' he replied sheepishly, then he emitted a low growl of laughter. 'What a shock I had waking up in the chair right next to him. He jumped out of bed in his nightshirt with his bare legs. I didn't know what to do.'

Lara glanced to Mrs Hewitt and saw her fighting to hold back a giggle.

'Did you laugh?' Marion asked, grinning.

'Yes, I couldn't help it,' he said again with a tiny guffaw of laughter. Then he was groaning, holding onto his sore head.

'Poor you,' Marion said.

And as Lara came to pat his shoulder and Mrs Hewitt put the kettle on to brew some strong coffee, Tiddles the cat trotted by, then stopped abruptly and ran to Angus with a miaow.

'What do you want, cat?' The young doctor grinned.

Then for the first time, ever, Tiddles went right up to Angus and brushed his back against his leg. Lara saw tears shining in Angus's eyes because there was no accounting for this. The surgery cat had never strayed anywhere near the young doctor till now. And as Angus picked him up and settled him on his knee, Tiddles snuggled down and began to purr loudly.

'Well, I'll be blowed,' Mrs Hewitt cried. 'I've never seen that cat sit on anybody's knee like that.'

Angus shrugged, stroked the cat, then gave him a good scratch behind the ears. And then the young doctor was beaming a smile and whatever had been fractured by the telling-off from Bingham appeared to have healed instantly.

18

It had already been a strange kind of Sunday with Lara's walk disrupted by Jimmy Diamond, then kissing Leo, and that row going on in the kitchen when she got back to the surgery. But thankfully, the rest of the day progressed quietly with Leo and Marion resting in their rooms and Lara settled in the parlour to catch up with her reading. Later, as they all gathered around the table for their customary Sunday roast lamb dinner. With Bingham tight-lipped at the head and Angus monosyllabic, Lara prayed an emergency call would come in to rescue her from the tension. So as soon as she'd finished her meal, she made her excuses and headed to the corridor to pull her coat, woolly hat and scarf from the hooks. Then she was out through the door to stretch her legs and breathe some air. The sky was clear but already, she could feel that sharper nip in the air as the late-afternoon light faded and the freezing cold began to bite.

It was quiet down the street, just one or two women at their doors chatting. As she set off walking briskly towards the bridge, she'd only just passed the curtained windows of the Taylors' house when a rough voice shouted from behind, 'Ah, Nurse

Flynn. We meet again.' It was Jimmy Diamond and it felt as if she were being stalked. Reluctantly, she turned to see him striding towards her with his young associate trailing behind, a skinny, brown lurcher at his side. The lad looked reluctant but also scared and right away, her heart went out to him.

'Well, nursey. Are you ready for round two with our young vet?' Jimmy grinned. Then he strode to Leo's door and rapped loudly with the gnarled stick he carried. Lara felt the sharpness of the sound go right through her and she walked quickly towards the door to be there for Leo.

Jimmy glanced sideways to her, a mean glint in his eye.

But she held her ground, readying herself for what was coming. Hopefully, Leo would be out, maybe called to an emergency. But in moments, the door opened and Lucky shot out towards her. Jimmy lunged for the little dog and grabbed him so hard, he yelped in pain. He had him though and he'd already clipped a metal chain to his collar.

'Let him go, right now,' Lara ordered, her whole body bristling with fury.

'I'm sorry, what?' Jimmy smirked, cupping a hand to his ear. 'As you well know, Nurse Flynn, this dog is mine and there are blokes here in the village who will support me on that.'

Leo had stepped out through the door now, his face like thunder. 'It's OK, Lara. I'll deal with this.'

'Yes, there you go, Lara. The brave young vet says he can manage.'

With her heart pounding as adrenaline pumped through her body, Lara felt fearless. She walked straight to Jimmy. 'Give me the dog,' she ordered, as the poor creature whined and strained against the metal chain.

'Just taking what's mine. That's all there is to it.' He glanced to the young lad standing sheepishly beside him. 'And this is my nephew, Luke Diamond. If you have any further questions, he will be able to confirm our ownership of the dog.' He glanced to his nephew beckoned him over. 'Luke, you take the dog, so I can put this nonsense to bed good and proper.'

Lara saw the lad swallow hard, and he barely looked up as he grabbed the dog's lead. Then he stood quietly to the side, looking scared.

Once Jimmy was free, he stretched his arms, began to limber up. 'Right, young vet. Like I said before, let's fight for the dog. Last man standing wins.'

'No, Leo!' Lara shouted.

'Oh, the little lady says no. Are you going to obey?'

Leo slowly shook his head, then he looked directly at her. 'Sorry,' he mouthed.

She sighed heavily, muttered under her breath, 'Oh for goodness' sake.'

Other villagers were gathering now, including Ed Cronshaw. 'Don't let him goad you, Leo. You step aside, let me have a go at him.'

'Nope,' Leo said firmly. 'This is my fight, no one else's.'

'This shouldn't be a fight!' Lara shouted, stepping between Leo and Jimmy. 'There is no proof this dog belongs to Mr Diamond. And most of you here will know that Leo saved him after he was injured.'

'Ha, I don't think that counts, given our young vet was the one who mowed him down in the first place,' Jimmy scoffed.

'It was an accident. I was witness to it,' Lara replied firmly, scanning the faces of the men who'd gathered, seeing a certain glint in their eyes and knowing there was little she could do to stop this happening.

Leo was already shrugging off his jacket, rolling up his sleeves. *Such a manly gesture*, were the words that popped into her head. But she'd seen enough fights on the streets of Liverpool to know that the young vet was very lacking in experience and way below Jimmy's weight and strength. So he didn't stand a cat in hell's chance.

'Come on, young vet,' Jimmy leered. 'Let's see what you're made of.'

Lara's heart sank; she'd already seen Leo smashed in the face by Vic Taylor. Bingham had been able to straighten his nose that time. But he was now facing a heavier and much more vicious opponent. Her heart picked up a staccato beat; all she could do was stay close so she could intervene if things got too violent. All the bad outcomes of the fist fights she'd witnessed on the streets of Liverpool came back at her, and she groaned painfully inside.

Leo's shoulders were hunched, he was shifting about, getting into position, whereas Jimmy just stood and waited. Leo was like a lamb to the slaughter.

Lara sucked in a breath as Leo swung the first punch. It missed, skimming past Jimmy's nose.

She felt her stomach twist, then gritted her teeth as Leo danced about a bit more. Then Diamond took two quick strides in his direction and punched him hard in the gut.

Lara heard the 'oof' sound, as all the air was knocked out of him. He groaned, staggered, then straightened up.

'A glutton for punishment are you, young vet?' Jimmy mocked as he drew back his right arm and landed another punch.

But then a shrill, loud whistle cut through harshly, and someone yelled, 'Police!'

Jimmy and his nephew scarpered, seeming to melt into thin air with the little dog.

'Nothing to see here,' Ed was shouting to the two uniformed police officers who were heading in his direction.

'We're not here on a reccy, Mr Cronshaw,' the older and sturdier of the two officers called back. 'We're here to arrest *you*.'

'What?' Ed croaked. 'What for?'

A familiar voice came at Lara. It was Inspector Stirling and he was saying out loud, almost shouting, 'Edward Cronshaw, we are arresting you for the murder of Victor Taylor...'

Lara felt the enormity of the words twist her gut. And as one of the constables handcuffed Ed, the rest of what the inspector was saying slipped into a blur of sound. This couldn't be happening; Ed was no killer... or had she got it completely wrong?

Glancing up to see the deep shock on Ed's face, Lara knew she hadn't misjudged him. Then Lizzie was shrieking in the background, 'It's not Ed. Ed wouldn't harm a fly!' She was shouting and screaming, trying to push her way through with baby William in her arms as a broad-shouldered, uniformed police officer stepped in front to hold her back. It felt as if two unrelated issues – a skirmish over a dog and Ed's abrupt arrest – had melded together to deliver nightmarish injustice.

Lara felt anger surge up from her belly. She ran after Inspector Stirling. 'What's going on? Surely you don't believe Ed killed Vic?'

He turned with a glazed, professional expression. 'We have grounds to arrest Mr Cronshaw... and right now, all else is confidential.'

Lara felt stunned. A flashback to finding Vic's body came at her then: she saw his frozen face, that fine, red mark around his neck. What were these 'reasonable grounds' that would make a young father of two children, a hard-working, honest man, end up being accused of murder?

Leo found her then, his breath coming quick. 'What's going on, Lara?' he asked, glancing to those in the street who were now rapidly dispersing as the police car pulled away with Ed in the back.

'I have no idea. But the police have arrested Ed for Vic's murder.'

'What?' Leo shouted, coughing, barely able to steady himself as he fought for breath. 'It's not Ed. He's a good bloke; he can't have done that. Surely this must be some terrible mistake?'

'Well, good bloke or not, the police seem to think otherwise, and they've taken him.'

Leo was straightening up now, but he was shaking his head. 'This doesn't make sense. Not Ed, it can't be,' he huffed, then groaned in pain and held his ribs.

Lara put an arm around his shoulders. 'Slow your breathing, that's it. Try to calm yourself. You were punched hard so your ribs will be sore. But breathe, just breathe.'

He was nodding, visibly calming. 'Good job I've got medical advice on hand. We vets aren't good at treating ourselves.' He straightened up, blew out a breath.

'Feeling better?' Lara asked.

He nodded. 'Yes, I think I'll live. But if we hadn't been interrupted, I'm damn sure that Diamond fella would've made mincemeat out of me.'

'He would indeed,' Lara replied firmly.

Leo knotted his brow and when he spoke again, his voice sounded steadier. 'This thing with Ed though, it's very troubling. But I suppose we need to trust the police will make sure they have the right man. He's probably being taken in for questioning, that's all.'

Lara didn't know much about policing, but she felt sure they'd have to have hard evidence to swoop in and arrest a man off the street like that. She sighed, reaching out to Leo. 'You might be right. We'll just have to wait and—'

In the next second, the high-pitched wail of a woman's voice cut through. It was Betty Cronshaw, out of breath as she ran up the street. 'Somebody said the police have taken my Ed for Vic's murder.'

'Yes, they've taken him in for questioning,' Lara said, fighting to keep her voice steady.

'First, they wrongly arrest Josh. Then they take Ed. Do these police know what the bloody hell they're doing?' Betty screamed.

Lara opened her mouth to reply but instantly, Lizzie ran to Betty, white-faced, still in shock, with baby William crying in her arms and little Sue wide-eyed, frightened at her side.

Betty put an arm around Sue, pulled her close and right away, she seemed to steady up. When she spoke again, it was with cut-glass precision. 'You get yourself back home with the children, Lizzie. I'll get a lift from Sam Collins in his butcher's van, and I'll go straight to Ridgetown Police Station and sort this mess out.'

'Right, yes. I suppose that makes sense,' Lizzie was saying but her eyes were wide, her breath coming quick. Clearly, she was in shock.

'You go home with the children, Lizzie. Let Betty deal with this,' Lara said gently.

'Right. Yes,' Lizzie croaked. Then she pulled Sue close and began to walk back up the hill.

The folks in the street who'd come out to watch the fight were rapidly dispersing, some of them casting sceptical or sympathetic glances in Lizzie's direction. Already it was easy to see the divide in opinion and Lara knew that unless Ed was released right away, this was going to be a very tough time for the Cronshaw family.

She glanced to Leo; he looked wrung out. When he spoke,

his voice sounded choked. 'I can't believe this is happening to Ed... He's a good bloke. And with all that stuff going on with Jimmy, I can't help but feel I'm partly responsible.'

'Don't be daft,' Lara said firmly, reaching out to him. 'The arrest had nothing to do with your fight... but it might have saved you from a nasty beating.'

He sighed a heavy breath. 'I'm inclined to agree with you, Lara. But I'd have taken my chances if it meant being able to keep the little dog.'

Suddenly panicked, Lara exclaimed, 'Lucky! Where is Lucky?'

'They took him, Jimmy and that nephew of his. As soon as the police arrived, they were away.'

Lara felt tears sting her eyes and the sorrow mixed up with the shock of Ed's arrest knocked her sideways. But seeing the state Leo was in – hunched over, white in the face and starting to shiver with cold – she knew she had no choice but to stay strong.

'Let's not give up hope, hey? For Ed and his family and the little dog...'

He nodded, offered a weakened version of his lopsided smile. 'You're far more optimistic than me, Lara. But I'll push my scepticism aside and hold on to what you've said.'

'That's good.' She tried to smile, but the moment was cut through by a familiar voice calling down the street. It was Philippa, striding down in her jodhpurs and leather riding boots.

'Leo, darling! One of the gamekeepers came back from the village with some story about you in a fight.'

'I'll leave you to it. See you later,' Lara said gently.

Leo offered a weary nod. He looked exhausted, especially now he had to rise to Philippa's questioning.

As Lara turned to walk back up the cobbled street, she

offered a nod and a good afternoon to Miss Harrington. Philippa reciprocated the gesture with narrowed eyes, then she was gushing over Leo, leading him to the vet's surgery.

'Well, well, it looks like the young lady of the manor has come to the rescue,' Mrs Hewitt was saying, then she pursed her lips as Lara approached the surgery door.

'Certainly seems that way,' Lara replied as she followed the housekeeper inside.

'Come on, I've just brewed a pot of tea,' Mrs Hewitt called over her shoulder. 'And we have scones fresh from the oven.'

'That sounds very welcome indeed,' Lara replied, but she felt as if her words were superficial, resting on top of boiling emotion. Her thoughts were mainly with Ed, Lizzie and the family but she sorely felt the loss of the little dog.

As Lara took her place at the kitchen table and Mrs Hewitt busied herself with tea and scones, she felt grateful for the calm and the quiet. The spit of the Aga, the clink of crockery, all helped to soothe her. And once the first cup of tea was poured and she'd stirred in some sugar and taken her first bite of a freshly baked scone, she felt as if she could breathe again.

'What a kerfuffle out there,' Mrs Hewitt offered, as she settled in her place at the opposite side of the table.

'I know, it was a horrible mess... All we can hope is that Ed will be questioned and released very soon.'

Mrs Hewitt drew a slow breath. 'It might not be as simple as that... There could be evidence that he did kill Vic Taylor.'

Lara pursed her lips, considering what Mrs Hewitt had just said. 'We'll just have to wait and see.'

After another sip of tea, Mrs Hewitt added, 'Well, the inspector seems a level-headed sort of man. He's sharp and professional and he looks like someone who'll do the right thing.'

Lara would have instantly agreed in the early stages of the investigation. But having witnessed what felt like a cold, professional side to the detective during the wrongful arrest of Josh and now Ed, she felt very unsure of him.

'All we can do is hope.' She tried to smile, but it must have fallen short because Mrs Hewitt's eyes filled with concern.

'Aargh,' Angus called as he staggered into the kitchen. 'I've always been a man who can be lured from his bed by the smell of freshly baked sweetmeats.'

He was stretching and yawning, then ruffling his unruly blond hair as he took his seat next to Lara at the table.

He frowned, cleared his throat. 'What's up with you two? Has Tiddles the cat been run over by the butcher's van?'

'No not that. But the police have just arrested Ed Cronshaw for Vic Taylor's murder,' Mrs Hewitt replied.

'What? Ed?' Angus howled. He was bolt upright in his chair now, casting his eyes around the kitchen as if searching for answers.

'He's just been taken in for questioning,' Mrs Hewitt tried to soothe him as she got up from the table to butter more scones.

Lara was already shaking her head. 'Yes, but they've arrested him on suspicion of murder.'

'Ed. Murder,' Angus called as he slumped forward in his seat.

Mrs Hewitt placed two buttered scones with jam in front of Angus and poured him a cup of tea as he sat, unusually quiet, with Lara filling him in on detail of the arrest. Angus was intermittently shaking his head, then tutting, but he listened carefully.

Once she was done, he sighed out a deep breath. 'I know Ed can get a bit out of hand when he's had a few beers. I've had to pull him away to stop him getting into a fight. But this doesn't add up because he's only aggressive like that when he's had too much to drink. So that doesn't fit with him being able to strangle Vic in a highly professional way, then slip him into the mill pond.'

'No, it does not,' Lara agreed, feeling buoyed up by what felt like Angus's support.

Mrs Hewitt continued to look sceptical as she sat quietly sipping her tea at the other side of the table. Almost as if the housekeeper had felt the heat of Lara's gaze, she glanced directly across the table. 'So, I've been listening carefully to what you've both been saying. And, as you know, I run a tight ship here at the surgery and part of that is having respect for others' opinions. So right now, I need to tell you that I don't believe Ed Cronshaw is innocent—'

Angus drew a sharp breath, opening his mouth to retaliate. But Lara reached out a hand to him. 'No, let Mrs H continue; she's entitled to her own opinion even if it differs from ours.'

'Thank you, Nurse Flynn,' the housekeeper replied. 'So, just to repeat. Right now, I'm thinking the police must have grounds for Ed's arrest. So that might make him guilty as charged.'

Angus tried to speak again but Lara held up her hand.

In the next second, a voice called from the door, 'What's this about police? What the heck's been going on?' Bingham stumbled through, his cheeks flushed, his trilby askew. 'I've just been up to the vicarage for a few glasses of port with Reverend Hartley and I come back to find folk out on the street and talk of police in the village.'

'Just sit yourself down, Dr Bingham,' Mrs Hewitt said gently. 'I'll brew some more tea, then we'll fill you in on the detail.'

But Angus was already in full flow. 'It's Ed Cronshaw: they've arrested him for Vic Taylor's murder.'

'What the blithering heck?' Bingham replied, glancing to the housekeeper. 'Is this true, Mrs H?'

'Yes, perfectly true,' she replied as she poured boiling water into the teapot.

Bingham blew out a breath. 'That's a shame. Ed's turned out to be a good, solid working man and an excellent father to his children.'

'Yes, that's why it doesn't make sense,' Angus replied. 'The police must have made a big mistake with this.'

Bingham slumped onto his seat at the head of the table. 'Well, there isn't much we can do right now except weigh the evidence, if we ever hear it. Then wait and see what comes.'

Angus was still restless, and he pressed further. 'What's your gut feeling, though, Dr Bingham?'

Bingham pursed his lips for a few seconds, then sighed out a breath. 'I've lived long enough to know that the unexpected does happen, more often than you think. But when it comes to taking another person's life... as we all know from our practice here at the surgery, that is a huge undertaking, a giant step for any human to take. So do I think Ed Cronshaw is capable of such a step? The truth is, I don't know. What I do know is that he can get into bother and be aggressive when he's had too much to drink. But now, especially after his son was born, he's shown himself to be a good, kind and caring father. So his profile doesn't fit that of a murderer. Then again, in moments of passion, tempers flare out of control. And none of us know what we're truly capable of until we're pushed into a situation where we need to act...'

The whole table fell silent and all that could be heard was the trickle of tea as Mrs Hewitt poured from the recently brewed pot.

The back door slammed open and with the sound of

running feet in the corridor, Marion burst into the kitchen. 'Ed Cronshaw's been arrested for murder. I've just got back from visiting my family in Ridgetown and I saw him being pulled out of a police car.'

'Yes, Nurse Wright, we are fully aware,' Bingham called gently from the head of the table.

Marion looked a little deflated as she removed her coat, hung it over the back of her chair and slumped onto her seat. Within seconds though, she was leaning forward, her eyes shining. 'It's all round Ridgetown. Ed's well known there from years ago. They're saying he's guilty, for sure.'

Lara opened her mouth to speak but the words wouldn't come.

'Let's wait and see,' Mrs Hewitt said, with a glance to Lara. 'There's at least two sides to every story; that's what I was taught growing up.'

'Hear, hear,' Bingham called from the head of the table, before lifting his teacup and taking too big a slurp of very hot tea. Then he was damn and blasting and rapidly blowing out air while the rest of the table held back their laughter.

19

Later, as Lara walked by the telephone table on her way to the stairs, the phone began to ring loudly. Knowing Mrs Hewitt had just nipped into the pantry to 'sort things out' as she always put it when stuff needed to be done, Lara had no hesitation in picking up the receiver.

'Hello, Ingleside Surgery, Nurse Flynn speaking,' she said politely. In response a loud, ranting voice came at her. She held the phone away from her ear and when things quietened a little, she spoke again, 'Hello, this is Ingleside Surgery. How can I help you?'

'Well, you could start by offering an explanation for why I've been questioned by the police!' a well-spoken male voice shouted back at her. Instantly, she recognised Patrick's voice, and a shiver ran through her. With all that she'd witnessed today, all she'd been required to do, she felt a building of tension in the pit of her stomach and had to ball her free hand into a fist to stay in control.

When at last he paused for breath, she felt her voice burst out of her. 'I have no idea what you're talking about, Patrick.'

He began to rant again about how well he'd treated her when they'd been together in Liverpool, how he'd never asked anything from her and of course, that expensive antique necklace he'd gifted her – the one she'd made sure to return. It was clear he'd had more than a few drinks, so she let him ramble. Once he'd run out of steam, she asked again, 'Why have you rung me? What do you want?'

'It's the police. You sent the police,' he raged, then his voice was sharp as he snarled, 'Don't you start thinking you can get away with this, Lara. You're nothing more than a jumped-up orphan girl. You might have told the police about me acting suspiciously around your pathetic village in the middle of nowhere. But you are wrong, completely wrong. I had to come there in person because otherwise, you'd never have given me back the necklace that was my family heirloom.'

She had to steel herself to keep her voice steady. 'Of course I would have given it back, you know that. So I still don't understand why you're so aggravated.'

He yelled again, 'The police took me in for questioning! You told them about the cigarettes I smoke – those with the gold band. Some stubs were found at the site of an arson attack at some mill apparently and in the pocket of that Vic Taylor, who was found dead. I met him briefly in your poky, little village pub, when I came quite rightly to reclaim that necklace. I barely knew the man, yet you told the police I might have had something to do with the fires and with the poor sod drowning or whatever happened to him.'

Lara had once known this man intimately so she could tell by the effort he was putting into protesting his innocence that he knew more than he was saying. But he'd already been interviewed by the Liverpool police, and he hadn't been arrested so currently, he wasn't a suspect. And in fact, all she'd told

Inspector Stirling were the names of those she knew who smoked that brand of cigarette.

'Look, Patrick, all I did was answer their questions as honestly as I could. Given this is now a murder enquiry, I thought it was absolutely the right thing to do.'

'Of course you did, Lara. Thoughtless as ever. And now they suspect Vic Taylor was murdered, where does that leave me? I've studied law, I'm a solicitor; this could badly damage my reputation.'

Lara felt the heat rising on her face as her grip on the telephone receiver tightened. Clearly, this was all about Patrick and his pompous but fragile self-importance. When they'd been going out together, he'd admitted that the line he trod as a solicitor was just this side of legal. And yes, she'd given his name to the police regarding the cigarettes, but she'd also mentioned Lord Harrington as well.

'I don't think there's anything I can do for you, Patrick. I haven't given the police any other information apart from the brand of cigarette you smoke. All I've done is tell the truth.'

'Ha!' he mocked. 'What you mean to say is you've twisted the truth for your own benefit. And you've landed me right in it.'

Lara felt her cheeks flush with more heat now and her grip on the telephone tightened. That was it. She was done.

'Goodbye, Patrick,' she said firmly as she replaced the receiver with a firm clunk.

For a moment, she just stood with her mind still whirring, her hand resting on the telephone. Then she pressed her lips into a firm line and instead of climbing the stairs, she walked to the kitchen.

'That sounded like a long call; was it a new case?' Mrs Hewitt asked, her cheeks flushed pink, and a single strand of dark hair stuck to her face as she straightened up from the oven.

'No, it was nothing. Just someone from the police asking questions.'

Mrs Hewitt twisted her mouth almost imperceptibly, and Lara could tell she wasn't entirely convinced. But Lara's white lie had come from a place where she had no energy left to explain about Patrick.

'Well, I suppose whoever it was needed to ask their questions. But you look tired out, Nurse Flynn... Why don't you go up to your room and have a lie down.'

Lara nodded. 'That's probably a good idea. It's been a very long day.' Then she offered a tight smile. 'So much for this being a Sunday; it's supposed to be a day of rest. I'd rather be back-to-back with patients.'

Mrs Hewitt barked out a grim laugh. 'I know, it's not fair, is it? Get some rest; you'll soon come to.'

But even before she'd reached the kitchen door, Lara felt a shiver of restlessness run through her. 'Darn it,' she muttered under her breath, as she turned back to Mrs Hewitt. 'Do you know what though, I think I'll head down to check on Leo. Jimmy Diamond gave him a couple of heavy punches to the stomach and he's all upset about the dog being taken.'

Mrs Hewitt offered a warm smile. 'Yes, that's a good idea. I know I've told you before what a soft spot I have for that boy. Make sure he's all right and report back to me with any concerns.'

'Will do.'

Lara was just about to leave when the housekeeper raised a delaying hand. 'Hold fire one minute. You can take some scones for Leo and his dad.' In moments, she was back with the baked goods in a brown paper bag. 'They don't eat properly, those two men living cramped up in the back of that surgery on their own.

So tell them these are from me and if they require anything else, all they need to do is ask.'

'Will do. And that's such a nice gesture, Mrs H,' Lara replied, as she beamed a smile.

It was almost dark outside as she walked down to the vet's, and it was still very cold. But the sky was clear, and the moon was full, so it boosted her. The lights were on in the cottages at either side of the cobbled street and as she passed by, she heard the murmur of voices within and the cry of a small child from behind the door of the new tenant with twin girls. She'd only briefly met Sophie Lampton and had been surprised to find she was quite well spoken and had once worked as a teacher. Her girls were a delight, but the thin, pale-faced, young mother had not been forthcoming with any detail of her husband. And Lara had been niggled by the wary look in the woman's eye. Anyway, the twin girls would be needing a check-up soon, so she'd be sure to follow up with the family.

She was at the door of the vet's now and about to knock when the door swung open and Arthur was there in his thick coat, woolly scarf and the deerstalker hat that had been a recent replacement for his battered trilby.

'Hello, Nurse Flynn,' he said with a smile. 'I'm just off down to the Old Oak for my Sunday-evening pint with Ted, the landlord. You'll find Leo in the surgery; he claims to be sorting things out for tomorrow.' Arthur lowered his voice, 'But between you and me, I can see how cut up he is about losing the little dog.'

'What's that you're saying?' Leo called.

Arthur offered a mischievous smile, giving Lara a brief pat on the shoulder. Then he was gone.

'It's only me,' Lara called. 'I come bearing scones from Mrs Hewitt.'

'Come forth and bring the scones,' Leo replied. 'And I

couldn't help but overhear what my dad was saying about me being cut up over the loss of Lucky. All I can say is, yes. He's absolutely spot on. Plus, as you were witness to earlier, I took a couple of heavy punches to the gut, delivered by our very own local ruffian. So, on reflection, I think it's fair to say I have not had a good day.'

'Yes, I agree.' Lara smiled. 'I hope the scones will ease some of that pain.'

He sighed out a breath. 'We can only try…' Then he gritted his teeth as he lowered himself carefully onto the chair beside his cluttered desk.

'You look like you're in agony. Are you OK?' she asked gently.

'I miss my dog,' he groaned as he slowly released his breath. Then glancing up with a sheen of what could have been tears in his eyes, 'It's made me feel extra sad, now he's gone. I'd have taken more punches to the gut just to keep him.'

'I'm sorry, Leo. I truly am. But I think it's a good job the police arrived because let's face it, that Jimmy Diamond would have beaten you to a pulp.'

He began to laugh, but instantly shouted out in pain and held his ribs.

'Straight to the nitty-gritty as always, Nurse Flynn,' he grunted.

'Always the best way. Don't you think?'

He looked directly at her, his eyes burning into her in the way she remembered from when they'd kissed.

She cleared her throat. 'So do you have any butter? You look like a man who needs a scone right away.'

He laughed, then clutched his ribs again. 'Please. You're a nurse; you're supposed to bring ease to injured patients, not torture them with more pain.'

'Ah, you'll mend up in a few days, or maybe a week… two weeks.'

'Aargh,' he gasped. 'Don't make me laugh again.'

An urgent knock sounded on the door and he groaned.

'Looks like we might have an animal emergency. You need to go to the door for me, Lara. I don't think I can make it.'

'Righto,' she called, going straight to the door and opening it wide. 'Oh!' she cried, shocked.

'What? Who is it?' Leo called from behind.

But Lara was too stunned to reply because right there, on the step, was Jimmy's young nephew with the little dog on its lead.

Lucky was already wagging his tail excitedly and Lara felt tears prick her eyes as she leaned down to stroke him.

'Don't tell anyone I came here,' the lad said, glancing over his shoulder. 'I waited till dark so I wouldn't be seen. But this little fella's been whining since we took him. I can't bear to see him so upset so I'm going to tell Uncle Jimmy he ran off.'

'Thank you, thank you,' Lara said raggedly, almost choking on tears as the lad thrust the lead at her. Then he was backing away, running down the deserted street.

Lucky was yapping and fussing. When Lara picked him up and walked back to the treatment room, Leo's face lit up with the broadest smile, then and instantly, he was dabbing tears from his eyes.

'He's back. Lucky is back,' was all he could say. Then he was wiping his eyes with the back of his hand and Lara couldn't stop grinning.

'Hello, Lucky. Welcome back,' she croaked.

Once they were settled with cups of tea and freshly buttered scones and Lucky had been fed and watered, Lara was sitting on Leo's desk chair, cradling the little dog on her knee. 'I can't believe he's back,' she said for the umpteenth time, and Lucky seemed to nuzzle closer as if he understood every word.

Leo pulled up a spare chair and sat down carefully, still wincing with pain. But he had a homely, satisfied air about him. 'We'll keep shtum about the lad bringing Lucky back. Neither of us want to see the young fella in trouble with Jimmy.'

'Yes, most definitely,' Lara said. 'It's odd though, isn't it, that someone like Jimmy Diamond could have such a gentle, caring nephew?'

Leo shrugged. 'There's no accounting for it. Even in the animal world, you have a reasonable idea what a calf or foal or puppy is going to look like, but temperament is another matter. It's impossible to predict.'

'Yes, you're right. And that's just as true for humans. I mean, some of the babies I delivered in Liverpool to rough-and-tumble families turned out to be just the opposite. And there were many gentle couples who ended up with right tearaways. So you never know what you're going to get.'

'Yes indeed.' Leo sighed, and she thought he was losing interest in their topic of conversation. But then she saw the brightness in his eyes that triggered her back to when they'd kissed, and she knew any repeat of that would be too overwhelming for the two of them right now.

'Oops, what time is it?' she asked, glancing to the clock on the whitewashed wall. 'I need to get back to the surgery for supper.'

'Yes, of course,' he replied, jumping up from his seat a little too quickly and yelping with pain.

After she'd gently placed Lucky down with a good stroke and a scratch behind the ears, she saw Leo looking so beaten up and sorrowful, she had no choice but to walk over and give him a brief kiss on the cheek. 'You steady on there, champ. No more fighting for a while… in fact, never again.'

He was nodding, then calling to the dog as the little fella trotted after Lara, 'Come on, come to me, you scallywag.' Leo had to walk all the way to the front door and Lara had to pick Lucky up and hand him over, so he didn't follow her outside.

'Now, you be a good boy,' she said to the dog.

Leo laughed, then groaned in pain, and said, 'I will.'

The moon and stars were on full display as she walked back to the surgery and before she went inside, she stood gazing up to the glory of the heavens. At the sound of footsteps behind, she turned to see Angus heading towards her.

'Just been for a swift half at the Old Oak,' he offered by way of greeting. Then he followed her line of gaze. 'Ah, look at those stars… how wonderful. There's a passage from Homer's *Iliad* we had to learn at boarding school, something about being on a battlefield at night with brilliant stars around a gleaming moon and clear light bursting down from the sky… or something like that.'

Lara felt surprised as she noted this other side to the young doctor and it intrigued her. 'Back when you were at boarding school, I bet you never thought one day, you'd be reciting Homer on a village street in a remote part of rural Lancashire.'

'Indeed not, Nurse Flynn,' he said, gently linking her arm and leading her into the surgery.

'Where have you two been? You're late for supper,' Marion called playfully as she bounded down the stairs.

Angus was straight back at her. 'Well, excuse me if I'm wrong, Nurse Wright. But aren't you, yourself, hastily making your way to the aforesaid supper?'

'Yes, but you were out. I was in.'

'Doesn't make any difference,' Angus quipped.

'Does,' Marion replied.

'Doesn't.'

'Enough now, you two,' Mrs Hewitt called as she bobbed out of the kitchen. Then she whispered urgently, 'Come on, hurry up. Everything's running late today and his lordship's on the verge of conniptions.'

'What exactly are conniptions?' Angus turned with an exaggerated frown and a glint in his eye to ask Lara.

'I don't entirely know,' Lara replied. 'But if we don't get in through that door, I feel sure we'll find out.' They bustled along the corridor, Marion with a hand clamped over her mouth to stifle a laugh.

Bingham glanced up sharply as they entered the kitchen together and took their seats. But instead of complaining about their lateness, his eyes crinkled at the corners with good humour, and he called pleasantly, 'Good to see you all, team. A little late perhaps. But after all, it has been a day full of incident.'

Lara tried to think of an appropriate reply, but nothing would come. Then Angus, smooth as anything, came out with, 'Sorry we're a little late, Dr Bingham. But have you seen the stars out there tonight? Nurse Flynn and I were just admiring them.'

Bingham offered a belly laugh. 'Good try, Dr Fitzwilliam. But I saw you heading down the hill to the Old Oak earlier.'

'Ah well, it was worth having a stab at it.' Angus sighed theatrically, then grinned.

And as Marion leaned across the table to tease Angus about his stargazing and Mrs Hewitt tutted over the vegetable soup that she thought had a little too much salt, Lara saw Bingham's proud glance around the table and knew for sure that it was good to be part of a team such as this.

'Oh, Nurse Flynn,' Bingham said overly loud. 'Up early, as usual.' Then he exchanged a guilty glance with the housekeeper.

Lara wasn't having any of this. She abhorred secrecy so she spoke out right away. 'Look, I can see you two are in the middle of some heated discussion. And given the way you're looking at me, it feels as if I'm the subject. So I think it only right you tell me what the heck is going on.'

Mrs Hewitt glanced to Bingham. He swallowed hard then said, 'Go ahead, Edith. Tell her. It's only fair and she'll find out soon enough anyway.'

Lara felt like everything she held dear was collapsing around her as she stood waiting for Mrs Hewitt to finish straightening her apron and look her in the eye.

'Right, so, Nurse Flynn. You might want to sit down for this. But it's best that you're told straight out.'

Lara's heart picked up a staccato rhythm.

'It's just that, well, Dr Bingham took a call from a police officer in Liverpool late last night. Apparently, some person has filed a complaint about you giving false information in a case related to the recent goings-on here in the village. This person said you'd lied to the police about some cigarette stubs and who smoked them, something like that.'

'What?' Lara cried, instantly outraged. Tiddles the cat yowled and shot past her.

Mrs Hewitt seemed to draw back.

'This is all a load of nonsense,' Lara almost shouted. 'I already know who this "person" is. It's my ex from Liverpool trying to stir up trouble. I should have told you yesterday, Mrs H, but it was him who I was having that long conversation with on the telephone. He was angry that I'd told the police he'd visited Ingleside and made a connection with Vic Taylor.'

20

Lara slept soundly and woke with a ping as soon as her alarm went off. It felt colder than ever in her room and her feet, having escaped from the covers, were icy despite her woolly bed socks. After such a hectic few days, it took her a few moments to know what day it was. 'It's Monday,' she muttered with steaming breath.

As she dressed, she felt glad of the woollen vest that didn't feel quite as cold as the uniform she donned at speed. Then she pulled on her thick wool stockings, hopping from one foot to the other on the icy floor. It was silent in the corridor, so she knew Marion hadn't roused yet, so as she jogged along the landing and down the stairs, she felt reasonably sure she'd be first as usual to the kitchen for breakfast. So it startled her, and she stopped just short of the door, when she heard Bingham's voice. He seemed het up about something and when she heard him mention the police, closely followed by her name, her skin prickled with concern.

It didn't feel right to stand there listening, so she pushed through and called a semblance of her usual good morning.

Bingham blew out a breath and he was vigorously nodding. 'Right, so that explains a thing or two. And if it is what happened and you're telling the truth, I don't think there's a case to be answered here.'

'What do you mean, Henry? Of course Nurse Flynn is telling the truth. Are you doubting that?'

'No, of course not. It just came out a bit formal, that's all. Bear in mind I was speaking at length to the police last night and it's all been very worrying. I mean, on reflection, what the blithering heck were they talking about?'

'Exactly,' Mrs Hewitt said, setting her mouth in a very firm line.

Bingham's face clouded as he turned to Lara. 'The only thing is, Nurse Flynn... we need to have you cleared by the police so we can reinstate you here at the surgery.'

'What do you mean, reinstate? When was I un-instated?'

Bingham looked sheepish. 'Well, it was last night, when I got a call from the police.'

'Oh for goodness' sake, this is all stuff and nonsense,' Lara said, feeling angry tears threaten.

'Yes, I agree,' Mrs Hewitt growled. 'Can we not do it right away, now Nurse Flynn has given her side of the story?'

Bingham frowned deeply, stood silent for a moment. 'I don't think we can, I'm afraid. But I'll telephone the Liverpool police right away and speak to the officer involved.'

Lara swallowed hard against a dry throat. 'Right, yes. Please do that because I have a full list of patients and I need to get out on my visits.'

Mrs Hewitt pursed her lips. 'Yes, there are plenty of patients to see.'

Bingham thrust out his chest like a man with a mission as he strode towards the telephone in the hallway. Once he'd dialled and was speaking, Lara felt reassured by his brisk tone of voice. 'Right, so you're saying we need to wait until I've spoken to Inspector Stirling, and he's given the all-clear. Yes. I understand. And just to confirm, you're going to call them now... Right, yes, all right. Thank you very much.'

Lara had felt her stomach tighten at the mention of Inspector Stirling. Knowing what a stickler for protocol he was, she wasn't altogether sure he'd clear her straight away. The thought of kicking her heels while the rest of her team had to take on her visits felt too much to bear. She cursed Patrick under her breath, vowed never to speak to him again.

'Damn and blast it. Why can't things be straightforward?' Bingham shouted from the hallway as he slammed down the telephone receiver. Then he was in through the kitchen door, his eyes bright, shining in Lara's direction. 'I'm not going to risk a telephone call; I'm going straight down to Ridgetown Police Station now, in person. I'll be ready and waiting when Stirling comes on duty and I'll make damned sure he clears you immediately so you can get on with your duties.'

Lara sucked a deep breath as she felt what had been tightly held inside of her begin to loosen.

'I'm so sorry, Lara,' Mrs Hewitt called sorrowfully from the Aga. 'This should never have happened.'

'It's not your fault, Mrs H,' Lara replied gently. She tried to smile but all she could manage was a twist of her mouth. 'There are forces at play here that we have no control over. But come hell or high water, I'll be back on my visits this morning.'

The housekeeper swiped at her eyes with the flat of her hand, then she was pulling a pan off the Aga and when she spoke again, her voice sounded back to business as usual. 'I've got your porridge, Nurse Flynn; it's almost ready.'

Lara nodded, walking to stand next to the housekeeper. 'It's been a funny old morning, Mrs H. So why don't I brew the tea?'

'Yes, that would be very nice indeed.' Mrs Hewitt smiled as she pushed the red teapot along the counter towards Lara.

Once the tea was brewed and Lara sat sipping a heavily sugared cup, Mrs Hewitt walked over with the bowl of porridge. It made Lara's breath catch when she saw the housekeeper had made the swirl of cream on top into a heart shape.

'That's so sweet. Thank you, Mrs H,' she croaked.

Lara was still sitting at the table with her second cup of tea and a round of toast and jam, waiting for Bingham to call back with news from the police station, when Marion and Angus ran in for their quick breakfasts.

'What's up?' Marion called right away as Angus, oblivious, slurped a mouthful of tea, grabbed his toast and ran.

'Just a bit of a nuisance, that's all,' Lara replied.

But Marion was still frowning as she took her first big bite of toast. And as she munched, she asked, 'What nuisance? What's going on?'

Lara knew Marion wasn't going to let it drop, so she gave a quick summary of what Patrick had done.

'That good for nothing piece of—' Marion hissed, then she dodged around the table, planted a big kiss, sticky with jam, on Lara's cheek, and called over her shoulder as she ran from the kitchen, 'I hope that call comes soon. But don't worry, I'll help out with your visits if need be.'

'Thank you,' Lara called after her, wiping the traces of jam from her cheek and feeling buoyed up enough now to chuckle.

Mrs Hewitt was also laughing, then she was dabbing at her eyes. 'What would we do without our Nurse Wright?'

'I have no idea,' Lara replied. 'She just meets everything head-on, with so much energy. Like a force of nature.'

Mrs Hewitt walked to the table with her own cup of tea. 'You do know, don't you, that you are the perfect colleague for our Nurse Wright? Just imagine if she worked with someone who had a matching temperament. Our patients would be dizzy.'

'Yes, that's true. And at times like these, it's reassuring to know that even if I am delayed for a while longer, Marion will catch up in double quick time.'

'She will for sure,' the housekeeper said. Then she frowned. 'I still worry about her, though. Out on her motorcycle in all weathers, especially at this time of year.'

'She'll be fine, Mrs H,' Lara replied, but sometimes, she had the same stab of concern, especially when her mind flashed back to Marion's motorcycle accident in the summer.

In the next second, the telephone jangled loudly. 'That'll be Dr Bingham; I'll get it,' Lara said as she ran to the hallway. Her breath felt stuck in her chest as she picked up the receiver and waited for the call to connect.

'You're free to go out on your duties,' Bingham reported triumphantly. 'Inspector Stirling could see immediately that this Patrick fella from Liverpool was up to no good. Apparently, when he'd rung the station in Liverpool, he'd been slurring his speech and sounded quite drunk.'

'That's such good news,' Lara replied. 'Not that Patrick was drunk, of course; that's how he sounded when he spoke to me too. But I'm so relieved I can get back out to see my patients.'

Then as Bingham began to ramble with a little too much detail of his conversations with the police in Liverpool and Ridgetown, Lara couldn't help but feel impatient. She was already behind time, so she urgently needed to get on with her visits. But he was still talking. In the end, she had to cut in and speak firmly, 'Right, Dr Bingham. Yes. But I need to go now to see my patients.'

'Righto, Nurse Flynn. I'll see you later back at the surgery,' he called jovially, as he put the phone down.

She was shaking her head, still smiling at Bingham's quirkiness, as she walked back to the kitchen.

'Well?' Mrs Hewitt asked, both eyebrows raised and a smudge of flour on her cheek from the pastry she was mixing.

'I'm all clear for duty.' Lara grinned. 'But I'll be on catch-up now for the rest of the morning, so I hope the roads aren't too icy.'

The housekeeper let out a yelp of joy. Then she said firmly, 'Go easy, Nurse Flynn; the roads will be slippery.'

But Lara barely caught the edge of it as she ran from the kitchen to grab her thick coat and district nurse's hat from the brass hooks in the hall.

* * *

The day whizzed by quickly and seemed to reflect the heightened state she was in as she ran late to all her visits. She needed to work through lunch, so she didn't get back till late afternoon. After a quick bite to eat, she was posted to the clinic with Dr Bingham, who was still revelling in his triumph over the Liverpool police.

It felt satisfying later to be back around the kitchen table for the evening meal. And given what had happened this morning, she still felt buoyed up.

'Well, you think you've had "one of those days", Lara...' Marion called as she leaned across the table, smearing a blob of custard that had escaped from a spoonful of jam roly-poly pudding up the sleeve of her uniform. 'Wait till you hear this. You know that American fella who bought Alice Taylor's farm? Well, I was on a visit up near Fell Farm this morning and he called by to borrow a big spanner. He's tall and broad-shouldered with a muscular build and he's got longish, wavy hair. He's so good-looking, like a movie star, and he has that American swagger about him. He's a bit too old for me, but wow, what a catch for an older woman.'

'Ooh, sounds interesting.' Mrs Hewitt giggled as she came to lean on the table with both hands. 'What's his name?'

'Karl, I think. I was a bit overwhelmed to take in the detail.'

Angus had been listening carefully to Marion's story, and he said, 'I think I saw him the other week when I was up that way. He's done all sorts to the Taylors' farm and he's building some kind of aeroplane or glider in the barn. All very exciting by the sound of it but I'm just wondering what he'll do with the glider when it's ready.'

'He'll probably fly it,' Marion said as she held out her bowl for the final scrapings of custard from Mrs Hewitt's pan.

The housekeeper narrowed her eyes as if she were trying to remember something. 'I heard something on the radio a while ago about those gliders... From what I remember, they drag them at speed, then they take off and soar up into the sky. I mean, how do they steer the things and how do they get them back down without crashing? It all sounds a bit scary if you ask me.'

'That's the future, Mrs H,' Angus said, his eyes shining.

Lara was shaking her head. 'No, it's not for me. I like to keep my feet planted firmly on solid ground.'

'Me too,' Mrs Hewitt said.

But Marion was staring into space with her custard spoon half-raised to her mouth. 'Just imagine, though. Floating up into the air like that, looking down to see everything laid out below. It sounds like heaven.'

There was a moment of silence as they all gazed to Marion,

still caught up with her imaginings. Then she dropped her spoon noisily into her pudding basin and the moment moved on.

Angus eased back in his chair with a sigh as he finished his second helping of pudding. 'I'm so full of roly-poly, I feel just like the aforementioned pudding.' He groaned theatrically and placed a hand over his belly. 'So much so, I might never be able to move from this very spot. I might have to spend the rest of my life, right here at the table, being fed Mrs Hewitt's puddings.' Then he had a twinkle in his eye. 'However, given our Nurse Flynn has successfully come through a tricky time, I'm just wondering if I might be able to persuade you all to move across the road to the Dorchester. So we can raise a toast to Ingleside Surgery and all who sail in her.'

'Sounds like an excellent idea.' Bingham smiled. 'But I have other business to attend to this evening.'

When the whole team glanced to him as one, he hastily added, 'I promised Arthur Sullivan I'd meet him for a drink in the Old Oak. I don't want to go into the detail but it's a date we mark from our war years. Something we do every year.'

'Yes, of course. That's fine,' Angus replied, his voice low, respectful. Then he glanced around the table and asked, 'So, are the rest of you up for it?'

'Yes,' Lara and Marion called at the same time.

Angus rose from his seat and held out an arm to Mrs Hewitt, who had just stood up from her chair to begin clearing the table. 'Look, I know you always decline these invitations, Mrs H. But if Dr Bingham's going to be here in the surgery for a while longer to answer the telephone, why don't you come with us?'

The housekeeper was already shaking her head. 'I've got these pots to clear and there might be calls coming in...'

Bingham stood up and when he spoke, his voice was gently

authoritative. 'I will clear the pots. So there's no excuse, Mrs Hewitt. In fact, I am ordering you to go. Even if it's just for one drink. And if I get called out to a visit, I can bob across the road and let you know. How does that sound?'

Mrs Hewitt blew out a breath. 'That sounds like a plan, but it would go against all my usual good sense.' Then she began to smile. 'But you know what, Dr Bingham? Blow it. I'll go this time, just for one drink.'

'Hurrah!' Angus called as Lara and Marion jumped up excitedly from their chairs.

Bingham was standing up and he was chuckling. 'Come on, Mrs H. It's time to let your hair down a little.'

'Right, so I just need to check the Aga first, see if it needs refuelling.'

'Oh no you don't,' Bingham replied, already blocking her access to the stove. 'I have lived with this Aga just as long, if not longer than you, and I'm perfectly capable of checking and refuelling the blasted thing. So go. Just go.'

Marion was already beside her. 'Come on, Mrs H. Off with your pinny... We're going to the pub.'

It felt delightful, mischievous almost, as they exited the kitchen with Mrs Hewitt in tow and Bingham calling after them, 'I'll be fine, absolutely fine,' as he opened the Aga door and a heavy puff of black smoke came straight out, making him cough.

'He's never been left alone in there for years. Not since I needed to visit my sister in Ridgetown when she had an accident on her bicycle,' Mrs Hewitt muttered. She still seemed tense, and she glanced back to the surgery any number of times. But once Angus had linked her arm and led her up the stone steps to the door of the pub with Lara and Marion following behind, she was snuggling up close to the young doctor and giggling.

21

The Fleece was quiet, and Lara was glad of that given this was Mrs Hewitt's first time out since forever. It felt strange to see the housekeeper in a different setting and it seemed to make her and Marion and Angus a little giddy. It was nice to see Ada raise a hand in greeting, then her eyes opened wide with surprise when she saw Mrs Hewitt.

'Well blow me down with a feather, I've never seen you in here before, Mrs H,' she said with a grin.

'No indeed. This is a new venture for me.' Mrs Hewitt smiled. 'In fact, I've only been in on a handful of occasions and that was well before your time behind the bar, Ada.'

'Well, let's not leave it as long next time,' Angus said.

The housekeeper gave his arm an affectionate squeeze. Then she spotted Betty Cronshaw with Josh, sitting at a corner table. 'Hello there,' Mrs Hewitt called, walking over to speak to them as if she'd been a regular in the pub for donkey's years. 'How are you doing with all that's happened to your Ed?' Lara heard her ask.

As Betty began to reply, Marion whispered to Lara, 'Look at her. It's like she's been coming in here every week for years.'

'I know,' Lara said, holding back a giggle. Stifling it immediately when Betty emitted a sob as she spoke of Ed still being held in custody and how he'd been moved to Preston prison.

'They're having a rough time of it, the Cronshaws,' Marion said under her breath. 'And there's talk that Lizzie's only a couple of weeks away from being evicted from their cottage because they can't pay the rent.'

'Really? Does the mill not provide anything at all?'

'Not if a man's unable to work because he's been accused of murder.'

It hit Lara with a punch. 'Right, yes... But Lizzie's got two tiny children. What will happen to the family?'

'They'll be evicted by the Harringtons, who are landlords for all the properties in the street. They're tough with non-payers so they'll have to pack their bags and go. And I suppose Lizzie and the children will move in with Betty.'

A picture of the cosy little home Ed and Lizzie had made for their children came at Lara and she felt tears sting her eyes.

Sensing her disquiet, Marion spoke gently. 'Don't be upsetting yourself, Lara. In this village, no matter what, the folks look after one another.'

Lara snatched at that information and once she had a pint of beer in her hand and she'd taken her first mouthful, she was beginning to feel better. Then, as Mrs Hewitt walked back from Betty and Josh, she pulled out a chair and sat down with a contented sigh next to the cheerfully blazing, open fire stacked with logs.

'You look like you've been doing this your whole life, Mrs H.' Angus smiled as he walked back from the bar, having stayed chatting to Ada after insisting he pay for all the drinks.

'Well, to some extent, that's true. When I was a girl, my father was the landlord of a pub in Ridgetown and me, my mum and older sister lived in the flat above.'

'Really?' Angus said, raising both eyebrows in surprise. He seemed to be fascinated by the detail of Mrs Hewitt's former life. 'So did you ever serve behind the bar, that kind of thing?'

'Oh, no. I was too young for that. But I did learn how to change the pumps down in the cellar. And of course there were a lot of glasses to be washed.'

'When did you leave there, Mrs H?'

Her face clouded a little. 'Well, we didn't so much leave as get evicted.'

'Oh dear, sounds daring.'

'It was. We had to do a moonlight flit. Pack all we had onto a horse-drawn cart and leave in the very early hours when no one was about.'

Marion leaned in then. 'That all sounds very dramatic, Mrs H.'

'Well, it was I suppose. But for me, it was upsetting because I loved that pub and the nice flat we had there. And you know what it's like when you're a child and you latch onto something.'

'Yes, I do,' Lara said straight out, thinking how unsettled she'd been at being packed off to boarding school from her aunt's house.

Mrs Hewitt reached out to give Lara's hand a squeeze, then she smiled. 'But we got by; we'd already left another property under cover of darkness, as had many other families we knew at that time. It was just how things were back then – lots of folk ran into money troubles.' She shrugged, gazed into the fire, seeming far away for a few moments. 'My father was arrested shortly after that, accused of stealing money from the till of that pub.

But he hadn't; he was an honest man despite his heavy drinking.'

Lara's head was reeling with all the unexpected detail of the housekeeper's early life. She'd never expected anything other than Mrs Hewitt's having been brought up in a very sober household akin to that of a Methodist minister.

'Less of this talk of the past, hey,' Mrs Hewitt said, raising her glass in a cheers. 'Here's to the here and now and our life and times at Ingleside Surgery.'

'Cheers,' they all cried, as Mrs Hewitt downed the remains of her whisky and dry ginger in one go.

Angus's eyebrows shot up as she plonked her glass firmly down on the table. 'Fancy another, Mrs H?'

'Yes, please. And I think I'll have a single malt this time, that's if they have one.'

'Coming up,' Angus called, with a wide-eyed glance to Lara and Marion.

Lara, Marion and Mrs Hewitt sat quietly then in their alcove by the fire and the warmth was making Lara a little sleepy.

'Are you OK?' Marion asked gently.

'Yes. In fact I'm feeling very relaxed.' Lara smiled as she tried to stifle a yawn. 'It feels like I might need an early night, though. I was pedalling as fast as I could on the icy lanes this morning and it still took ages to get to my visits. And I had to dismount many times to wheel my bicycle. I can't stand that feeling of being on catch-up; it wears me out.'

Marion chuckled. 'That's my resting state. And I know I should be more conscious of the time. But you know what? I like the boost it gives me. Except I hit a very icy patch and nearly skidded off on a sharp corner. I was all over the place and thought I was going to lose Gloria.'

Lara had an instant flashback to the accident Marion had

had in the summer and she groaned out loud. 'For goodness' sake, please, Marion, will you slow down. I'm not ready to deal with the stress of you having another smash.'

Marion twisted her mouth, seemed to shrug.

'I mean it,' Lara growled. 'You have to slow down... for me.'

'Don't be cross with me, Lara,' Marion whispered mischievously.

'I'm not cross. I just need you to be safe, that's all.'

'Well, you might be pleased to know that a wise, old farmer I visited this morning told me that heavy snow is on the way. So nobody'll be able to go anywhere in a hurry.'

'That suits me,' Lara replied, sitting up straighter now. 'At least if you're confined to the village I can rest much easier... But how could that farmer be so sure? Isn't it the case that when it's very cold and freezing, it's too cold to snow? Or something like that.'

'People say all sorts of stuff, especially out here. But believe you me, from the winters I've done here and in the Highlands of Scotland, it's damned cold just before, during and after heavy snow.'

'Oh, I hope it doesn't come tomorrow.' Lara sighed. 'I've got some urgent cases to follow up.'

Marion pulled her close. 'We'll manage, you know we will. And if your bicycle's frozen up or it's too slippery on the lanes, I'll get you on the back of Gloria and we'll sail away.'

'Slide into a ditch, more like.' Lara giggled.

Mrs Hewitt leaned in with a warm smile. 'It's so good to see you two nurses out together. It warms my heart, it truly does.'

'It's good to be here,' Marion was saying. Then a blast of cold air came at them from the door, making woodsmoke puff from the fire.

'What the flipping heck?' Marion called as Lara coughed.

Then she heard Leo's voice and in the next second, Lucky came running at her with his tail wagging.

'Hello there,' Lara beamed, already stroking the little dog and pulling him onto her lap.

'Well, you're a fine-looking fella with that patch of brown over one eye,' Mrs Hewitt cooed, reaching out to give him a scratch behind the ears.

'That's it, I've lost my dog yet again,' Leo said with a grin as he walked over to their table on his way to the bar.

'It's not my fault he prefers me to you,' Lara replied, delighting in the warmth of the dog and the softness of his fur.

Leo was shaking his head. Then Angus called from the bar to ask what he wanted to drink, and the spell was broken.

Lara noted Mrs Hewitt's glance as she looked from her to Leo, and back again. Then she leaned into Lara with a twinkle in her eye. 'I've always said it, and I know it to be true... He's a lovely lad, our young vet.'

'We know what you're up to, Mrs H,' Marion whispered. 'No matchmaking, please. I get enough of that from my mother every time I go home.'

Mrs Hewitt held up both hands. 'Guilty as charged. I'll say no more.'

Lara was about to whisper to Marion and tell her it was perhaps a bit late for matchmaking when the pub door burst open again and another gust of freezing-cold air came at them. A rough voice growled, 'I thought I'd find you here, young vet.' It was Jimmy Diamond with his pale, scared-looking nephew, Luke by his side.

Lara saw Josh MacDonald bristle and he got up from his seat to close the door. Then he walked towards the bar to stand beside Leo.

'Looks like you've got the big guns with you tonight, young

vet.' Jimmy grinned. 'But no need. We're here on peaceful grounds to recover our rightful property.'

He glared directly at Lara and the little dog whined pitifully. Then Jimmy turned to the stricken-looking lad by his side. 'My young nephew here lost his grip on the dog's lead, and the little blighter ran back to where the dog thief lived. So, Mr Sullivan, let's set this straight once and for all.'

'You'll have to deal with me first,' Josh said, stepping between Jimmy and Leo.

'Well, if that's the way you want it, Mr MacDonald... However, from what I hear, you're still not entirely cleared by the police. So I'd be careful if I were you.'

Betty was on her feet now. 'That's a load of rubbish, Jimmy Diamond. And you know it.'

'Oh, so the mother of another murder suspect speaks up. That's novel.'

Josh emitted a low growl and strode towards Jimmy.

'Right, that's enough,' Ada called, stepping out from behind the bar. 'Out you go, Diamond. You're already barred from here, so no argument. I'll call the police if you don't make a move.'

Jimmy pressed his lips together as if were stopping himself from laughing. 'As if a little girl like you could tell me what to do.'

'She might not be able to. But I certainly can,' Sid Lightfoot called as he stepped around the bar with a shotgun. 'Out, right now. Before I fill you full of shot.'

Jimmy tipped his head to the side, clearly weighing the situation. And as Sid moved closer and gestured with his gun, he shrugged, then beckoned for Luke to follow him.

'I'll be back for my dog, Sullivan!' he spat as he exited, leaving the door wide open to a blast of freezing-cold air.

The tension in the pub eased once Josh had closed the door.

'Phew, I wasn't expecting that on a Monday night out,' Mrs Hewitt breathed.

'Sorry about that,' Angus replied. 'I hope it didn't scare you, Mrs H.'

'No, not me. I mean, it's never good when men are waving shotguns about. But more often than not, it's just bravado. That Jimmy Diamond needs to be watched carefully, though; he's part of a family that were terrorising Ridgetown folks when I lived there years ago.'

'Yep, you're spot on there, Mrs H,' Marion offered. 'And my mum's been saying the Diamonds are getting even worse. Word is they were the ones who killed Vic Taylor... but it's a case of innocent until proven guilty and of course, they've got folk who can be persuaded to give them alibis.'

Angus tipped his head to the side. 'But maybe we're just judging them on past conduct?'

'Nah, that lot are guilty as hell,' said Mrs Hewitt as she knocked back the remains of her whisky.

Lara saw Angus stifle a laugh and Leo's mouth dropped open.

* * *

Later, after Mrs Hewitt, at her own request, had been escorted back to the surgery by Angus and another round of drinks had been consumed, Lara sat gazing into the fire with the little dog sleeping on her lap and she felt at peace. Then as Marion gave her a gentle nudge and murmured, 'It's time to get moving,' the dog stirred, and Lara lifted him from her knee and handed him back to Leo.

'Come on, you little traitor,' Leo said as he tucked the dog under his arm.

'You're just jealous,' Lara quipped. And in that moment, as he grinned back, he looked so warm and handsome, she felt like kissing him again.

Marion linked her arm as they called their goodbyes to Ada behind the bar, then to Josh and Betty, who were still deep in conversation.

'Goodnight, goodnight,' echoed gently around the pub and it made Lara feel even more sleepy.

As soon as the biting cold hit her, however, she felt her eyes snap open as she followed Angus carefully down the steps.

'Watch your step, it's very sliiiippy…!' he called as his foot skidded, and he slid all the way down the steps and part way down the street on his backside.

'Oh my God, are you OK?' Lara called, stepping carefully after him, as Marion and Leo both cracked up laughing.

It took a few moments for her to reach him, and he was laughing and groaning with pain all at the same time. But he said he was all right, and was more concerned about anyone else falling.

'Try to stand up, Angus,' she instructed. But he didn't seem to be able to get a foothold.

'Step back. Let me take him,' Leo called authoritatively from behind, nudging Lara for her to take hold of the dog. He slipped on ice even before he got to Angus, then as Angus crawled over to try and heave him up off the street, they both fell together and slipped even further down the hill.

Marion was doubled over with laughter now and Lara was trying to hold it back, but it was like a scene from a comedy sketch.

'Hang on, let me see if I can help,' Marion called, taking tentative steps towards the two men.

'Are you OK? Are you hurt?' Lara called.

'No,' they both replied.

'Just a few bruises, that's all,' Angus added.

Marion was there with them now and she gave clear instruction of how to proceed. 'Right, so see that low wall over there? Shuffle over – that's it, just like that. Now pull yourselves up. That's good,' Marion encouraged. 'Now get your footing... It looks like somebody's spread some ash there at the side. Go there, get a foothold.'

'I think we're safe,' Angus called, just as one foot slipped again, wildly out to the side, and Lara and Marion just couldn't stop laughing.

'Sorry, I can't help,' Lara called between bursts of giggles. 'I can't risk hurting this little fella.' She snuggled her cheek to Lucky's warm fur.

Later, after both men had steadied up and the dog had been handed back over, they all watched as Leo tentatively made his way back down to the surgery. 'Thank you,' he called, raising a hand before going in through his door.

Lara linked Marion's arm as the young doctor tentatively led the way back to the surgery. 'It's a bit like being Scott of the Antarctic out here in the winter,' Angus called over his shoulder.

'Oh, of course it is,' Marion replied. 'Except that the Antarctic is not a village street.'

He turned with a mock-frown. 'Oh, is it not? Well, from what I've experienced out here in the wilds of Ingleside, I think this might be just as perilous.'

'Oh, yes. I can see where you're coming from with that,' Marion quipped, then she was laughing and grabbing Lara's arm as one foot skidded out from under her.

'All OK back there, team?' Angus called merrily.

'All good, Mr Scott,' Marion replied breathlessly.

'The door to the surgery has never seemed so far away,' Angus mock-wailed, then laughed. 'Ow, my ribs are hurting. Hope I've not punctured a lung.'

'I think not,' Marion replied just as they reached the surgery door. 'Because you're talking and talking, Dr Fitzwilliam. You've got enough breath for all three of us put together.'

He was shaking his head and laughing as he pushed through the door. 'But what you don't know is how much pain I'm in.'

'What's this about pain?' Bingham called down the corridor.

'Oh, just our junior doctor being melodramatic as usual.'

'Dr Fitzwilliam, dramatic? Never.' Bingham laughed as he walked up to meet them. 'But I must say it is very icy out there tonight. I nearly slipped on my backside coming back from the Old Oak.'

'See, I told you.' Angus turned to Lara and Marion with both eyebrows raised.

'Right, so what I don't understand,' Marion said, tipping her head to the side, 'is how me and Lara managed to stay on our feet when you men were all over the place.'

'Well, you've got smaller feet,' Bingham replied, a flash of mischief in his eyes.

'Mmm, forgive me if I'm wrong, but wouldn't that be a disadvantage?'

'No, not really, because you haven't got as much surface to slip with.'

Mrs Hewitt shouted through from the kitchen, 'Well what about those snowshoes that the explorers wear? They make their feet bigger so they can move more easily.'

'Mmm, good point, Mrs H,' Bingham mused, and he was just about to open his mouth to offer something else when a loud knock came to the door.

'Whatever's that?' Mrs Hewitt said, frowning, as Bingham moved briskly to open up and Lara, Marion and Angus stood waiting.

'Come in out of the cold,' Bingham said, ushering a man in a smart overcoat, plaid scarf and black Fedora hat into the surgery.

It was Inspector Stirling, out of breath and needing to collect himself. 'Sorry,' he croaked. 'I've had a hell of a journey up from Ridgetown and I've had to abandon my car and walk the final distance. I tried telephoning but the ice must have brought the phone lines down.'

'Come in, man,' Bingham called. 'In there, in the sitting room where you can get warm by the fire.'

All, apart from Mrs Hewitt, who was checking whether the telephone was working, filed into the sitting room after the detective.

'Ahh, that's nice,' Stirling said, removing his leather gloves and warming his hands by the fire. When he straightened up, he pulled off his hat and although Lara didn't know him all that well, she could tell by the brightness of his eyes he was here to deliver unexpected news.

'Sit down, Inspector,' Bingham offered, indicating a chair by the fire.

'I'd rather stand if you don't mind,' Stirling said. 'And I'm sorry to come here at this late hour but I didn't know what else to do.' He swallowed hard, gazing directly to Lara. 'It seems that we've arrested the wrong man for Vic Taylor's murder. You were right, Nurse Flynn, in your support of Ed Cronshaw. Two reliable witnesses have come forward to say they saw Ed in Ridgetown late that night. He looked aggressive, he'd had a few drinks, and he seemed to be looking for Vic Taylor because he asked one or two if they'd seen him. But there is no way Ed could have made it all the way back to the mill pond before it froze over. So, he's in the clear.'

'Phew, thank goodness,' Lara breathed. 'Does his wife Lizzie know?'

'No, not yet. I need to speak to her and his mother urgently.'

'I'll come with you,' Lara offered right away. 'Lizzie and the children live in a cottage just across the street. And we've just come from the Fleece and his mum, Betty, she's in there.'

'Right, so the sooner, the better,' Stirling said.

As Lara followed the detective out to the street, she felt her heart soar with relief. That was instantly undercut by the knowledge that Vic's killer was still somewhere out there. But she'd never thought Ed was guilty and she hoped now that the detective would question Jimmy Diamond more thoroughly.

It took a while for Lizzie to come to the door and Lara daren't knock too loud because she didn't want to wake the children. As Stirling shivered beside her in his overcoat, she sensed his urgency.

'She's coming now, I can hear footsteps on the stairs.'

In moments, Lizzie had the door open, and was standing there in a white nightgown with a plaid blanket wrapped around her shoulders. 'What is it?' she called raggedly. 'Is it Ed? Has something happened to him?'

'It's good news, Lizzie. Can we come in?' Lara asked. She'd seen the fear on Lizzie's face when she'd clocked Inspector Stirling. 'Come on, let's go inside,' Lara said gently but firmly, and at last, Lizzie turned and they followed her into the warm kitchen. Lara turned to Inspector Stirling. 'Tell her straight, just tell her.'

'What? Tell me what?' Lizzie almost sobbed and Lara stepped to put an arm around her.

The inspector sucked a sharp breath then he spoke quickly with no preamble. 'Ed's been cleared of all charges. He'll be back home with you and the children in the next few days.'

Lara felt Lizzie almost buckle at the knees. 'What? Are you sure?'

'We're certain. There are two credible witnesses who saw him in Ridgetown that night at a time when it would have been impossible for him to make it back to the mill pond before the water iced over.'

Lizzie slumped further and Lara needed to guide her to a chair. She was crying now. Big, deep, gut-wrenching sobs. 'I don't believe it,' she croaked.

'It's true, Lizzie,' Lara said, needing to hold back her own tears.

The inspector appeared increasingly uncomfortable, his eyes flitting around the tiny kitchen. 'I'm so sorry for all the trouble this has caused, Mrs Cronshaw. But we did have some other witnesses from Ridgetown who'd reported Ed had been in a heightened state and he was on the hunt for Vic that night. Probably to give him a good hiding after that fight they'd had in the street.'

Lizzie cut in then. 'I think you need to stop making excuses, Inspector. Have you any idea how hard this has been for us with Ed locked up? No money coming in and two young children to look after?'

Stirling bowed his head, murmured an apology.

'It's not enough just to say sorry. You need to be much more careful in future.'

He nodded. 'I will. I'll take all you've said into account.' As he opened his mouth to speak again, a piercing wail came from upstairs and he sucked a sharp breath.

In moments, Sue was pottering down the stairs and she was

sobbing. 'Where are you, Mummy? I thought you were gone as well.'

'I'm here, my baby. I'm not going anywhere,' Lizzie croaked as she got up to put an arm around her daughter. 'These people have come to tell us that your daddy will be home soon.'

'Daddy?' the little girl said, her eyes opening wide.

'Yes, he's coming home.'

Then as Lizzie picked Sue up and held her tightly, they were both crying.

There was a tap at the door and Betty walked in, scowling immediately when she saw the inspector. 'Lizzie, is everything OK?'

'Yes, everything's fine. They've cleared Ed and he'll be home soon.'

Betty clutched at her chest; she couldn't speak for a moment. 'Are you sure?' she asked, turning to the inspector.

Stirling looked her straight in the eye. 'Your son has been cleared of all charges, Mrs Cronshaw. All we can do is apologise for his wrongful arrest. But at the time, we did have enough evidence to charge him.'

'That's what they always say,' a deep voice called from the door and Josh stepped in, bowing his head as he came through the low doorway.

'Ah, Mr MacDonald. Yet again, I can only apologise to you too.'

'Well, that's all right, given you're letting Ed go. But that leaves a guilty man out there wild and free.'

Stirling nodded. 'Yes, we're fully aware of that. And of course, we'll continue our enquiries.'

Josh heaved a sigh. 'Well, let's hope the next time you arrest some fella, it'll be third time lucky.'

'Yes, that is our intention,' Stirling said, and in that moment,

Lara saw the man's humility. She knew he would pursue this case even more rigorously and he wouldn't give up until it was solved.

Just as they made to leave, Josh grabbed Stirling's arm. 'Remember, Inspector. Some of us who've done prison time go on to lead good, honest lives. So don't go locking us up for no reason.'

Stirling nodded, apologised again, then he followed Lara out of the cottage and back across the street. He only slipped on ice once and Lara was able to grab hold and steady him.

'I don't know how you're going to get back to Ridgetown tonight, Inspector,' she was saying as they staggered in through the surgery door.

'Oh, don't worry about that,' Marion called up the corridor. 'Mrs Hewitt is insisting the inspector stay overnight. She's already made up a bed in the sitting room.'

He opened his mouth, probably to politely decline. But with his car left way back on the road to Ridgetown, he seemed to realise he had no choice. 'Well, all I can say is thank you for your hospitality.'

'We don't want to see you in a ditch, Inspector,' Marion offered with a grin. 'So, come on, let's get you into the kitchen. The Aga's stoked up and we've already poured a glass of single malt whisky, thinking that might be just the right thing to warm the cockles of your heart.'

The inspector sighed out a breath. 'Ah well, that's very welcome and it's perfect for a night like this.' Smiling as he removed his hat, he then shrugged out of his thick coat and seemed to relax.

Lara noted Marion's wicked smile and she remembered how taken her colleague had been by Stirling when he'd called to the surgery in the autumn to ask questions about the fires at the mill. She stood for a moment slowly shaking her head as her colleague grinned, then mouthed to her, 'He's so good-looking.'

'Don't get carried away,' Lara hissed in her ear. But it was too late; Marion was smiling deliciously, and Lara could already see that dreamy look in her eyes.

22

Lara needed to hide her amusement the next morning as she sat alone at the breakfast table and Stirling wandered through dishevelled in his shirtsleeves and braces. Bleary-eyed, stubbly-chinned, his dark hair sticking out at angles, he walked to Marion's place at the other side of the table and gently lowered himself onto the chair. 'A bit too much of the single malt last night,' he called raggedly. 'But a brisk walk back to my abandoned car should wake me up.'

Lara wasn't too sure on that score; he was heavy-eyed and had now slumped forward to cradle his head in his hands. She'd left the table for her bed at a reasonable hour but even from upstairs, she'd caught bursts of lively chatter between Bingham, Angus, Marion and the inspector.

Stirling groaned and slumped further forward.

'Here's two aspirin for you, Inspector Stirling,' Mrs Hewitt called brightly as she emerged from the pantry with bacon, eggs and sausage. She placed the tablets and a drink of water down beside him, and asked, 'Full English breakfast?' which made him laugh, then moan, then cradle his head again. Mrs Hewitt placed a reassuring hand on his shoulder. 'I've seen far worse than you at this table, so I know you'll get through this, Inspector. And I'm thinking some buttered toast and plenty of coffee might do the trick.'

'Aye, that would definitely fit the bill. Thank you very much, Mrs Hewitt.'

It felt odd to see the detective in Marion's seat opposite, but it helped Lara to balance up her shifting opinions of him. He'd frustrated her during the enquiry into Vic's death but that had probably all been down to it being a police investigation with guarded confidentiality. At least now Ed had been cleared, she could detach herself a little from the case. But even as she thought it, a flash of Vic lying in the mill pond came at her strongly enough to make her breath catch.

She was shaking her head, and she might have been muttering under her breath because she heard Stirling ask, 'What was that, Nurse Flynn?' Then he was rubbing his forehead with the heel of his hand.

'There you go, Inspector. Nice, strong cup of coffee,' Mrs Hewitt called, 'and given it's still iced up and bitterly cold out there, I'm thinking a small helping of warm porridge with a scattering of sugar might be another option.'

'No, not the porridge. I'm good with toast and coffee... maybe even just the coffee.'

Lara felt a tickle of laughter in the pit of her stomach, but she couldn't, she just couldn't give in to it because the man was in such pain.

Mrs Hewitt saved her from losing control by producing her list of visits. 'It's terrible out there and with everything frozen up, there's bound to be black ice. So you need to be very careful because until they get more grit on the roads, it'll be like a death trap.'

Lara startled at the housekeeper's extremely descriptive language.

Sensing her disquiet, Stirling glanced up and said gently, 'You'll be fine, just take your time.'

Mrs Hewitt was back again from the Aga and leaning on the table. 'As you can see from your list, Nurse Flynn, we're cutting right back to visits within walking distance or those who can get themselves to the surgery. So, on your list, you've got the usual checks on Mr Makepeace and a visit to Robin Taylor. Then the Valentines aren't too far out of the village so you should be able to make it on foot to young Izzy. Her mother called yesterday to report now this harsh weather's arrived, the little lass has that nasty cough again, the one hanging over from diphtheria.'

'Oh, that's a shame, I thought we had it all cleared up. But right, yes. I can get out there to check on her,' Lara called as Mrs Hewitt retreated to the Aga.

Inspector Stirling spoke up. 'You should be proud of what you do here in this community, Nurse Flynn. It's not the same for us police; we're always pulled in different directions and chasing our tails. And let's face it, the police are never the most popular public service. But your work is like a safety net. It's everything for the people of this community.'

Lara felt a little stunned by his eloquence. 'Well we do what we can,' she replied.

He offered a slow smile. 'You medical folk always dodge away from praise. We police hardly get any. So, please, take on board what I've just said because it's well deserved. And what's more, we police and you medics, we often work closely together.'

'I'd never really thought about it like that but yes, it would seem so,' she said, as she rose from the table. 'What with the arson attack at the mill in the autumn, closely followed by the

Lennox children going missing, then Vic's body in the mill pond. Thinking about it now, this isn't the peaceful, rural idyll I'd been expecting.'

'It certainly is not,' Stirling replied with a twist of his mouth. 'I'm thinking I might apply to go back to Edinburgh for a quieter life.'

Lara began to chuckle.

Then Marion's voice called from behind, 'No, you can't possibly do that, Adam. You've only just got started here.'

He was shaking his head and smiling, then groaning and clutching his head again. And as Marion bustled in and swept around the table to grab the slice of jammy toast Mrs Hewitt had already prepared, Lara shot her a wide-eyed glance and mouthed, 'Adam?'

Marion was grinning and nodding behind the inspector, and it was a good job Stirling couldn't see her because she was all gooey-eyed.

'Nurse Wright,' Mrs Hewitt called abruptly. 'Here's your list of visits. Now, off you pop to your duties.'

Marion giggled, then flashed a smile to Lara.

'That Nurse Wright, she's here, there, everywhere. She's like a whirlwind,' Mrs Hewitt said loudly. Clearly trying to cover for Marion's boldness.

'Aye, she's a good lass,' Stirling chirruped, a mild flush to his cheeks which may or may not have been from his hot cup of coffee.

Mrs Hewitt exchanged a wide-eyed glance with Lara as she got up from the table and called to Stirling, 'I'll no doubt be seeing you around, Inspector.'

'No doubt at all, Nurse Flynn.' Then he chuckled softly. 'At this rate, I might still be here nursing my hangover when you get back from your visits.'

Lara laughed.

Then Mrs Hewitt called from the Aga, 'Don't you worry, Inspector Stirling, I've fettled far worse hangovers in this kitchen. We'll have you up and running in no time.'

'I hope so, I truly do,' he groaned as Lara picked up her medical bag and slipped out of the kitchen.

She donned her scarf, gloves and her brimmed nurse's hat and was ready to face the icy roads. Stepping gingerly out of the front door, she noted that the street had been gritted and even as she stood collecting herself, Herbert Threlfall's black horse and milk cart plodded slowly by.

'You're doing well to get out and about today, Mr Threlfall,' she called after him. 'Our bicycles and motor vehicles aren't an option in this.'

'Well, I can only get as far as the grit takes me, Nurse Flynn. I daren't risk my horse's legs on this ice,' Herbert called over his shoulder as his horse walked steadily on with a jingle of harness.

Lara felt heartened by the man's spirit and set off down the hill to Daniel Makepeace's cottage with a spring in her step. She soon steadied up though and needed to take shorter strides when she slipped on an ungritted patch of cobbles and almost slipped flat on her back. It didn't daunt her; in fact, it made her feel more alive.

Her visits in the village all went to plan but she needed to spend extra time at the Taylors', especially with Robin. He would have been back to school after the diphtheria if Vic's death hadn't delayed things. But today, Lara saw the first signs of him coming back to life. For once, he was up out of bed and sitting at the kitchen table, with the beginnings of a twinkle in his eye.

'You're doing well, Robin,' she told him after she'd checked his temperature, pulse and respirations.

'He is, isn't he?' Uncle Josh called from the sink where he was washing the pots. Then he said to Robin, 'We'll have you back to school with your new friends soon. Won't we, matey?'

'Yep, I hope so. I'm missing the lessons.'

Josh groaned theatrically. 'Oh, it hurts my head when you say that. How can anyone enjoy sums as much as you do?'

'I don't know, I just do. In fact, I've been working on my maths while I've been in bed.' He lowered his voice then. 'Don't tell Mum but I've done some working out in pencil on the wall behind my pillow.'

'Don't you think I haven't seen that, you scallywag.' Alice grinned as she bustled into the kitchen with a large wicker basket full of the freshly baked bread she sold to the villagers. She went over to Robin, put an arm around his shoulders and gave him a snuggle. 'You can do your calculating over every single wall if you like; I'll soon have them whitewashed. It's just so good to see you more like your old self.'

'Yes, it certainly is,' Josh said, grinning as he turned from the sink and dabbed at his eyes with a tea towel. He cleared his throat then. 'Right, so, Alice... Do you want me to deliver the bread for you?'

'Yes, that would be very helpful because I could knead another batch and get it in to rise.'

'It's good to see you all busy. I'll leave you to it,' Lara called. Then with a steady hand on Robin's shoulder and a few gentle words, she picked up her medical bag and went back out to the icy street.

There were only one or two women out and about in the village and they raised a hand and shouted a good morning with steaming breath as Lara returned their greetings. She glanced up the hill over the route she'd need to take to the Valentines' farm and her heart skipped a beat when she saw the frail, elderly retired schoolmistress, Miss Frobisher, beginning to make her way down from the top. As the thin, white-haired woman began to tap down the hill with her walking stick, Lara felt a sharp stab of concern. A slip and a fall at the woman's age might prove fatal.

'Miss Frobisher,' she called urgently up the street, increasing her pace. 'I can go down to the shop for you if you tell me what you need.'

'Oh no, dear,' the elderly woman grinned mischievously. 'You'd spoil my fun.'

'But it's a bit risky and some parts are very slippery even with the grit.'

'Please, Nurse Flynn, do not fret. I've negotiated this street in all weathers since I was a young teacher at the village school. I am perfectly aware of the risk. In fact, I enjoy it. When you get to a certain age, there are few things that get the heart racing.'

Even as they stood talking, Miss Frobisher began to weave her way around Lara, and it was obvious she wasn't going to stop. So with a final, 'Please be careful,' Lara had no choice but to let her go.

She couldn't watch; it would make her too anxious. But as she reached the top of the street where she'd need to turn left for the Valentines' farm, she glanced back to see Miss Frobisher competently negotiating the final few steps, then opening the post-office door. In the next second, Lara's foot slipped and she almost went sprawling. It gave her a jolt and made her laugh when she clicked that she might be more at risk than the elderly schoolmistress. Knowing she should have been more vigilant in this shaded spot close to where Angus and Leo had slipped on the ice last night, she made sure to follow the line of grit that had been spread at the side of the road.

Izzy Valentine was white as a sheet and coughing violently when Lara arrived and it made her anxious till she'd been able to check her observations. But she was happy to report that there was no fever, no racing pulse and when she listened in with her stethoscope, Izzy's chest sounded clear.

Sally sighed with relief. 'That's good news, Nurse Flynn. Sorry to bring you out here on such a bad day, but me and Harry hardly slept last night, she was coughing so much. And you know what our Peter's like; he's always fretting about his little sister.'

'I told you I was all right,' Izzy croaked, then she began to cough again. A dry, hacking bark that left her breathless. Once she'd recovered, she said, 'I sound like my dog, Fly.'

'You do.' Lara smiled. 'Oh, and where is Fly? I didn't see him in the yard and I kind of miss his menacing growl.'

'He's in the barn,' Izzy replied. 'Dada says it's too cold for him in the kennel right now.'

'I agree; everything's frozen out there, even the cow muck.'

Izzy piped up then with her husky voice, 'I like it when the muck's frozen, because it doesn't stick to my welly boots.'

'Yes, good thinking,' Lara replied, then she turned to Sally. 'Right, her chest is clear so that's good. But call again any time if you're worried.'

'Many thanks, Nurse Flynn.' Sally smiled as Lara made to move. 'It feels like you're our guardian angel.'

'Well, it would be good if I was. Because I'd have wings and I could fly to my visits and avoid the ice.'

Izzy began to giggle, then she was hacking with a cough again.

'I'll see myself out,' Lara said gently with a quick glance and a smile to Izzy. 'But please ring if you have any further concerns.'

'Will do, Nurse Flynn,' Sally called over her shoulder.

As Lara picked her way carefully back across the slippery yard, she heard a menacing growl from inside the barn and knew it was Fly making his presence known. Then he emitted a thin whine, and it felt as if he was expressing his concern for Izzy.

The air felt even colder as she made her way back to the village, but she'd begun to have a better eye for the black ice now. Maybe if she wintered here again next year, she'd be very adept in freezing conditions. Just as she thought it, both feet skidded violently, and she was forced to revise her expectations.

'Good to see you out and about,' Leo called as she nudged carefully around the corner of the Fleece.

'I'm still a beginner out here in the wilds but I think I'm getting used to it.' Then, realising Leo didn't have the little dog, she asked, 'Where's Lucky? Is he OK?'

'Yes, sorry. He's fine. I didn't want him freezing his paws off in this and I don't trust myself to carry him, not after mine and Angus's performance on the ice last night.'

'Yes, you were both a bit all over the place.'

He laughed, nodded, but she could still see the tension in him.

'Are you sure you're all right?' she asked, taking a careful step towards him.

'Yes, I mean, no. Not really.'

'What is it? Can you tell me?'

He heaved a weary sigh, began to shake his head, then glanced to her with a mournful expression. 'Blow it. I might as well get it off my chest... It's just that... Well... I think I might be going out of mind because I can't stop thinking about you, Lara.'

She hadn't been expecting that one bit, so it felt it like a punch and instinctively, she took a step back. 'I'm sorry, Leo... I mean, I like you and I think we get on. But there are so many things to consider.'

He was nodding. 'Look, if it's about Philippa... we're just friends, she'd like it to be more but—'

She was shaking her head. 'No, Leo... it's not that. And I can't talk about this now out here on the street.' What Leo didn't realise was that for a professional woman, getting into a relationship wasn't straightforward. She'd always known that what she'd had with Patrick wasn't going to last so it hadn't been an issue. This already felt very different... and here in this village with everybody knowing everybody's business, it needed to be handled carefully.

Leo grimaced as if he were in physical pain and he was about to speak again when a loud voice shouted from the surgery. It was Angus, bursting out through the door and skidding on ice. It felt as if he'd been summoned to her rescue.

'Hello there, you two!' he called, and Lara felt relief flood through her as Angus strode, then slipped, then strode again in their direction.

'How are you doing?' Angus asked with a grin as he punched Leo on the arm. 'What's up, Sullivan? You look like you've seen a ghost.'

Lara offered a smile and raised her hand. 'I need to get back to the surgery, so I'll leave you to it.'

'Righto,' Angus called, jovial as always. But she could feel Leo yearning after her even as she left him in the street.

As she approached the door, she met Sam Collins, the butcher, stepping gingerly out of the surgery with his head bandaged. He called, 'You need to be careful, Nurse Flynn.'

For a split second, she was thrown out because she thought he was referring to her and Leo.

Then he added, 'I'd only taken two steps out of my shop door when my feet shot from under me and I went straight down and cracked my head open.' He pointed to his bandage for emphasis.

'Sorry to hear that, Sam. Hope you didn't knock yourself out.'

'Nah, just split the skin. Doc Bingham's done a good job of stitching me up, so I'll be right as rain in no time. You need to watch your step though in this ice. I consult my barometer every day and it's telling me things are going to get worse. There'll most likely be heavy snow tomorrow or the day after.'

'I'll be careful.' She smiled as he raised a hand and stepped cautiously down the hill to his shop, leaving Lara at the surgery door with the sound of Leo and Angus's conversation behind her. They were laughing together now, and it helped to dispel her own tangled feelings. She liked Leo, she really liked him... but it was straightforward for him because nothing would change if he got engaged or married. Whereas she'd have to make a choice between her career and marriage. Even now in the twentieth century, nurses still had to give up their registration if they decided to marry. And she certainly wasn't prepared to do that yet for any man, no matter how good-looking. So right now, it felt as if Leo was out of bounds... unless they had an understanding of what they could and could not be. It all felt way too complicated, and in the long run, the best option might be to stay as friends. Then she remembered those tender kisses and felt a jolt of pleasure.

'Oh for goodness' sake,' she said out loud as she walked down the green-tiled corridor.

'Is something up?' Mrs Hewitt called as she poked her head out of the kitchen.

'No, it's fine. I'm just a bit cold and things are too slippery outside.'

'Well, it's a good job I've just baked some scones, and we've got plenty of strawberry jam... A real taste of the summer, that's what we need on cold, winter days like these.'

'Sounds like heaven,' Lara replied as she slipped off her leather boots, thick coat and nurse's hat. Then she hung them on the brass hooks in the corridor as if she were leaving her thoughts about Leo with them.

'Good news,' Mrs Hewitt called as Lara walked into the kitchen. 'There'll be wagons coming out to spread grit on the roads, so we should be able to restore our visits to the farms in due course. That's if we don't get snowed up in the meantime.'

'Oh that's good, or maybe not, depending on the weather,' Lara replied as she slipped into her seat at the table.

'Well, at least we still have the phone lines open. Dr Bingham's been ringing around to patients who might struggle to get to the surgery due to the icy roads and asking them to check on their neighbours who don't have telephones. There's been nothing particularly worrying so far, so fingers crossed it'll stay that way.'

'Let's hope so,' Lara replied as she took her seat at the table and reached for her cup of tea. 'But if a true emergency does come in, goodness knows how that'll pan out.'

'It'll be touch and go, that's for sure. Especially if it snows. So let's hope for the best, Nurse Flynn. That's all we can do.'

Mrs Hewitt walked to the table with the scones and placed them down in front of Lara. And as she took her first bite, it brought back the warmth of summer, the green-leafed trees and wildflowers out on the lanes and her first days at the surgery when she'd tasted these scones for the very first time.

'I'll be glad when it's spring,' Lara murmured.

'Me too, Nurse Flynn. I can't wait to feel the sun warming my bones,' Mrs Hewitt replied as she settled in her place at the table.

23

Even by the afternoon, there was a gathering of dense, grey-white cloud in the sky and Lara shivered as the deep cold met her when she stepped out to the street.

'There's snow coming; I can smell it,' Marion called from behind.

'I'll be guided by you,' Lara replied, twisting to see her colleague dressed for the weather with the collar of a bright-blue, woolly jumper poking from her thick coat and a long, multi-coloured scarf wrapped around her neck. 'You look cosy,' she said with a grin.

'My mother knitted me this scarf last winter. She said if she can't be with me when I'm going out in all weathers, at least she can offer motherly love in knitted form.'

'I like the sound of that,' Lara said, but it made her feel like a sparsely clad orphan in her own coat, with just a thin scarf and woolly gloves. At least she had her district nurse's hat, pulled down low. She'd not needed anything other than what she now wore when she'd worked in Liverpool and there'd been some very bad winters there.

The two nurses stood together at the door for a few moments, ready to make a start on their much-reduced lists of visits. Lara was to check on Daniel Makepeace and Marion to follow up on the Ryans' baby, Cara's recovery from a nasty chest infection.

Even as they stood there, a few big flakes of snow began to drift down and one landed on Lara's nose.

'Ooh, that's a good omen, a snowflake to the nose.' Marion giggled.

'Is it?'

'According to my mother... but she has all kinds of sayings and beliefs. Most of them she's made up herself.'

'Well, I'll take it as a positive,' Lara called over her shoulder as she stepped out carefully onto the icy street.

This was a follow-up visit to Daniel because his niece, Esther, had been there this morning and she'd pulled Lara aside, tears shining in her eyes. 'He's sleeping much more now and sometimes, his breath's barely above a whisper.'

Lara had known for a while her elderly patient was losing ground. He'd always been very poorly with heart failure, so the changes were a worsening of what was already there. But with her trained eye, she'd noted the increased cyanosis that made his lips a darker blue and he was profoundly fatigued and sleeping even more. So she'd promised Esther she'd bob down and check on him again.

'I'm off this way,' Marion called, turning to head towards the sawmill.

'See you soon,' Lara called, as Marion trudged away.

She began to pick her way carefully down the icy street, and caught sight of a tall, ragged figure, hunched over as he walked round the corner by the Fleece. His head was down, his breath steaming and he had a piece of sacking pulled tightly around his shoulders against the cold. Lara saw him stagger and she went straight to him, slipping a little on ice as she walked.

'Can I help you?' she asked, her voice breathy.

The hunched figure let out a low chuckle. 'Nah, that's all right, Nurse Flynn, I'm right as rain.'

'Ed?' Lara cried, recognising his voice. 'Ed! Is that you?'

He straightened up, offering a ragged smile. But his bare hands were tinged with blue and his face ruddy with cold. He tried to speak again but his voice broke, and he gasped as if he'd taken a punch to the gut. Then he croaked, 'Yes. It's me. They've let me out.'

She gulped a breath. 'It's so good to see you, Ed.'

He grabbed her, pulled her into a hug and she could feel the deep sobs he was trying to hold back. Then he swallowed hard. 'I thought they'd never get that I didn't kill Vic, and they'd keep me inside for good.'

'I always knew you were innocent,' she said firmly.

He offered a deep, bitter laugh. 'Well, not everyone was of that mind, or I wouldn't be standing here now in the freezing cold with a sack round my shoulders... Your mind starts to play tricks when you're locked up like that. In the end, I was starting to think I *had* killed Vic... and maybe I'd just blotted it out.'

'I can't even imagine,' Lara breathed. 'But the only thing that matters right now is that you are home and you've been cleared of all charges.'

He was nodding. Then he began to shiver so violently, his teeth were chattering.

Lara was all action. 'You need to get moving, Ed. I'll see you to your door.'

He gulped back a sob. 'What's my missus and my children going to think, seeing me like this?'

'They'll just be delighted to have you back.'

He swallowed hard, offered a bitter laugh as his body shuddered.

'I'll walk you down to your cottage,' she repeated gently.

He was already setting off, but she could see the sheer exhaustion in his slumped shoulders and the way his feet almost dragged. Even before he reached his cottage door, he began to sob: a deep, heart-wrenching sound. 'I can't do it, Nurse Flynn. I can't go in there looking like this.'

'It will be fine, trust me. Your family will be delighted to see you. I'll come with you, wait at the door till you're safely inside.'

He was nodding his head, blowing out a steaming breath as one or two voices were shouting now from down the street, 'Good to see you back, Ed!'

Lara knocked at his door, then stood aside.

It took a little while for Lizzie to open up, but Lara knew she'd heard the knock because her voice was getting louder as she soothed baby William.

As soon as the door opened, Lizzie stood rigid, speechless, with the baby squirming and babbling in her arms. Ed doubled over as if he'd taken a punch to the gut. Lizzie reached out to him then, calling raggedly as she swiped away tears, 'Come on, Ed. Don't be standing there all day. Let's get you inside.'

As he stepped into the cottage, he was saying, 'I'm here. I'm back.'

Lara watched with a glow of satisfaction as he hugged Lizzie, then pulled his baby son from her arms and held him as if he never wanted to let him go.

Little Sue came to him, clinging to his leg, 'Daddy, Daddy. Where have you been? I cried when you were away.'

As Ed reached down to stroke her hair, he said gently, 'I'm back now, my baby. I'm back.'

Lara stood by to make sure all was well, then she turned to walk on to her visits. But even as the cottage door began to close, a rousing cheer came from the women on the street. And as she passed by the post office, Miss Shaw flung open the door. 'Is it right? Is Ed Cronshaw back?'

'Yes.' Lara grinned, and the postmistress smiled and clapped her hands.

The joy of Ed's homecoming seemed to infuse the whole village, and even as she tapped on Daniel's cottage door, she heard more excited chatter from behind. Walking in to find Daniel blinking awake and looking perkier than he'd done for a while, it felt as if he'd already been told the news. His pulse was still weak though and his breathing barely above a whisper, but he offered a smile when Lara told him the story of Ed's return.

'I always knew that lad was innocent. And I've always liked him... He had a tough time growing up, but he's a good, kind soul.'

Daniel was soon closing his eyes and drifting back to sleep and after another quick check of his thready pulse, Lara left him secure in the knowledge that he was holding his own. She still felt heightened by Ed's return and as she stepped out to the street, the snow began to fall more heavily, with a brisk wind whipping it up, making the snowflakes swirl around her in a delightful pattern. It made her feel even more exultant, and she couldn't wait to get to the surgery to tell Mrs Hewitt the story of Ed's return.

As she slowly made her way back up, the street was rapidly emptying as snow gathered against the cottage walls. There were still some women out and about, though – dashing to the post office and queueing inside Sam Collins's butcher's shop, probably stocking up in case the cold snap worsened.

Lara pushed on, but as she walked in through the front door, an unusual silence met her. She could hear the rumble of Bingham's voice in his consultation room, so she knew he was seeing a patient. But even before she reached the kitchen, she knew Mrs Hewitt wasn't there.

The room was neat and tidy as always, but the only sign of life was Tiddles the cat stretched in front of the Aga. He raised his head and held her gaze for a few seconds before stretching his paws, then promptly falling back to sleep. All seemed as usual, apart from the absence of Mrs Hewitt. Lara had never known this to happen and it unsettled her. So much so, when the phone jangled in the hallway, she felt the shock of it go right through her.

She was straight there to pick up the receiver. 'Hello, Ingleside Surgery, Nurse Flynn speaking,' she said briskly.

'Oh, Nurse Flynn. I'm so glad it's you. This is Moira, Tom Douglas's wife, and I'm so worried about our little Poppy. As you know, she's got a heart murmur, and she's only just properly recovering from being in hospital with the diphtheria. Well, this morning, she looked a bit peaky, and it worried me. But she's even worse now and she's lying on the settee, and I can barely rouse her and—'

The phone cut out then. Lara pressed the two buttons on top repeatedly, but no dialling tone came. 'Damn,' she swore out loud. She replaced the receiver then picked it up again. Still nothing. She felt very concerned for Poppy and it felt as if there was only one option: she'd have to go out on foot to the Douglases' farm. She calculated the distance; it wasn't all that far out of the village. So, quickly, she scribbled a note and left it by the telephone:

Moira Douglas telephoned re Poppy. The child sounds poorly but call cut off as we were speaking. I'm setting off on foot to assess, might be a while.

She hadn't even removed her coat, so she quickly pulled the relevant equipment out of her medical bag and pushed it into a rucksack. Then she was back out to the street with snow swirling thickly around her as she scrunched her way back down the hill. She could see lights still on in the butcher's and the post office but only a very few folk were still out on the street. She dismissed any concerns she might have about the weather because all she could think of was getting to Poppy as fast as she could. And as she trudged through the snow, images of the little girl who'd almost lost her life to diphtheria flashed through her head. Poppy was very vulnerable and might need hospitalisation, but it panicked her when she realised the lanes would be impassable. So it felt even more important to get out there to assess, especially given Poppy had a heart murmur.

As she crossed the bridge and began to walk along the lane, the gusting wind threw thick flurries of snow right at her, making her eyes sting. She'd seen snow in Liverpool but out here in the open, the way it swirled so fiercely and was already sculpting into drifts felt like a whole different thing. She could barely see and had to use the dry stone walls and bare hedges as a guide to keep her on the narrow lane. Way before she'd reached the turning that led up to the Douglases', she was shivering violently and up to the knees in drifting snow. She trudged on, her legs and hands numb with cold, the flurries so thick, she could barely see ahead.

'Just keep going,' she said out loud. But the snow was rapidly deepening, and it was becoming so much harder to walk. She gritted her teeth, kept moving even when her face began to feel like a frozen mask and her hands in their knitted gloves were completely numb. The further she walked, the harder the snow gusted in her eyes, making her slip and stumble. She fell to her knees once, twice, but she growled under her breath, picked herself up. All the while fixing in her head an image of Poppy lying poorly in bed.

The wind was stronger now and laced with stinging snowflakes that fired straight in her face. And worryingly, the light was beginning to fade. She felt increasingly disorientated in this changed landscape and had little idea of how much further she needed to walk. She paused for a few moments, trying to identify any landmarks, but she was completely lost in a blizzard. All she had were glimpses of bare hedge or what now felt like the trusty drystone walls that bordered the lane. She had no choice but to keep going, using the walls as a guide.

The further she walked, the colder she became, and she was needing to use more of her fading energy to cover a short distance. *Don't give up, you can't give up,* ran through her head but she couldn't feel her feet now inside her thick, leather boots. Still, she pushed on. Then with a heavy lurch to the side that took the breath from her body, she felt her ankle twist, and she sank up to her waist in snow. She cried out in pain, clawed at an icy drystone wall, trying to pull herself up. But each time, she slipped and fell back further. She kept struggling until she'd crawled into shallower snow, but she had nothing left to give and she didn't even have the breath to cry for help.

Then as pure cold seeped further into her bones, she knew she'd have to use every bit of her strength just to stay conscious. She fought to keep her eyes open for as long as she could, urging her brain to be aware of why she was here on a lonely country lane, why she needed to get to the Douglases' farm to assess Poppy. An image of the little girl with her blue eyes and fluffy, brown hair flashed through her brain... She was still struggling to regain the ground she'd lost after the diphtheria. *It's her heart, she got a heart murmur,* floated through the remains of Lara's consciousness and hot tears came from the frustration of not being able to get to her patient. She felt sorry for herself then, out here all alone in the middle of a snowstorm. This was no picture-postcard scene with fluffy flakes slowly drifting down. It was harsh and potentially life-threatening. She felt a shudder deep inside the core of her body. Then it stopped, as if that was it, there was no more that could be done. She tried to smile at her predicament, but her face was set numb, like a mask.

Ah well, she thought. *At least I've tried my best to get to my patient.*

A bit too much, you eejit, Marion's voice whispered in her ear, and she felt comforted by the almost presence of her colleague. She fought for a little longer with the whispers of her consciousness. It even made her smile to recognise that right here, she wasn't far from Tom Douglas's shippon where she'd helped deliver a calf on her first day at the surgery. In the next moment, she lost the thread of that thought and she tried to draw a breath, but it felt stuck. Tears stung her eyes when it dawned on her that she might be dying and might never sit around the table in the warm kitchen again. Wistfully, at the tail end of her consciousness came the awareness that she'd never find out what could happen between her and Leo and if she could have cried, she would have done so at the thought of little Lucky pining for her.

She couldn't even feel the snow as it swirled over her, but she had a sense of the weight of it. It almost felt comforting, like being tucked up with a thick eiderdown by her Aunt Matilda when she'd been poorly in bed. No, that wasn't going to help her get out of this. She needed to act and not snuggle down. But she couldn't move her limbs and right then, she felt like wailing and crying. She was stuck. And even as she sucked in another tight breath, she could feel her heart slowing to a dull, sludgy thud. It filtered through to her slowed-up brain that she had no strength left to fight. And as her chest became heavier and her breathing slowed even more, the world went completely black.

24

Lara had no sense of time as her muddled senses tried to feed back to her. She was sure she could hear voices, but they faded in and out. Her body still felt numb and when she tried to open her eyes, she couldn't. Then, a flash of searing, white light came at her, and she was sure she was in heaven because she couldn't feel her body, and she felt as if she were floating on air. She had no choice but to go with it because right now, she knew she couldn't do anything to break free from this limbo state. And strangely, she didn't feel afraid because she was prepared to meet whatever came next.

'Lara,' a gentle voice called. A kind voice. A man's voice.

She tried to answer, but her mouth wouldn't work.

More floating, and her fingers were tingling now as if they were coming back to life. She sighed heavily.

That voice came again; she was sure she recognised it now and it was asking her if she was all right.

In her head she answered, *I'm fine, just fine.*

But then, more light came, and it felt as if a transition were happening. *This must be what comes next*, she thought matter-of-factly. She could feel her tongue resting in her mouth, her lips pressed lightly together. She moved the tip of her tongue, drew in warm air and tried to force her eyes open so she could see what might be celestial light.

'Am I in heaven?' she whispered hoarsely.

She couldn't properly hear the response, but she felt the warmth of it and thought she could hear gentle laughter. Whatever place this was felt safe and she knew she'd be all right.

Then a man's well-rounded voice replied, 'Well, if heaven is a bed in Ingleside Surgery's clinic room, you're right there.'

She felt her eyes blink, but she still couldn't see properly. She tried to lift her head, but her body wasn't working.

'Who is it? Who are you?' she whispered.

'I'm Angus,' said a ragged voice, breaking with emotion.

As she blinked open her eyes, she saw him, clearer than she'd ever seen any human face before. Angus was smiling, his blond hair sticking out at all angles. Then tears were streaming down his face. He twisted away from her for a second to call brokenly over his shoulder, 'She's awake.'

'What?' another male voice called. Then she felt firm fingers at her wrist palpating her pulse. 'Nurse Flynn. Lara. How are you feeling?' It was Dr Bingham, and he sounded het up.

She tried to prop herself on one elbow to reassure him, but fell back.

'Lie still, my dear,' Bingham murmured soothingly. 'You're going to be fine. But right now, you need to rest up.'

'Is she awake?' a female voice called urgently, then Marion's face hovered over her and Lara reached up to touch her cheek.

'Marion. My friend Marion.' Marion began to sob, and Lara felt the tears dropping on her face as she asked, 'What happened to me?'

'You went out to see a patient in the snow, you numpty,' Marion hiccupped. 'I know you did it for the right reasons, but you weren't wearing the right clothes. So you must have slipped and fallen or something and you got too cold.'

'Oh, I thought I was in heaven.'

'You nearly were.' Marion laughed raggedly. Then she was upset again. 'Don't you dare do anything like that again, ever. I can't lose you, Lara. I won't function as a nurse or a person without you.'

'I'm so sorry you were worried,' she croaked gently. Trying to smile but it felt like too much effort, so she reached out to pat her friend's arm.

Marion heaved a slow breath. 'Oh, I'm just glad you're alive,' she murmured. 'And from now on, you're not going anywhere in adverse weather conditions without me by your side.'

'I'll try,' Lara breathed, as she pulled Marion closer. 'What happened to Poppy Douglas, the patient I went out to see?'

'She's fine. Mrs Hewitt saw the note, not immediately, but a little while after she got back from the butcher's – buying extra meat because she knew we were going to get snowed in.'

'Ah, right. So did someone visit Poppy?'

'No, we couldn't get there because of the snowdrifts. But the telephone started working again and we managed to ring. Poppy will need a visit at some stage but soon after that call you took, she began to vomit. It sounds like she was so pale and poorly-looking because she had a tummy upset. Not heart related, we think. When this weather clears, we can check her out properly.'

'Oh, that's a relief.' Lara groaned. 'I'm sorry I put you all through this and made you worried.'

'No, don't be sorry. You were only doing your best for your patient. And you're new here so you weren't aware of what drifting snow on the narrow lanes can be like. I don't think you'd get many roads blocking up so quickly in Liverpool.'

'No, not really. The city is completely different. That was quite something out there. I've never felt so cold and so alone in my whole life.'

'It can be very scary when you're out on the lanes or up near the fells and bad weather comes in. But the snow's easing up now and if you're well enough to go out through the door tomorrow, the village will look like a picture-postcard scene – all the roofs of the cottages covered in snow and rosy-cheeked children throwing snowballs and building snowmen.'

'I hope I can get out there to see it.'

'Mmm, you'll do as you're told, milady... And first things first, let's get some of this warm sugar water into you that Mrs H has prepared.' Marion dropped her voice. 'I have never seen Mrs H in such a state over anything as she's been about you getting lost in the snow. She couldn't function; she couldn't even make a cup of tea.'

'Oh, that's a shame. I feel bad for causing that.'

Marion swiped at her eyes, then said firmly, 'Don't feel bad; it's just a sign of how much we surgery folk care about each other, that's all.'

'Even me, do you care about me, Marion?' Angus's voice called from behind.

'Even you,' Marion quipped. 'And given you helped carry Lara on a blanket stretcher in blinding snow all the way back from a certain death by hypothermia, well, I suppose I could say you've gone up in my expectation to the level of "hero".'

'Oh, thank you very much,' Lara heard him reply.

'So, Angus helped to bring me back on a stretcher, but who else?'

'Oh, that was me and Josh MacDonald. Angus and I were tearing down the street as fast as we could in a heck of a panic after we found your note. Josh came running out of Alice's and you should have seen his face when we told him that you were missing. He was out in his boots and his woolly hat in a flash. Me and Angus could barely keep up with him.'

Lara needed to swallow hard to hold back tears at Marion's vivid account.

'Where is Josh? Is he OK?'

'Yes, he's fine. He went straight back home as soon as he knew Bingham was happy with your vital signs and he was confident you'd live.'

Lara swallowed hard. 'Was I that bad?'

Marion pressed her lips together and nodded solemnly.

Lara felt the impact of that news and lay quietly for a few moments to process it. When she spoke again, her voice was throaty. 'I'm sorry for causing so much stress. But I'm so glad to be back safe and sound.'

'You and me both,' Marion said with a wobbly grin. 'But right now, I need you to be a good patient and take some spoonfuls of this sugar water or Mrs H will have my guts for garters.'

Lara felt the sweetness on her tongue and did as she was told but exhaustion began to hit again, and she had to fight to keep her eyes open.

'Just relax, Lara,' she heard Marion's voice soothe. 'Dr Bingham said you'd need to sleep after the exertion your body's gone through.'

She caught the tail end of what Marion was saying just as she sank into a deep sleep.

Then blinking her eyes open a while later, she startled awake, sucking in air.

'Marion?' she called, surprised by the edge of panic in her voice.

'I'm here,' Marion replied instantly.

'And me too,' Mrs Hewitt's voice called. 'I can't tell you what a shock I got when I found that note of yours, Nurse Flynn. I only wish I'd seen it sooner, but I thought you were still out on your visits in the village.'

'It's all right, Mrs H, please don't trouble yourself. I was the one who made the decision to walk to the Douglases'… I'll know better next time; I won't get caught out again.'

Mrs Hewitt was nodding, then she cleared her throat. 'I wanted to go out with the search party, but Dr Bingham wouldn't hear of it. I was mad as blazes at first but when I saw Angus and Josh and Marion so exhausted when they got back with you, I knew of course it would have been too much for me.'

'You did the right thing, Mrs H,' Lara said firmly, propping herself up on one elbow. 'Just imagine if we'd both needed carrying back.'

'Yes indeed.' The housekeeper laughed, then hiccupped on a sob. Then she dropped her voice theatrically and whispered, 'But if there'd only been me in the surgery, I'd have damn well got on with it and hauled you back any way I could.'

Lara began to chuckle; she couldn't help it. 'You're a spirited woman, Mrs H. I hope I'm like you when I get to your age.'

Marion spoke then. 'Well, it would seem you're already like that, given you set off all alone through the snow like Scott of the Antarctic.'

'I did, didn't I? But it was not the right decision.'

Mrs Hewitt grasped Lara's hand and gave it a squeeze. 'Well, Nurse Flynn, as usual, I've got something in the oven – one of those rice puddings you love so much – so I'll get back to the kitchen. But it feels better than Christmas having you back home safe.'

'Thank you, Mrs H,' Lara called after her. Then she glanced to Marion. 'I think I'm ready to get up now; I'm feeling much better. What do you think? Shall I see if my legs will hold me?'

'Go on, let's have a go,' Marion said and grinned.

Lara was already swinging her legs out to sit at the side of the bed.

'Go easy. Take it slow. Do you feel steady enough?'

'Yes.' Lara nodded. 'I'm a bit dizzy but that might be down to lack of food.'

'Right, so when you're ready, let's see if you can stand up.'

Lara glanced down the length of her body and felt startled. 'I'm in my nightie. How did I get into my nightie?'

'Me, I did it.' Marion grinned. 'There was no choice; you'd been lying in the snow and you were soaked through, so I stripped everything off. I even changed your undies.'

'What?' Lara said, wide-eyed.

'Nah, course I didn't, just teasing. Your navy-blue bloomers were dry as a bone.'

Lara began to giggle, and she was shaking her head. 'You, Marion, are supposed to be looking after me and not tormenting me like that.'

'I know, sorry. What can I say? I grew up teasing and being teased by my brothers. So I blame those boys for what I've become.' Then Marion spoke with a gentler voice. 'So, are you OK? Do you think you can stand?'

'Yes,' Lara replied firmly.

'So, one, two, three, go.'

Lara pushed up from the bed and instantly felt woozy.

Right then, there was a tap on the door and a man's voice called, 'Can I come in?'

'Yes,' Lara said.

'No,' Marion called at the same time.

The door clicked open, and it was Leo with the little dog in his arms.

'Oh, it's you,' Lara said, mildly shocked and needing to sit back down. But most of all, she was delighted to see Lucky wagging his tail furiously and already struggling free from Leo's arms.

'All right, all right, you little rascal,' Leo called as he deposited the dog on the bed right next to her.

'There you go, little fella,' she called, already stroking him. Tears welling in her eyes as he wagged and wagged his tail.

Leo was standing back, looking on, and when he spoke, his voice sounded throaty. 'You gave us all quite a shock there, Lara. I'm so glad they found you.'

She swallowed hard to hold back tears. 'Yes, I don't remember much about it but it's so good to be home safe and sound.'

'Probably best if you don't remember it,' he said, offering a wobbly smile. 'You're back now and that's all that matters.'

Marion piped up then. 'Yep, she's doing well. But you know what she's like: a law unto herself. And I bet my bottom dollar she'll be thinking she can get back to work tomorrow.'

'No, you can't do that. You need to rest,' Leo was already saying, his voice shot through with concern.

'Maybe just light duties then?' Lara asked.

'Oh, you try and talk some sense into her, Leo,' Marion cried. 'I'll go and get some cups of hot, sweet tea and when I come back, I want to hear that she's compliant.'

Leo was shaking his head. 'Not much chance there.'

Lara was grinning now and with Lucky snuggling against her, she felt warm and well cared for.

'Seriously, though,' Leo said as Marion clicked the door shut behind her. 'You need to rest up. Listen to the advice.'

'Mmhmm, I hear what you're saying, Mr Vet.' She smiled. Then gently, she moved Lucky to the side and stood up from the bed. 'I know this might seem improper, given I'm in my nightdress, but I just need a hug.'

His eyes flashed with warmth as she reached to put her arms around him and snuggled close. Then he murmured, 'I was sick with worry when I heard you were missing. I didn't know what to do with myself.'

He pulled her against his body, seemed to breathe her in.

As she drew in the warm, musky smell of him, she kissed him gently on the cheek. Then they stayed in each other's arms until they heard the busy tap of Marion's shoes out in the corridor.

'We'd best keep this to ourselves for now,' Lara said, drawing away from him, sitting back on the bed beside Lucky, who was now sleeping.

'There you go. Two good cups of tea and some of Mrs H's shortbread.'

'Thank you, Marion,' Lara and Leo said together.

Marion narrowed her eyes, opened her mouth to speak again but seemed to think better of it. 'I'll consult with Dr Bingham, but I think you're ready to move from the clinic room – in fact, Lara, you've got a nice flush to your cheeks now.'

Lara gulped back a giggle. Of course Marion knew exactly what had been going on. 'Well maybe me and Leo, when we've had our cups of tea, could move through to the front room to sit by the fire for a while.'

'Sounds good to me.' Leo grinned.

Then the telephone in the hallway rang shrilly, cutting through.

'I'll get that,' Marion said, stepping briskly out through the door. She was back in moments. 'I'm sorry, Leo, but it's your dad from the surgery. He says he's not feeling too good, and he needs you to go out on a call. One of Lord Harrington's gun dogs, apparently.'

A shadow seemed to pass over Leo's face, and he sighed heavily. 'Right. It looks like I need to get off.'

'Yes, I'm afraid so,' Lara replied, gathering the sleepy little dog and passing him to Leo.

'I'll see you again soon,' he said firmly, Lucky fully awake now, wagging his tail and struggling to get back to her.

After Leo had gone, Marion came to perch on the side of the bed. 'Well?' she said, her eyes round, like saucers.

'Well, what?' Lara teased.

'You know exactly what. And it's probably the reason why you've got such rosy-pink cheeks after passing out cold in the snow.'

Lara grinned. 'I must be made of strong stuff.'

Marion put an arm around her. 'Mmm, there is that. But I think it's the heat of passion that's warming you right now.'

Lara began to giggle, and Marion was chuckling. And as the dregs of Lara's narrow escape began to loosen, they were soon talking of other things.

* * *

A few days later, when the snow had melted away, leaving waterlogged fields and lanes splashing with water, Lara cycled out to check on Poppy Douglas. Bingham had already visited, and he'd reported that the little girl was making good progress, but he needed Lara to follow her up. She knew what he was up to; he wanted her to complete that circle of care that had nearly cost her life. She could see the sense in it and given he'd put her on restricted duties, just for few days, she knew she'd be able to take her time with the visit.

As she cycled by the winter fields, a fresh breeze made the clouds scurry. And when she came to the spot where she'd fallen into the snow, not far from the track that led up to the Douglases', she stopped for a moment to give thanks for her rescue. Then, as she was about to push off, a lively, yellow-beaked blackbird began to sing in the bare hedge and it lifted her spirits, made her sure she could smell the earth coming back to life. Spotting a patch of white by the side of the road and thinking it was un-melted snow, she dismounted, needing to look closer. It was a clutch of snowdrops, the first she'd seen out here in the countryside and the delicacy of the tiny, white flowers, and the promise they held for warmer days ahead, brought tears to her eyes. She reached down to touch the delicate petals, saw them dance as the cold breeze caught them. 'There you go, my beauties,' she murmured, smiling as she remounted her bicycle.

Before she pushed on towards the turning to the Douglases' farm, she gazed up to the sky as a mass of grey cloud slid across, skimming the tops of the fells. The vast sky above and the dark earth below made her feel like an insignificant figure. But knowing what a near miss she'd had out in the snow, her body began to sing with joy as she felt the strong beat of her heart and knew how lucky she was to be alive. She gave thanks for the land and the plants and trees that would soon be bursting back into life. And she looked forward this year, more than ever, to the brighter, warmer days of spring. Then, just as she pushed off on her bicycle, a hare bobbed out from the hedge right in front of her. The creature turned, almost nonchalantly, then hopped off in front as if leading the way. It made her smile, and she kept smiling as she pushed against her pedals to make her way at a lolloping hare's pace to her first visit of what felt like a fresh start to her life.

* * *

MORE FROM KATE EASTHAM

ACKNOWLEDGEMENTS

Courage for the Country Nurse is my third book in this series, and it feels as if I'm living and breathing Lara's nursing experience. The more I write, the more vivid my memories of being a nurse on the Nightingale Wards of Preston Royal Infirmary become. I'm sure I sometimes catch a whiff of that strong carbolic disinfectant which gave hospitals their unique smell. It's such a privilege to draw on my nursing experience, especially for this book with its emphasis on sick children. Memories of night shifts on Children's Ward have come tumbling back. And one case in particular – a critically ill boy with pneumonia who I nursed in an oxygen tent – has always stayed with me. In the late 1970s, ward visiting for relatives was restricted to afternoons and evenings, so the nurses had full charge of their young patients outside of those hours. The emotional toll of dealing with sick children who were often crying, upset and missing their parents was significant. In addition, there were no intensive care units, so all critically ill patients were nursed on the wards with an allocated nurse who sat by the bed to give special care. I stayed beside my very sick child all through the night amid the hiss of oxygen and the restless cries of other children. I'd been told not to open the oxygen tent except for observations of temperature, pulse and respirations. But when the little boy became distressed, I had to unzip it, just a little, to hold his hand. It worked like magic and thankfully he stayed settled for the rest of the shift. And as always on any ward during the night, renewed energy came when the first rays of light peeped in through the tall windows and the birds began to sing their morning chorus. That's when my poorly patient rallied and as soon as he offered a tiny smile, I knew he was going to pull through. It was a privilege to have those experiences, and I will always be grateful for that. Even more so now I'm drawing on the memory of them for my writing.

I am already excited about the next book in the Country Nurse series and, as always, so grateful to my readers. I'd also like to thank my agent, Judith Murdoch, for her ongoing support and advice. And of course my lovely editor – Francesca Best – and all the wonderful team at Boldwood Books.

And, as ever, I want to say a special thank you to my family – especially my husband Joe who battles his Parkinson's every single day and never gives up.

ABOUT THE AUTHOR

Kate Eastham is the author of heartbreaking wartime historical fiction. Before this, she was a trained nurse and midwife, and spent 20 years working in palliative care. During this time she had the privilege of listening to stories from patients of all ages and backgrounds, many of whom were veterans of the world wars.

Download your exclusive bonus content from Kate Eastham here:

Follow Kate on social media:

x.com/eastham_kate

ALSO BY KATE EASTHAM

Diary of a Country Nurse

A Fresh Start for the Country Nurse

Changing Seasons for the Country Nurse

Courage for the Country Nurse

Printed in Dunstable, United Kingdom

83729194R00179